The Child Healers

The Child Healers

by Murray Kappelman, M. D.

DAVID McKAY COMPANY, INC.
New York

THE CHILD HEALERS

LIBRARY OF CONGRESS CATALOG CARD NUMBER: 76–165088
MANUFACTURED IN THE UNITED STATES OF AMERICA

Dedicated to Joan and my four children
And to the Allisons whom I have touched in my life

The Child Healers

I

HE knew that it was almost time to get up but he resisted, moving deeper into the mattress. The sounds outside of the room told him it was morning; the increased tempo of the paging, the voices rising in volume, the firmness of the heels as they proceeded down the long corridors. How long had he been asleep? Christ, it couldn't have been more than three hours. A sound erupted loud, familiar, insistent. Instinctively his hand reached over his head and picked up the phone. But the loud interference continued; and all he was listening to was a dial tone.

The alarm stopped abruptly, leaving a silence more alive than the intrusive ringing which preceded it. He opened his eyes. There was no moment of adjustment. He knew immediately where he was as he had known each morning for the past six months when he had been awakened at every conceivable hour of the night and day. The two bunk beds came quickly into perspective, crowding out all of the other furniture which had been shoved haphazardly around the small, narrow room. Nothing adorned the walls. The other beds were unoccupied and unmade. The sheets had all been pushed down by angry, tired feet. The beds never seemed to be made; they were either being briefly occupied or awaiting the next occupant. He knew that sometime someone must make these beds and pick

I

up those white pants and shirts off the chair and floors but his constant impression of this room was one of frenzied disarray.

He glanced backward and saw the retreating figure of a young man in jockey shorts making his way to the sink in the corner of the room. As the man moved away, he shouted to Mike.

"Get your ass up. It's twenty to seven and rounds begin at eight."

Mike moved over the edge of the bed and swung his legs to the cold linoleum-covered floor.

"I'm beat. I didn't get to bed until four last night."

Ed looked back from the sink, his face half covered with shaving cream.

"Is it just you and me in here today, Ed?" asked Mike, still not moving.

"Uh huh," Ed replied between calculated downward arm movements of the razor, carefully engineered to prevent shaving his growing sideburns.

"You know, I sometimes think nobody else works every other night like we do. I know the surgeons are on every fourth night and the medical boys must work every three because Alan and Bert are here at night only once or twice a week at the most."

Ed had finished and moved away from the mirror.

"You better hurry up or you'll miss breakfast. Andrews is always on time."

"Oh, man, how well I know." Mike began to lather his face and his actions unconsciously quickened as he thought back over the mornings this last month when he had been late for rounds on the floor below. Sometimes he had had a damned good reason but Andrews never waited for explanations. He merely paused, turned to Ed or one of the senior residents and quietly murmured, "Let us go back to the beginning of the case history so that we can bring Dr. Hillman up to date." His tone would be sad, creating waves of guilt at the thoughtless

2

misdemeanor, recalling memories of past mistakes and bringing on firm resolves not to get caught in the act of such disrespect in the future.

Mike checked his watch and calculated that he had enough time to have a cup of coffee and a roll. He picked up a pair of white canvas pants. They were so heavily starched that he had to pry each leg open. He began to curse softly at the time he was wasting trying to get the pants on. The arms of the starched white shirts were stuck together; and he spent more time than usual punching his fists through the sleeves. When fully dressed and picking up his wallet and stethoscope, he became aware of the fatigue in the muscles of his arms and legs. The exhaustion was part of the pattern that made up his days and nights as did the stiff, fresh, clean feeling of the starched white uniform brushing against his skin.

As Mike finished dressing another noise interrupted the intent silence of the room. The phone gave two long, insistent rings before the two men could focus on the meaning of the sound. Ed walked back from the doorway where he had been standing about to leave and quickly picked up the receiver. Mike stood watching Ed's face closely.

"Hello."

Ed gazed at the floor as he listened to the long outpouring of words. Finally his forehead wrinkled in exasperation. When he spoke, his tone was more controlled than was usual, his words without any variation in rhythm.

"Hold on a minute, Sheila. I'll ask Mike."

Ed turned to Mike who now stood facing him with his arms folded, waiting for the inevitable.

Ed placed his hand over the phone receiver.

"Sheila Plotkin has a kid down in the Emergency Room with a hundred and five degrees. She can't find anything and wants one of us to take a look before she sends the kid out."

Mike grimaced. "Damn it, that's the fourth time in the last two weeks we've had to go down there and bail her out. Why in the hell doesn't she call the resident? Christ, Todd's on duty now. He won't bite her."

"Mike, you know damn well it's not Todd she's scared to death of. It's the chief. If he keeps hearing about all of her calls about nothing, she'll be out on her ass. She's smart enough to know that much."

Mike nodded. He turned and tossed the towel onto the nearest bed.

"Okay, Ed, tell her that it's my turn." He paused and took a deep breath. "Tell her I'll be down in a few minutes. And tell her to make me some coffee, damn it, maybe she can do that much."

Ed took his hand off the receiver. "Sheila, Mike's coming right down." There was a brief pause. "You're welcome. Don't apologize. We understand." Ed put the phone back on the cradle and looked up at Mike. He shrugged his shoulders and smiled. Before walking out of the room cluttered with the wrinkled residue of a hospital night, he turned to Mike.

"Don't show off. Make a quick diagnosis and you'll have time for coffee." He chuckled and left the room.

She stood staring down at the dark, restless infant lying on the disturbed sheets of the hospital stretcher as Mike approached the doorway. Her body was rigid in contemplation. The long, dark brown hair was decisively pulled back with a large leather barrette, the thick strands hanging limply down to the middle of her back. Wisps had escaped during the long night of bending over sick infants and lay loosely against her ears. Her hands mindlessly stroked the black rubber tubing of the stethoscope which dangled from her neck. She was short and slender enough to appear frail. She started slightly at Mike's voice.

"Morning, Sheila."

Mike walked over to the desk where the single page chart lay clipped onto the metal board and picked it up. He read

4

the child's name and then turned toward Sheila and waited. He was acutely aware of the child's mother sitting on a chair directly across from him, watching his every movement, eyes darting from the whimpering infant to the two strange figures in white. Mike continued to wait. When Sheila made no attempt to introduce him, he reread the child's name and took several steps toward the large black woman who sat continually smoothing down the already folded edges of a child's unraveling cotton sweater.

"Mrs. Turner, my name is Dr. Hillman. I would like to look at Phillip also and help find out why he has this high fever." There was a brief pause for Mike to catch his breath. The woman did not move. "May I check him?"

The woman shifted the weight of her large body on the chair and ran her tongue quickly over her lower lip. The infant's whining cries never ceased and the woman's voice was so thick with sleep and fatigue that one word slid into the next in a slurred mumble that required careful attention.

"My name's not Turner. It's Greene. The baby is Turner." Mike nodded. "Yeah, check the baby, Doctor. Do anything but please find out why he's off his food and burnin' like that."

Mike smiled briefly with his mouth; his eyes not changing. "We'll do our best."

He read the chart quickly, noting the history scribbled on the yellow Emergency Room sheet. He had some difficulty reading the age. He turned to Sheila who stood next to him, one hand resting easily on the squirming infant.

"Nine months?" Mike questioned.

"Yes." Sheila looked toward the mother, whose head shook up and down affirmatively as if repeating the answer to a backward child.

Mike picked up the otoscope from the table and pulled his stethoscope out of his pocket. Sheila stepped back and eased herself slowly into the chair next to the desk, studying Mike's movements.

5

The chubby infant lay tossing restlessly, eyes open, mouth forming a constant whimpering cry. His knees were drawn up almost to the stomach wall in a regressed, fetal response. Mike touched the hot, moist skin and gently stroked the baby's stomach for a few seconds, hoping to make a physical contact that might lessen the child's agitation.

"It don't do no good to love him," said the mother. "He won't stop bawlin'."

Mike nodded and stopped patting the baby's abdomen. His hand quickly ran over the baby's head, feeling for the anterior fontanelle. The covered opening in the bony skull was still present and was flat and still. No fullness, or pulsations, or depressions. He watched the incessant restlessness for a few more seconds and then began his examination.

When he had finished, he handed the equipment to Sheila who still sat motionless at the desk. She assembled it. Mike reached down and slowly brought the baby up to his shoulder. He rocked back and forth talking quietly, almost singing soft words of reassurance. His left arm supported the heavy buttocks of the infant against his left shoulder and his right hand rubbed the moist back in a gentle, circular fashion. The baby's movements did not cease and if anything the crying intensified.

The mother rose and stretched out her arms. "It ain't gonna work. I tole you. He's jes' too sick." She accepted the infant and cradled him against the pendulous flesh covered by the shabby print of a faded housecoat. Still standing, she stared at Mike. "Thanks, though." A brief silence. "Doctor, can you tell me somethin'?"

Mike frowned for a second in concentration as he stared at the baby and answered. "We're going outside to talk about the baby. There may be a few tests that we want to run, Mrs. Greene, before we'll know. Please wait for a few more minutes."

The woman closed her eyes and nodded slowly. She reached

her free hand up from the child to wipe the perspiration away from her forehead.

"Doc, please tell that little nurse what to do. I been here almost all night before she would call you. Jes' tell her how to make the baby well so's we can go home."

Mike was exquisitely aware of the small figure sitting hunched over the chair next to the desk. He did not turn around. He continued to stare at the woman pressing her sick baby against her full breasts.

"She's a doctor, Mrs. Greene," he said. "And a very good one. I'm here to give another opinion on your baby so we can be sure. But Dr. Plotkin will be back in to finish the tests."

The woman's expression did not change. She continued staring at the blond-haired young man waiting for him to finish. When there were no more words and the two interns were about to leave, the woman said quietly but firmly:

"You please come back too, Doctor. Before I go out of here with my baby, would you please come back too?"

Mike turned to look at her. Sheila walked out of the room leaving them alone. Mike swallowed and paused a second as the woman's eyes pinned him against the door. Finally he answered.

"I will come back if Dr. Plotkin asks me to. I promise. But only if she asks me."

The woman sighed and sat down heavily, the whining infant still in her arms.

Sheila Plotkin stood leaning against the cool tile wall in the hallway outside of the Pediatric Emergency area. Her head was bent and she stared at the floor, waiting for Mike. When he came into the hallway, and she finally spoke, there were months of despair and frustration in her voice.

"She knew damn well I was a doctor. I must have told her a hundred times during the night. Mike, she knew damn well."

Mike did not answer. There was nothing more to say and he

7

wanted to move ahead and not linger on the embarrassment of the moment. He leaned up against the opposite wall and started talking about the infant in the room—the irritability, the fever, the failure to find much in the physical examination, the insignificant history, the restlessness, and again the irritability.

"Sheila, the kid needs a spinal tap. That much irritability can't be just written off to the fever. Even the mother couldn't quiet the kid down." Mike paused to collect his thoughts. Sheila waited for him to continue, trying to push the tail of her crumpled white linen blouse into the starched white skirt which hung loosely around her thin hips. After a minute Mike said, "The white count is up, way up . . . there has to be an infection, Sheila. If the tap is negative, get a clean caught urine or do a supra-pubic tap, but get urine. That kid has a hidden infection. Try those tests and see. If that doesn't tell you what you want to know, call for help, but smarter help than me next time. Ask Todd or one of the other assistant residents." Sheila stood quietly absorbing his instructions. Suddenly she moved away from the wall and said briskly,

"Thanks, Mike. That was a help." And she disappeared abruptly into the Emergency Room.

Mike entered the cafeteria, checked his watch, and walked through the line picking up a plastic cup and filling it with coffee. Stretching his very tall body over the counter he grabbed the last roll which had slid into a crevice of the metal tray. Then he searched the cavernous room. Ed's arm shot up into the air attracting his attention. Mike walked over and settled into an empty chair.

"Did she have a real problem?"

Mike nodded. "Yeah. She had a real problem. A sick kid with nothing announcing what was wrong. Sheila stops just short of making the right decisions. It's painful as hell because she knows that she hasn't gone far enough but gets hung up and can't move. I told her as much as I know. We may call you in next before we call in God."

Ed laughed and didn't answer.

They sat at a long table in the brightly lighted basement room where the slow, low-pitched murmur of voices suggested the hesitant acceleration of the early part of the day. Mike tilted the disposable paper cup and finished the last bit of the hot, bitter brew.

"Don't start again about the damn coffee. It's as bad as usual, I know." Ed leaned toward him so that Mike could see the sharp outline of his roommate's profile. Ed's dark, thick hair tumbled over the high forehead with its incipient furrows. His eyes were always half shut in contemplation; the broad, slightly irregular nose and the full, firmly set lips were steady trademarks. Ed's chin was the only feature which changed with his moods. It could be firm when confronted with a difficult problem, but it softened in the rare moments when Ed would talk seriously about something he deeply felt. Mike had been living with Ed in the same apartment for the past nine months and had learned to respect his silences.

"We'd better move. You know that you're presenting this morning? The Rollins kid." Ed picked up his tray.

Upstairs as they walked down the narrow hall into which the various rooms opened, the ever-present sounds of the children filtered into their consciousness without disturbing their thoughts. In the distance one could hear the loud crying of the babies in the infant ward. Small voices hollering for the nurse vibrated over the general din of plates being placed onto or removed from trays. Mike heard the hoarse coughing of a child on the ward for whom he was responsible and made a mental note that its deep, croupy quality was subsiding. As they passed another room the loud voice of a television comic desperately trying to get the morning attention of the children was competing with the firm voice of the floor nurse demanding that the television set be turned down. Mike suddenly realized that Ed was no longer beside him. He had turned into one of the large rooms on the right and was bending over the railing of a bed in which a young girl of about five was quietly sobbing. Mike paused for a moment and watched. The railing went down. All he could see was Ed's back as he talked in low tones to the rocking, crying child. She inched over toward him. Ed did not move but continued talking and suddenly Mike recognized Ed's soft, throaty laugh. Then the girl moved toward Ed's crouching form and threw her arms firmly around him. Ed talked a bit longer, looked at his watch, and stepped away from the youngster. She looked at him with her face tear-stained and pleading. As he raised the railing he continued talking as she sat in the center of the bed quietly crying. He stopped, said something, and the girl attempted a small, trembling smile. The tears continued but the smile did not disappear.

Ed seemed somewhat surprised to find Mike still standing in the hall.

"Hey, you're going to be late."

"And you're not? That kid. Isn't she the one with renal mass?"

"Uh huh."

"When does she go up?"

"This morning. She was crying because she couldn't have breakfast."

"Jesus, if it were me I'd be crying because I was scared and my folks weren't here."

"Mike, she's been scared since she came in three days ago, so today is just another day to be scared. Her mother hasn't been in since she brought her to the clinic. And remember, we think we know what's wrong with her but the kid doesn't."

"What do you think she's got?"

"Wilms's tumor."

"She's old. That's a bad prognosis, Ed."

"Maybe, maybe."

10

"No metastases?"

"No spread that we can find now. We'll see when she goes up and is opened."

The dialogue was quiet, without emotion, detached from the rocking, huddled child they had just left.

At the nurse's station, Mike slipped away to make a last-minute visit to the child he was to discuss on rounds. Ed stood by the chart rack and ran his fingers down all the charts until he came to the one for the five-year-old girl. The chart was empty. The contents were already on their way up to the operating room. It was almost as if what had been written about her would approach the scalpel first and the danger, the futility, the pain of the words would be evaluated and dissected before she was. She was about to take her place in the operating-room procession following behind the impressions, the diagnosis, the temperature charts and the blood pressures. Ed stood there for a second, wondering what was real; the child with the tears and the wondering expression or the writing on the missing papers that described her body in the way that the doctors saw her in their educated but imperfect way.

Slowly and methodically, the other interns and residents had begun to gather around the nurse's station. Mike returned smiling, looking at his watch. As soon as he had slipped into the crowd, a tall, slightly bent older man walked briskly into the station. He wore a long white coat over his street clothes. The coat was tightly buttoned; but because his frame was so spare, it hung in folds around him. His hair was a dull brown flecked with strands of gray. His face was lined, without the firmness of youth or the slackness of age. His whole stance and attitude was that of someone bending over ever-so-slightly to listen carefully to a smaller, younger person.

"Morning, gentlemen. Where is our young lady doctor this morning?" referring to Sheila Plotkin who was missing from morning rounds for the first time.

"Good morning, Dr. Andrews," said the senior resident. "I

think Dr. Plotkin has a problem in the Emergency Room. She'll be here momentarily."

"Shall we begin?" Andrews did not wait for a response as he turned to the senior resident standing next to him and indicated that the morning rounds had indeed begun. "Who are you presenting to me today, Todd?"

The senior resident, short, dark, and intense, looked hurriedly around to make sure that Mike was present. His expression of relief was brief but unmistakable. "Dr. Hillman will present a new admission of two days ago." Todd turned toward Mike and waited. A rustle on the outside of the group signaled Sheila's arrival as she murmured her unheard apologies to the group as a whole, and to Dr. Andrews in particular. Mike palmed his notes and began his presentation.

"Charles Rollins is a six-year-old white male whose chief complaint of abdominal pain began six months ago, according to both parents who were present at the time of the interview. The pain was described as being peri-umbilical . . ." As Mike talked and outlined the case, his audience began to assume individual postures. The senior resident tensed and stood still. Ed listened quietly with his hands folded behind him unconsciously nodding his head when an area he thought important was being covered. Sheila Plotkin stood quietly rubbing the painful index finger of her left hand that she had cut attempting to remove the plastic covering of the disposable spinal tap tray while hurrying so as not to be late for rounds. Standing next to the nurse's desk with one knee resting on the soft seat of the chair was Sandy Breslow, the floor nurse. Her concentration alternated between the speaker and the speech. She watched Mike carefully, and listened intently; her eyes traveling over his tall, compact frame. Sandy had managed to attend morning rounds on this particular ward for over three years. She had listened to presentations from many of the men standing there as well as the men who had finished training and left to practice or to teach elsewhere what they had learned on this ward. She was able now to anticipate when an intern was about to experience a particularly difficult question and answer period with Dr. Andrews. Mike seemed to have his material down cold.

Gradually his words ebbed and Andrews began to speak, eyes moving from one staring face to the next. When he was finished he knocked his cold pipe into the ashtray on the desk, indicating that rounds were over. Sandy walked toward the medicine cabinet in the hall. As Mike passed, she said,

"Very good, Dr. Hillman." She was smiling broadly.

"Thanks, Sandy. Andrews was easy on me this morning."

"You're fishing for a compliment. You did a good job and you know it."

She laughed softly and moved from behind the medicine tray toward him. The top of her head reached his chin. He noticed how her blonde hair curled on her shoulder. Her hair was her best feature. Sandy wasn't a beautiful girl but she tried harder to be appealing than most beautiful girls would. All of her features were individually good but when put together they lacked distinction. However, her blonde hair transmitted a glow that transcended the plainness of the features and hinted of undiscovered beauty. There was a sadness in her face that caught Mike's attention, a suggestion of secrets withheld. He had always had the need to conquer the unknown, and then when successful to move on, leaving only the memory of his performance behind.

Sandy calmly waited for him to speak.

"How about going out tonight, Sandy?"

The blonde eyebrows wrinkled. "Anywhere in particular?"

"Leave the details to me. Will you go?"

Mike saw her pause for the briefest moment, look up with interest and smile. "You've aroused my curiosity. I'll go."

Mike mentioned the time, took down her address and moved down the hall. There was still a long day to conquer.

13

II

THE late winter wind injected tiny gusts between the crevices where her heavy green coat had pulled away from her small frame. She shivered and leaned closer toward the man walking briskly at her side, holding his hand more tightly, skipping every third or fourth step to keep up with him. She saw his brown shoes striding firmly on the gray concrete, heels hitting hard with each purposeful step.

The three people moved silently along the sidewalk, the child thrusting her shoulders forward as if determined to force her body into the next step. The man looked straight ahead, his expression maintaining an unchanging grimace despite the furtive upward glances of the child. His free hand gripped a small, multicolored overnight case, his knuckles whitened by his fingers' tight grip on the handle. The small, elegant woman walking on the other side of the child held her face still, wrapped in her own thoughts. Together they approached the glass doors that led into the lobby of the modern brick and steel hospital.

Allison Reddy felt cut off. This loneliness, frightened loneliness, had become her constant companion during the last two days. The anxiety had begun first in the doctor's office. After listening to the doctor suggest that she come into the hospital for diagnostic tests, she had been sent out of his consultation room to get her coat. Her parents had remained behind the closed walnut door for almost half an hour. When they had emerged, Allison detected a difference in their manner, a desire to avoid questions which exceeded their usual wish not to be bothered. And now this hospitalization . . .

Her mother stood off at a distance looking around at the doctors in front of the elevator.

"Aren't they young, Don?"

"It's hard to tell behind some of those beards."

"Oh, but they are young."

"Sometimes I think it's my eyes that are getting old. It's hard to imagine them as doctors."

"Well, I think they're only students, but even so . . ." Her voice trailed off as the elevator arrived and the assembled group moved through the open doors. Allison reached out and wrapped her fingers around her mother's hand, suddenly fearful that she might be left standing alone.

"Which is the children's floor?" Her father's hard voice questioned the stooped, elderly man standing at the controls.

"Five." The wrinkled hand touched the proper button and the operator turned a lined, dark face back to the oncoming crowd, waiting patiently for the next voice to command him into action.

"We're supposed to try and locate a Dr. Hillman," her father said when they reached the fifth floor.

An information desk was placed directly in the center of the fifth floor lobby. Seated on two chairs behind the chipped yellow wooden counter were two uniformed volunteers talking excitedly to each other. They continued their conversation, despite the fact that the Reddys stood waiting to be recognized.

"Would you excuse me? We're looking for a Dr. Hillman. Our daughter is being admitted here today. Where will we find him?"

The two women stopped talking abruptly and surveyed the

16

imposing figure of the man addressing them. Their eyes glided over Allison's head and she wondered if they had even seen her. She could tell that they had seen her parents and were duly impressed. The woman with the sleek blonde head smiled and pointed a jeweled finger down a hallway.

As the Reddys moved off, Allison waited tensely for the explosion. She had observed enough of her father's outbursts to know that his temper rose quickly and subsided slowly. The air was still for a second. She realized that she was pulling very hard on her skirt with both fists clenched. But all her father said was, "What in the hell are they doing in those goddamn uniforms if they can't help?" No fury, only petulance. What was going on within her that could cause such a change in the past few days?

Her parents moved steadily down the hall, gradually pulling away from her as she lagged slightly behind. Her father approached a blonde nurse who emerged from one of the rooms lining the end of the hallway. She stopped, smiled, and bent her head slightly to the side as she listened and glanced at the paper that Mr. Reddy automatically opened and showed to her. Then she walked slowly over to Allison, smiling.

"Hi. My name's Sandy Breslow. I'm the daytime nurse in charge of this hall. I think you'll be staying here while you're with us."

"Hi. I'm Allison." She suddenly perceived her imminent separation from all that was familiar to her. Conversation was impossible.

Sandy noted the girl's reticent withdrawal and moved silently back toward the nurse's station. She remained intensely conscious of the blonde child mutely leaning against the corridor wall staring at the floor. Finally, after several minutes, she walked back and stood quietly at Allison's side.

"It scares you, doesn't it?"

Allison nodded and turned her face toward the wall.

17

Sandy extended her right arm and allowed it to rest gently upon the child's shoulder, pressing down so fleetingly that Allison was barely conscious of the action.

"I'll try and help you get over that."

Allison smiled weakly. She wanted very much to believe this woman but she was finding it difficult.

"Thank you." Allison watched as the hand was removed easily from her shoulder.

"Your parents are waiting for you in the examining room next door. Your doctor is in there. You'll meet him first and then he'll want to examine you. Does that worry you?"

"No." Allison appreciated the nurse's approach, the honesty, the interest, the desire to make her comfortable but she suddenly felt very young and vulnerable and on the brink of being taken advantage of.

She walked slowly through the door of the large sunny room where her mother and father sat talking earnestly to a man in a white uniform seated on a stool directly across from them.

"How old is Allison?"

"Eleven," her mother replied, staring intently into the young man's face which Allison could not see because he had his back to her. However, she had the distinct sensation that he knew she had entered the room despite the fact her parents were so involved in answering his questions that they had not noticed her entrance. His back straightened and he glanced over his shoulder. Then he swung all the way around until they faced each other. Allison stood framed in the doorway, her long, streaming blonde hair absorbing a few rays of reflected sunlight, circling her face like a shining halo.

She immediately focused on the smiling eyes that were carefully surveying her. The remainder of the young man's features were individually clear and distinctive but his overall appearance suggested refinement rather than strength and composure rather than intensity. He was as blond as she was with clear, calm blue eyes; and he had lids with blond lashes that lowered to half cover the intense blueness underneath. His complexion was fair with only a faint imprint of last summer's tan remaining.

"Hi, Allison, we're talking about you. Do you want to listen or would you rather go around to the playroom?" He spoke easily and she suddenly felt less afraid and decided to stay. "What's your name?" Allison asked as she lifted herself up onto a stool which was placed next to a long, high table covered with a tightly pinned sheet.

"Michael Hillman." He smiled. "My friends call me Mike. Take your pick." Her parents sat still, their heads jerking back and forth as they followed the brief exchange.

Dr. Hillman winked and turned back to her parents. He glanced down at the few ink marks on the clipboard perched in his lap refreshing his memory and began again asking about Allison's past history. Her mother began to rub her fingers together as she described Allison's nosebleeds, the profuse bleeding, the fright, the rush to the Emergency Room, the gradual subsiding of the blood. Allison listened and frowned, remembering that unpleasant night in vivid detail. Both of her parents looked over at her and smiled tight, thin smiles. Boy, are they worried. She hugged herself as hard as she could and failed to hear the doctor approach.

"Hey, Allison, what gives? You trying to crawl inside of yourself?"

She looked up sharply and saw her fear in the same way that he did. Her knees unbent, and her legs slid down and touched the floor.

"How about getting undressed so I can examine you?" Allison stood up.

"Do you want us to wait outside?" Dr. Hillman asked as she began to unbutton her blouse. She shook her head and continued undressing.

"Please stare at that mark on the wall, Allison." Mike pulled down the shades and flipped off an overhead light.

19

"I'm going to look into your eyes now. It won't hurt." He was so serious and thoroughly involved with her at that moment that she wanted to laugh and say, "I've only been fooling. There's nothing wrong with me." But all she could manage was a simple statement whispered into his ear as he leaned over to look into her eyes.

"I like you a lot. I'm going to try and make you like me."

The lights went on and she looked into the doctor's face. Instead of seeing him smile and acknowledge her remark or wink at her like she had expected him to, his eyes were clouded and his lips were thinned. He seemed to be in pain.

III

Ed walked away from the nurse's station, hands pushed into the pockets of his stiff white trousers. His mind was beginning to race in time with the accelerating activity of the ward. Unconsciously he hummed to himself. His thoughts leaped ahead, allowing the immediate problems to surface and take precedence so that he could maintain a minimum of order in the chaos of his usual day. His humming became unintentionally louder.

"Somebody's happy."

Ed turned to face Sandy. He smiled, having become acutely conscious of the loud sound bouncing off the high-ceilinged walls.

"Me, I feel great. It's crazy. I shouldn't. Christ, I had four hours' sleep last night, but for some reason I have a new, fresh feeling inside of me this morning."

Sandy continued smiling, but closed her eyes very briefly. "Oh, God, I'd love to feel like that for a change. I seem to remember what a great feeling it can be, but somewhere I lost it. All of my feelings are the old, used ones." She stopped smiling with the last remark and assumed her usual detached, wary attitude. This was the woman she presented to the world of adults; the children never saw this guarded person. She had no protective coverings around the young; the pain they gave her was unintentional and against which there was no predetermined defense. She picked up little plastic glasses with lines and numbers marked on them, filled them carefully with pills or liquid, and jotted down notes in a small book as she talked.

"Mike did well this morning, don't you think?"

"Uh huh, he really was good today. Even Andrews thought so. You could hear every word that Andrews said today—that shows he was impressed. Last week when Plotkin presented, Andrews only moved his lips. I thought I had gone deaf."

Sandy continued working, screwing the tops onto bottles, filling syringes, and stacking small blue cards behind each plastic glass. She stared at the top of the filled medicine cart and spoke softly. "When he graduates as a human being, he'll make a good doctor."

Ed glanced at her, looking for some change in her expression but the set lines did not move. Without realizing it, he raised his voice.

"What in the hell do you mean by that?"

"Damn it, Ed, I don't know. It's just that sometimes I think that something very serious is missing in Mike. I watch him on the ward. I wonder if he really cares about anybody but himself. I think he knows it too. He stands so far back from the children that he misses so much of their beauty. He seems to be only searching for their pain. Somehow he keeps reminding me of a hand with only four fingers, and the one that's missing is the one that feels. I just don't know . . ." Her voice trailed off as she stared down the hall as if searching for the answers to her questions in the empty sterility of the hospital walls.

Ed didn't respond because there was nothing to say. Sandy finished with her medicines and moved off, pushing the metal cart in front of her. "Here comes the medicine lady," she called, entering an open doorway. The voices in the room ebbed for a brief second and then built to an excited, high-pitched ripple.

Ed watched her retreating form with a mixture of respect

and admiration. She was a damn good nurse and he had learned a lot from her.

"Ed, do you have a minute? Can I ask you a question?" One of the junior medical students assigned to Ed's ward was standing directly in front of him.

"Of course, Alan, what's up?"

"I've been rereading the chart on the Bronson kid in Room Four. He's the Mongol with the heart lesion who's in for a catheterization. You noted on his chart that he has something called Brushfield spots in his eyes. I've never heard of that before. Do you have time to show them to me?"

"Right. They're the white spots in the iris of the eye that you can see in some Mongols. Come on, let me show you."

Together they walked down the hall and entered a ward distinguished from the others by the number four painted in black over the entrance. Looking at the rows of cribs lined up side by side, painted the same color, with the bars at each side and the same thin mattresses covered with the tightly drawn white sheets, Ed had the uncomfortable thought that they resembled cages. The gurgling, crying, sucking sounds of infants filled the air. Sun streamed through the windows lighting the chrome poles over the tops of each bed and reflecting off the metal spigots on the wash basins. As always when he entered these rooms, Ed had an intense desire to pull down the shades so that the children would not feel so exposed and so vulnerable.

The two men stopped at the last crib on the right and moved around to the side of the bed. Ed leaned over and slowly lowered the metal side. The six-month-old infant who had been staring at the ceiling when they had arrived, turned his head toward them. His arms lay passively at his side. The undershirt and diaper were unusually clean and free of stains, suggesting that they had been changed recently. Sitting in the corner of the crib was a large stuffed rabbit. The blue, furry

23

body with the long folded white ears rested back on its tail. It was untouched and unnoticed. A red and white plastic rattle lay ignored about three inches from the baby's left hand. Ed spoke softly causing the baby's eyes to cease darting between the two men and come slowly to rest on his face. He reached into the crib and picked the baby's head up very gently and tilted it back. His even voice continued talking steadily to the baby as he carefully opened the eyelids wider while the medical student's slightly unsteady hand guided a flashlight toward the baby's face.

"Man, he sure doesn't cry very much." Alan shook his head, puzzled at the child's passive nature.

Ed nodded. "Mongols are often very placid . . . almost like that extra chromosome has given them an extra defense against all of us. . . ." The student grunted and peered into the eye. Finally he stood up and smiled. "Gee, that's great. I saw just what you saw . . . those white flecks. . . . How in the hell could I have missed them?"

Ed recognized the self-flagellation that every medical student endures before realizing that there is never time enough to learn everything in the four years assigned to that task . . . that the learning continues indefinitely. He smiled inwardly. How well he remembered the medical school days when he was ready to give it all up . . . when a particularly bright fellow student had made a diagnosis or answered a difficult question and he had felt crushed, uncertain that he would ever be able to accomplish what he had admired in the other student. The feelings for human beings came later when you suddenly realized that you were susceptible to sharing the pain and the suffering of those under your care.

Ed often longed to be released from the seemingly unending barrage of maimed and feverish children, and wondered if he was alone in wanting to treat and guide the healthy. That was his eventual goal, but this early pathway was littered with the prostrate figures of the desperately ill and deformed.

24

Alan was still watching the infant rolling his head back and forth in the bed. "I better be going. Thanks, Ed. I'll be ready for Todd on rounds tomorrow."

Ed found himself observing again the infant's distinctive facial features which clearly announced his genetic defect to the outside world. Standing back from the crib, Ed watched as the small, oddly shaped head moved slowly searching for him. Ed thought, he's looking for someone, anyone, to touch him, hold him, to right the wrong that nature has dealt him. But no one, no matter how hard they tried, could ever really help this infant. Even the most devoted care would never bring him further than the lowest levels of achievement taken for granted by most others; and even to this limited end there was no guarantee. Ed stood staring at the baby, now lying quietly in the center of the crib, next to the unused rattle and the unloved, untouched rabbit; and Ed felt the peak of his previous sense of exhilaration recede.

The phone was ringing on the nurse's desk. Ed noticed Sandy hurrying down the hall. As he walked out of Room Number Four, he saw her pick up the receiver. He tapped his fingers on the metal chart rack as she listened to someone on the other end and then saw her motion him over.

"Who's next up for a patient?" she said, her hand covering the receiver. "Cliff has a bad meningitis down in the Emergency Room."

"Yours truly . . . Mike is in admissions with a new elective." Ed picked up the phone. "I have a child down here, Ed, three years old, sick as shit, with a spinal fluid count of eleven hundred cells—all polys . . ." Ed listened, jotting down the details as he held the phone squeezed in his neck, hoping that it wouldn't fall in the middle of a sentence. Each figure, each word that he wrote down accentuated the seriousness of the child's condition.

"What's the kid's name?" Ed asked at last.

"Anthony Mazetti."

"Send him right up and send the parents to admissions. Cliff, if you could do me a favor and smear and gram stain the fluid for me while I start the I.V."

"I'm awful busy down here. Plotkin left me a kid with a urinary tract infection. Mike had told her to test the urine and she found pus, but she took off before starting treatment. Where's Todd?"

"Tell you what—just smear the fluid so it won't spoil and Todd'll stain it before we take a history."

"Okay, sorry, but the dam broke in this hellhole. Every sick kid in the city came in here today just to see me."

"That's because you're so pretty, Cliff."

Cliff was laughing. "Shit on that." As Ed hung up the phone he looked for Sandy. She was standing by a crib in Room Two counting the pulse on a sleeping child. Ed called out to her. His voice had an urgency that made her come immediately to the nurse's desk without questioning him.

"Who's on treatments today? I've got a bad meningitis coming up and I'll need help."

"Alston, but she's busy with the tracheotomy that the ENT boys just did in intensive care. I'll finish my meds and come in and help you."

"Hurry up. This kid sounds bad."

She raised her eyebrows slightly. "You go into the treatment room and get the fluids mixed and I'll be there before the child."

Ed picked up the phone, dialed the operator, and put in a page for his resident. Almost immediately he heard the shrieking sound of "Dr. Greenberg" bleating out of the loud speaker. He walked briskly over to the treatment room, opened the cabinets and took out several bottles of fluid. He fished inside his shirt pocket, found a blank index card, and began figuring and calculating and finally decided on the proportions of the fluids he was to prepare for the unseen child. He methodically began mixing the liquids and pouring off the amounts that would not be used. When he was finished, he shook the final solution thoroughly and covered it with a sterile piece of gauze. At the same moment the door burst open and Todd Greenberg hurtled into the room followed by Sandy who closed the door firmly behind her. Todd moved nervously around the room, eyes darting over the equipment and hands finally settling under the flow of warm water in the basin in the corner of the room. The small, dark resident's constant kinetic energy put many of his interns on the defensive. He always seemed to have the job done before anyone else had organized himself sufficiently to begin. His movements were staccato; his actions seemingly without pause. Ed deeply respected this senior man. He found in times of crisis Todd's aggressive tension fused into totally effective action.

"Sandy tells me we've got a bad meningitis coming up. What's on the smear?"

"I don't know. Cliff hasn't had time to stain it. He and Lem are busy as hell in the pit. I told him we would take care of that part up here. Maybe you could do it while I start the intravenous fluids."

"Okay, but let me first take a look at the kid when he arrives. Then if everything is fairly stable, I'll stain the slide and see what bugs we are dealing with."

Sandy moved quietly around the room, shifting the metal intravenous pole closer to the table and raising it higher. After a pause, disturbed only by the deep breathing of the three still figures, the door opened slowly and a tall black man pushed a stretcher ahead of him into the room, its wheels squeaking slightly. The aide's bleached white uniform contrasted sharply with his glistening dark skin as he brought the mobile bed level with the treatment table. He glanced over at Sandy.

"Miss Breslow, would you like me to put the kid on the table?"

"Please."

All of the waiting people had seen the frightened face of a

27

woman framed in the doorway with her mouth half open as if wanting to call out, her right arm partially raised, and her fingers clenched as if ready to knock on empty air. None of them questioned her presence; she was the child's mother. Todd turned to the aide and spoke rapidly.

"The kid's mother is standing right outside. Didn't Cliff send them down to Admitting?" The aide picked up the flaccid boy as if delicately protecting a leaf against a disturbing wind and laid the child onto the table. He didn't speak until the boy had settled listlessly onto the unwrinkled paper. "The father went downstairs but the mother insisted on following me." The child had eased into the bed, unconsciously twisting and curving his body. Sandy quickly straightened his arms and legs into a more natural position. It was obvious that the child was stuporous and unresponsive. His face was flushed; his blond hair was matted with perspiration. Occasionally the gray hospital gown which covered his body moved and rustled slightly as he trembled after a breath.

"The doctor down in emergency said to tell you that he left the slide in the lab down there ready to be stained." The aide paused. "Is there anything else you need me for?"

Sandy shook her head. The aide leaned forward and glanced at the child's face. Ed could see his lips moving wordlessly as he bent over the empty stretcher and pushed it steadily through the door.

Todd was sitting on the edge of the table attempting to move the child's head in several directions and manipulating his arms and legs. There was decided resistance in all areas. He looked at Ed, frowned, and Ed understood. Sandy had placed a blood-pressure cuff around the child's left arm and was slowly pumping it. As Ed hung the intravenous fluid bottle up on the overhead pole, Todd said sharply, "His neck is stiff as hell. So are his legs and arms. He's just about hanging on. I'm going to tell the floor nurse to give his mother something and take her to the conference room to wait for us." He pulled the door open revealing a wide pair of moist eyes. "I'll be right back." Sandy saw him slip his arm around the woman's shoulder gently to guide her away from the door where she had been standing vigil.

The mercury finished falling and Sandy looked up, relieved. "His pressure is stable, 90/50."

"Good. How about helping me get this I.V. started?" Ed picked up the child's arm and taped it to a wooden board. The child didn't move. His arm was hot and the muscles tight and tense. Ed slipped a rubber catheter above the elbow, tied it tightly, and began feeling with his finger for a vein into which he could slip his needle. He picked up the alcohol sponges, wiped off a small area and then accepted the needle which Sandy offered, uncovered it and inserted it quickly into the child's arm. For the first time the child moved but Sandy had anticipated the reflex and was firmly holding the boy's body. A shrill, high-pitched cry erupted from the child's throat. The eerie, piercing quality caused Ed to stop briefly and glance at Sandy. Her expression didn't change. The child's feet began to tremble and his free arm began to rise. Sandy leaned over, holding the child in position as Ed guided the needle toward the vein. His lips tightened and perspiration beaded his forehead. An itch developed in the small of his back. What a hell of a time to have to scratch myself, he thought. But his attention focused intently on the small, hot arm. He knew he was very close to the vein and gave a shove, sighing, as the tubing from the needle suddenly filled with the bright red color he was waiting to see.

"We're in."

Sandy handed him the tape as he fixed the needle in place. He opened the stopcock on the tubing and watched the blood as it returned into the child's vein followed by the clear fluid that made its steady way along the tubing.

29

"I wish to hell Todd would come back. I want to get some stuff into this kid." Ed sat on a stool next to the table. The room was still. The spigot on the sink in the corner of the room was leaking. The sound of the water dropping into the sink, loudly amplified in the waiting tension, drummed against Ed's ears. Time seemed to be caught in slow motion. Ed contemplated the still form, his eyes moving upward to regard the soft, full features which moved very little with each labored respiration. The gown had been pulled away during the cannulation revealing the flushed, soft skin of the boy's chest. Ed placed his stethoscope in his ears and listened to the boy's heart and lungs. The child's pulse was racing and the respirations, deep and slow.

The door swung open and Todd was back. The two men discussed what Todd had seen on the slide and agreed on the treatment. Sandy opened the cabinet and removed two small bottles; she quickly prepared them and Ed injected the drugs into the child's tubing—medicine that they hoped would do a job that they alone were powerless to do. They were the interpreters; they deciphered the message and only prayed that their translation of the code had been correct. The final action was not theirs; that belonged to the drug they were injecting and to the child who was receiving it. Todd turned toward Ed and placed a hand on his shoulder. "Let's get him into his bed, put him on special orders, calculate his fluids, and watch him." One sentence . . . how futile. Ed lifted the boy onto the bed that Sandy wheeled into the room. Suddenly the weight of the small body seemed almost impossible to carry. As he removed his arms from underneath the child Ed noticed that his fingers had begun to tremble slightly.

"I'll watch him," said Sandy. "Let Todd take the history . . . go and lie down . . . you look exhausted."

Ed was completely drained. He stood in the corner, leaning back on the metal cabinet, listening to the dripping water and the ticking of his watch; wondering in how many hospitals, in how many rooms like this, how many other people stood and questioned as he did now . . . why they were where they were, doing what they were doing, and if they could hold out until the uncertainty was resolved.

IV

SANDY'S finger rhythmically moved up and down as she accentuated each tiny drop of fluid as it fell into the clear tube. She counted her automatic movements and measured the number against the slowly circling second hand of her watch. The child did not stir. The fluid continued falling into the tubing. The room was quiet.

"Sandy, somebody is on the phone for you." An aide came into the room. "He said he didn't mind waiting."

Sandy nodded. She had the feeling that she knew who it was and was fully prepared for the resolute male voice that greeted her as she picked up the receiver.

"Hi, Sandy . . . It's Bert . . ."

"Hello, Bert . . . I'm sorry if I kept you waiting very long." Her voice was casual and distant. She stared impassively at the multiple colors in the painting of a clown dancing crazily on the wall opposite her.

"Sandy, I wondered if you might like to go to a movie tonight." Bert spoke rapidly but softly. She pictured him holding the phone tightly, somewhat embarrassed that he might be refused. And she realized that she would have to turn him down again despite the fact that she honestly didn't want to. She was seeing Mike. Sandy was familiar with the slight but perceptible change in Bert's resigned voice; it became softer and more controlled in answer to her refusal. She was not concerned that Bert wouldn't call back; she knew he would. It was just that he was so damned vulnerable.

As she walked down the hall to prepare the afternoon refreshments she smiled. Bert Gordon was only an inch or two taller than she was. His black hair was threatening to become gray and was thinning, particularly above the high forehead; and his attempts at growing the rest had only resulted in thick, bushy, and unmanageable temples. Bert was a man who at thirty-three could not deny the passage of time. He had put on just enough weight in certain areas to lose the tightness and resilience that one associates with younger men. However, the real key to his age lay in his eyes. They were clear and brown but settled. There was no sparkle of inwardly imagined excitement, and no intensity of emotion. They were the constant eyes of a mature, gentle, affectionate man.

Sandy often wondered why she hadn't been able to accept the reality and permanence of what Bert seemed anxious to offer her. She had slept with him on several occasions out of curiosity, later out of affection, but never out of honest sexual desire. The harder she tried to remember those evenings in her apartment with Bert, the more she remembered a lulling sensation of an anchored boat in gently rippled waters.

As she stood in the cold hospital kitchen pouring orange juice into small paper cups, Sandy thought back to when she was a student nurse. As if gazing at a forgotten snapshot, she could visualize the plain face flushed with excitement, lips parted and moist, attempting to taste every new sight, sound, activity whirling around her, causing her to seem almost beautiful in the afterglow of the discovery.

At that moment, an all too recognizable face intruded into her conscious thinking. She stopped and painfully turned her head as if to try to escape; and when she realized that retreat from this memory was impossible, she put down the orange juice can and stood with her hands tightly clenched in front of

34

her and her eyes squeezed shut. She saw his face wearing every expression that she could remember. She recalled his laughter as they ran along the streets after a house staff dance, drunk on cheap sherry which was all that they could afford. She cringed as she saw him scream in protest over the injustices, no matter how small, that he refused to tolerate in either man or God. She remembered his face, pensive, relaxed as they lay close together in his narrow bed after having made love, the boy talking endlessly and she listening through most of the night. His talking—volatile, excited, enthusiastic; his love-making—quiet, tentative, considerate. She shook her head violently from side to side; Oh, God, no more memories. But his face kept returning and she knew that before she could be free again she would have to remember it all and end by seeing his face as it had been that last time; flushed, feverish, pale and smiling weakly as she and his mother stood mutely staring down at him as he lay in bed, a dying patient on the floor that he had been in charge of only a few months before. She knew that that was the final face that she would be forced to remember because she had refused to look the last time that she had had the chance.

Sandy vaguely remembered walking into the large funeral home with the glass doors and high-ceilinged lobby with the marble columns, watching David's family and friends standing in groups talking in hoarse voices strained to remain low, with the rumbling din of whispered conversation rising like a mist over the crowd. She stood for a moment and allowed her hovering mother to slip her heavy brown coat from her shoulders; obeying without resistance as she had done many years before, suddenly feeling herself helpless and dependent again in this strange and ugly room. Somehow sensing this regression, her mother firmly grasped her arm and gently forcing Sandy forward, they had walked down a long corridor to a little room on the far side of the main funeral hall where David's family was receiving the condolences of the other mourners. People were waiting in a makeshift line, quietly talking, marking time until their turn came to visit the family, women with handkerchiefs strategically placed in gesturing hands, men with hats clenched in sweaty fists, murmuring, shifting their feet. Sandy recalled some violent inner anger welling up inside her toward these mourning people, these almost strangers who only knew the visible man, the external David, who could recognize the young doctor if they had met him but would never have known the man that she had loved, the boy with whom she had shared her body, the future she was to have married. Her anger was fleeting. Her own grief gave it no resting place. She had broken away from her mother's hold and slipped ahead of the waiting people. Many in the line recognized her, her name traveled audibly from one to the other until the sound of it whipped her body into the darkened room where the shadows competed with the black clothes for somber effect. She remembered nothing about the following seconds; only that within minutes she was standing facing David's mother. The two women looked steadily at each other. They said nothing, silence bridged their distance; no tears were shed—the words, the crying, the agony of dying were over. Together they had lived the last months of his illness, the final weeks of standing helplessly by as that growing part of his body that was foreign, intrusive, and painful had replaced the David that both she and this resigned, grieving woman she stood facing had shared, each in her own way. Sandy leaned back against the hospital refrigerator as the silent documentary of her loss continued. She recalled that David's mother rose shakily from the leather sofa into which she had wedged herself, stood up firmly, offering Sandy her cold, trembling fingers. Sandy took the woman's hand into her own, clenching it tightly, saying nothing, staring blindly into the empty eyes. They had remained there for a short time when Sandy's mother gently took her by the shoulders and guided her toward the funeral hall.

36

As she reached the doorway and saw the open casket and the slow procession of men and women filing past, the months of fulfillment followed by the weeks of agony came together and exploded. She began to cry in deep gulps. Her shoulders shook, her body rocking back and forth, and she began to run. She ran up the side aisle, averting her face from the coffin, and kept running, aware that her mother was trying to catch up with her, aware that heads had turned and surprised eyes were following her flight but she felt compelled to escape the unflinching, unalterable truth exposed in that open casket.

In the small kitchen where the partially filled refreshment tray sat unnoticed, Sandy felt her thigh muscles contract. She was reliving the effort to push open the heavy wooden doors at the back of the long funeral hall, her flight, sobbing, out into the street, coatless, close-cropped hair lifting slightly in the wind. She ran until her breath gave out and she sat down on the lowest step of a public library that she had never noticed existed. Spent, she stared vacantly out at the busy, moving traffic.

Gradually her gaze had traveled downward and settled on her abdomen which she knew was beginning to distend with the fetus that David had implanted during his last, very brief remission when she had begged him to take her to bed and hold her. How weak he had been, how helpless, how ashamed at how much she had had to do for him that night. Sandy rubbed her stomach and kept repeating, "David, I'm pregnant. Oh, David, I'm pregnant. Help me. I only want you. If I can't have you, I don't want this reminder. David, I'm pregnant and you're gone." They had found her sitting there and someone silently drove her home.

The next week she had told her mother about the pregnancy which had gone on too long to do anything about. She found an apartment for herself, moved out of her mother's home, as her mother watched without questioning. Sandy took a leave of absence at the hospital, retired into the interior of

37

her apartment and into herself and passively traversed her pregnancy, gradually becoming determined not to permit her life to be changed by this residue of a dead lover. After all, he was gone. And she was alive. What was the use of hanging on? She went through her labor stoically, hoping that the pain would erase her memories, delivered a healthy female infant whom she had carefully arranged ahead of time to have taken by the Jewish Welfare Board directly to the agency when she left the hospital. She had never seen her baby. But she could not help thinking of the child each time she thought of David. They went together and they haunted her. She had tried to replace them with the restless, driving force of life but felt the battle still raging within her as she stood in the immaculate, uncluttered kitchen on the Pediatric floor pouring juice for other people's children.

Sandy rubbed her eyes with the knuckles of her hands and straightened her body; she was not surprised by this interlude. It happened less often now than before but often enough to resemble a familiar dream.

As she pushed the cart down the long aisle listening to the wheels whispering on the tiled floor, Sandy wondered whether she wasn't moving slowly toward the day when she would finally be forced to accept the fact that time had the same meaning for her as did the children to whom she gave so much. Whether the outcome of any momentary connection was good or bad, they all left her standing in the same place and moved on. For one lacerating moment she realized that she had been attempting to make time the central focus in her life and force people into a peripheral orbit around it. Suddenly she understood how little life had infiltrated her hard outer shell. The lid to her casket wasn't even open for passersby to mourn her absence.

She entered the room where the new elective admission had just settled herself into bed after watching her parents leave. The child sat on the edge of the bed, her legs dangling.

38

"We have snacks every day. Would you like some orange juice?"

The girl looked at her closely, scanning her face so avidly that Sandy felt slightly uneasy. Finally she said, "Yes, Ma'am."

Sandy handed her a cup and held up a cookie. The girl shook her long blonde hair. Sandy placed the cookie back in the tray and moved closer. "My name is Sandy. We met before in the hall. Remember?" The youngster nodded her head. "I'll be your nurse during the days. Since you're here just for studies and don't look very sick to me, how would you like to help me with refreshments each day? I could use a helper."

Allison perked up. "I'd like that a lot. I've thought about being a nurse but people who hurt make me want to cry. How do you stop from crying?"

Sandy smiled. "You train yourself not to get upset but to help. It's not easy."

Allison peered at the woman standing in front of her. "Do you ever forget and cry anyway?"

Sandy shook her head. "Not often."

Allison probed. "But you do once in a while?"

Sandy shrugged. "All right, once in a while."

"Like today?"

Sandy frowned. "What do you mean?"

Allison reached back and brought a miniature leather purse from behind her and opened it, extracting several pieces of pink Kleenex. She handed them to the puzzled nurse. "You've been crying. Your mascara is smeared and several tears are still on your cheeks."

Sandy took the tissue and wiped carefully. She hadn't realized that she had cried. Was it the memory or the self-analysis that had followed?

"Thanks, Allison. You were right. . . . I do cry once in a while . . . and today was one of those unusual days."

"Was it someone in pain?" The child persisted.

39

"Yes, Allison, someone in a lot of pain but she's much better now." Sandy pushed the cart to the other side of the room and handed a paper cup to the thin, wispy hand that was sticking out from between the sheets in the only other bed in the room. She bent over as the hand pulled in the drink and whispered several words of greeting.

Sandy took the empty cups and tossed them into the waste can and started pushing the cart out of the room, acutely aware of Allison's eyes riveted to the back of her head, trying to reach out and keep her from leaving.

V

ALLISON tied the belt of her bathrobe tightly around her body and looked at her parents who had just returned from their lunch downstairs. Her mother smoothed down the sheet on the elevated bed for the third time in the past hour while her father moistened his lips and walked aimlessly about the room alternately staring at the ceiling or out through the open door. Allison bent down and pushed the cloth overnight bag under the iron bed. When she straightened up she noticed her mother restlessly fondling the cloth on her coat.

"I'm fine. It's all right if you have to leave. I know Daddy has a lot to do at the office and I'll be all right here." Allison watched the erratic ballet of these two people with concern. The purposeless shifting of her father's body and her mother's unaccustomed concentration on Allison's immediate house-keeping gave the scene a fictional aura. What was familiar to Allison was the sight of them leaving to go anywhere, bags packed standing in the hallway, a strange figure tightly holding her younger brother's hand and encouraging him not to cry, and Allison throwing the departing pair an offhand kiss as they breezed out of the apartment. When he was younger, her brother would weep despite the entreaties of the foreigner staying in their house. Later as he grew, he would whimper angrily; but in the last few years, he had stood stoically shout-

41

ing the list of items he expected to be brought him at the end of their trip. Her parents came and went in her life as relatives might who lived nearby but not within.

Now her mother said, "Well, Allison, we really do have to go. Your father has an appointment and I have several things that must be done. We'll be in to see you every day, dear, so save up all your stories for us." Her mother was slipping her coat on her shoulders, talking rapidly, hoping to cut away any recriminations from the child and any guilt from themselves. She walked over to the bed, placed her smooth, cool lips against Allison's cheek. Allison's father grinned foolishly and patted her on her shoulder. Finally he stood still and stared at the child.

"Just think of this as if you were going on a holiday this time and not us. Like it's your turn."

Allison stared at the man standing uncomfortably in front of her bed, not knowing what else to say to the girl in the unspoken silence that followed. The girl reached over and grasped his hand.

"I'll be fine. Go ahead. You'll be late." The two people paused momentarily and then turned and hurried out of the hospital room.

Allison focused her attention on the bed across the room from where she was sitting. She became aware that its occupant was watching every move that she made. The girl's deep, vivid eyes seemed to occupy most of her thin face. Allison pushed herself toward the bottom of her bed and leaned over the railing.

"Hi, my name is Allison. What's yours?"

There was a pause, not long, but long enough for Allison to become aware that her roommate was deciding whether to enter into a conversation, wondering whether to risk the dangers of becoming a friend. The moment passed and a reedy voice said,

"Regina . . . everybody calls me Reggie around here."

"Do you like being called Reggie?"

"Yeah, it's all right. I've been here so much and so long, it's really become my name."

"Do you like it here?"

"Oh, it's all right. They treat you pretty good, but they hurt you sometimes."

Allison paused and hugged her shoulders at the thought. "Do you think they're going to hurt me?"

"Dunno. Maybe. Whatcha got?"

Allison shrugged. "I don't know. I had a nosebleed last week and it was so bad I had to see the doctor and they put me in here." Allison decided that she wanted to see her roommate more closely; she slipped down off the elevated bed which was higher than she was accustomed to, and padded over to the other bed. She realized that she might have some trouble climbing onto it without disturbing the girl, so she pulled the stool over, stood on it and lifted herself up. She had taken her roommate by surprise. The girl had not expected this immediate contact and had pushed herself a little further back into the many pillows that propped her head up so that the wan face was almost lost in the billowing folds around her.

"You have a swell bunch of books," said Allison. "Can I borrow some if I want?"

"My uncle brought them to me. Sure, you can read them. I've read most of them twice."

"Golly, twice. How long have you been here?"

The small mouth curled in thought. "I'm not too sure but I think this time I've been in here three months."

Allison took a deep breath. "Three months, Wow. You must really know how to get around this place and what to do."

"I do."

Allison's voice was exceptionally bright. "Well, maybe you can help me and tell me what to expect and what I should do and how I should act."

Allison could see her new friend sit up a little in the bed and

43

look at her with a smile slowly beginning to crease the corners of her mouth. "Sure, I can do that. I know all about this place."

"Why have you been here so long?"

Reggie closed her eyes and spoke in a very low voice. "Well, I was born with this thing on my back and I've had a lot of operations. And they help me some but I still got a coupla big problems."

Allison stared at the girl and persisted. "Like what?"

The answer was clear and challenging. "I can't walk." At this point Reggie reached down and lifted the cover on the opposite side of the bed and pulled it over to show Allison her right leg. Allison had never seen a leg that looked like this one did. It was excruciatingly thin, the bones were outlined and protruding. A pillow was propped under the withered calf. Allison gazed at it for a moment and then turned back to look at her friend.

"That's something."

"It's pretty ugly, don't you think?"

Reggie looked carefully at Allison to see what her response would be. Allison knew that she was being evaluated, an evaluation unlike those she experienced at school or at home. She knew that her remark might make a difference between the two of them and was uneasy—she didn't really know quite what to say. Finally she said,

"You know, I've seen all kinds of funny legs around—some fat, some thin, and most of them on people I really like, so it doesn't make any difference to me." Allison experienced a lessening of tension. The strained moment was over. Something softer, more comfortable, remained.

"The only trouble with those legs is that I can't walk on them. Can't get around."

Allison grabbed the other girl's hand briefly. "Tell you what let's do. You do me a favor. You tell me exactly how to act and

44

what to do around here so I don't get hurt so much and so everybody likes me like they do you."

"Okay, that's easy. It's a deal, but what are you going to do for me?"

"I'm going to walk for you. I'm going to go where you want me to go and get what you want me to get."

The other girl smiled and pushed herself upward from the pillows in the bed, leaning toward Allison. "It's a deal." The two girls shook hands very soberly as if their ultimate survival depended on the pact they were making.

"Another thing bothers me," Allison said, "bothers me a lot. What do you do before you go to bed at night? Do you worry?"

"Some nights I cry."

"I was worried about that. I thought I might cry, too." Allison lied. She had been certain that she wouldn't cry. But she suspected that when night arrived she might become frightened. "Reggie, I've got an idea."

"What?" The voice was guarded.

"Every night before we go to bed you and I are going to say something we think is funny and we're going to laugh out loud. That way we won't be frightened, we'll hear each other laughing and we'll go to bed without being afraid."

"Do you think it will really work?"

Allison nodded vigorously. "I think so. Tell you what let's do, let's practice."

"Practice?" The head moved backward.

"Let's try now. Let's just look at each other and start to laugh and see how we feel." Allison began looking at Reggie, trying to think of something funny and after a minute she began to giggle. Soon they were both laughing, and the cheerful noise billowed out from the bed, filled the room, and escaped through the open door.

They were laughing so intently that they didn't notice Sandy's blonde head as it poked through the doorway quizzically perusing the scene—one child perched precariously on the end of the long, high bed, the other child propped up on two pillows, their hands clinging, eyes lit up, heads thrown back, both giggling happily. Not knowing why, Sandy began to smile to herself as she turned from the door, and moved back into the hall in time to greet a rapidly moving stretcher.

VI

Ed had decided not to go to his room to attempt sleep. He lingered in the Treatment Room, carefully washing his hands at the sink and splashing cold water over his face. A nurse came in and began efficiently tidying the disarray. She was conscious of Ed standing silently staring at her.

"You all look like you were busy while I was gone." Her statement was pleasant and inquiring. Ed didn't respond. The Negro woman stopped her concentrated housekeeping. "Can I help you, Dr. Erikson?"

Ed blinked and looked around for a bewildered moment and then smiled wanly. "No, I don't think so. Thanks. I'm just a little tired." He paused, collecting his thoughts. "Did you see where the parents of the new child went with Dr. Greenberg?"

She nodded. "Yes, I think so. All the rooms were crowded so he took them to the conference room. He must have just left because he waited so Sandy could give the mother some phenobarb. She was crying so hard, poor soul. I don't suspect he can still do too much talking to her."

Ed grunted his appreciation for the information and walked down the hall to the conference room.

Todd was bent over a long sheet of paper writing while the two parents sat huddled uncomfortably in chairs with large, confining writing arms. As Ed moved into the room he was struck by the terror in the woman's face. Her skin was pale, her hair was pushed back and tangled, her hands were visibly trembling, one resting uneasily on a crumpled handkerchief. The man was short, stocky, and balding. His chair was turned around halfway so that he seemed removed from the other two people in the room; and he was staring blankly out of the closed, streaked window.

Ed slipped into one of the chairs and listened, taking short notes to use in his history. Todd's rapid-fire questioning continued, and the tentative, halting responses returned mixed with threads of grief. Once Ed wanted to turn to Todd and suggest that they stop and let these people suffer in peace. But he said nothing and the questions continued.

Finally Todd was done. There was a long, tense silence in the room as no one got up to move. The father slowly turned in his chair and stared at Todd, glanced quickly at Ed and then back at Todd again.

"Is he going to live, Doc?"

There was a pause while Todd looked over at Ed. The two young men in their wrinkled white uniforms sat quietly, one looking at his hands, the other moistening his lips. The man spoke again.

"Is he going to live?"

As each second passed without any answer from the two suddenly hesitant doctors, the man and woman appeared to sink more deeply into their chairs. Their bodies lost some of their firmness and they gradually settled into the wooden slats as if their bony skeletons were slowly dissolving into the fluid silence. For the first time since entering the room, Ed noticed that these were not young people. He recalled the small size of the child. These were not the parents he would have anticipated meeting.

At that moment the child's father leaned over slightly, reached out his left hand and placed it over the woman's. He simply allowed it to rest there. The woman looked at her husband. Her face did not change expression but there seemed to be some relaxation of her trembling, a diminution of her terror.

"We can't be sure," said Todd at last. "We really can't be sure if he is going to live or not." A pause. "But we promise we'll do everything we can."

The child's parents were the first to move. The father stood up slowly, shook himself as if trying to remove something unpleasant from his skin, and calmly helped his wife to rise. She stood up slowly, leaning on him. They smiled hesitantly at the doctors still sitting in their chairs and the wife whispered a thank-you so silently that they could only be aware of what she was saying by looking at her lips. The couple seemed to fade out of the room.

Todd shook his head slowly. "Every Goddamn time I have to go through this, it's a real bitch. Sometimes I wonder if it's ever going to get any easier." His intense, swarthy face had lost the usual excited readiness.

"Christ, if it's still that hard for you . . ."

"It is." Quiet, almost ashamed.

"Damn, I can't face this with each tough case."

"I guess it's a matter of your makeup. This part doesn't move some guys an inch; they say a word or two, give a pat on the back and keep right on moving. Me, I'm a schmuck. . . . I've got to suffer with everybody." Todd rose, his resilience dampened.

Ed glanced at his watch and realized that it was time to go to the Emergency Room to check on any new admissions. In the corridor downstairs he passed the procession of stretchers laden with sprawled bodies. The sounds of suffering blended with the noises of equipment and staccato talking to create the unnatural din that so typified the Emergency Room. Groups of people were waiting in line to see the women seated behind the counters taking down names and addresses, insurance numbers, and complaints. The line moved very slowly as each

49

person finally waited through each of the three copies of each notation and the clerks' frequent pauses and repeated absences. Some of the people leaned against the wall, some rested against a companion, others stood slumped over looking at the floor. None seemed to notice the intermittent frenzied activity as stretchers pushed rapidly past them into the surgical emergency area. The patients would part to let the moving bed slide quickly past and then silently move together again.

Ed noted a tall black man standing straight upright in the middle of the crowd. He's crying, Ed thought. He kept his attention focused on the glistening dark face. The expression did not change, the lips did not move, the chin was firm. But as Ed watched he saw tears running down the man's cheeks. As the lines shuffled forward and reestablished their spaces, Ed glimpsed the man in his entirety. He was supporting his right arm firmly with his left, holding it level and close to his body. Ed moved a little closer. The twisted shape of the arm and its frail appearance became obvious. The man was standing in line with a broken arm, crying, moving quietly ahead, waiting his turn.

Ed insinuated himself between several of the people who grumbled until they looked up and recognized the white uniform. He approached the tall man and motioned him over toward the wall. The man looked around him unsure why he had been singled out. He pointed to his spot in line and Ed had to reassure him that he would not lose his place, before the man would move. Then just as the man was within several feet of Ed, a young nurse came rapidly through the swinging doors looking over her shoulder and calling out to someone behind her. Ed could see that she was going to collide with the man. He started to call out, but she came on too quickly to stop and struck the man, her shoulder at the level of his cradled arm. His lips parted but no sound emerged. He stood transfixed in pain.

"Goddamn it, watch out," Ed shouted at the nurse.

"Jesus, I didn't see him. Why isn't he standing over there in line?" She turned her face toward Ed, her expression changing from surprise to anger. She was holding two packages containing disposable syringes in one hand and a long rubber tube Ed recognized as a tourniquet in the other. Ed could see her knuckles whiten briefly.

"I called him over. Next time don't come barreling out of those doors without looking." Ed was rather surprised at his anger. He knew how hard the girl worked, how harassed she was, how important she was to him and to this man standing between them, but he still felt a need to berate her, as if in apology to the black man for a system that made him stand in line with a broken arm.

"Yes, sir." She spit the words out and turned quickly toward the injured man. Then she too could see the pain and the limp arm. She glanced up quickly at his face and could see the agony tightening the lines around the gleaming eyes.

"Forgive me. It was an accident." Her tone had changed. For a moment she stood there not knowing what to do. She hesitated and then leaned over and simply patted the man gently on the shoulder, and walked away.

"Come with me." Ed led the way toward the back of the cubicle and together they walked into the interviewing room. One of the ladies looked up quizzically as she saw the two intruders enter the sanctuary of typewriters, coffee cups, and detachment.

"I'm taking this man to Orthopedics. His arm is broken and he's in a lot of pain. One of you'll have to come back and get the information after we have made him comfortable."

For a moment the woman was about to argue. She turned toward her neighbor who looked quickly away, refusing to get involved. The woman smoothed the flowered print that hung over her ample, girdled abdomen and looked up at Ed. He stared at her, his jaw set.

"I said I'm taking him back. Are you coming later to get the information?"

The woman nodded. Ed eased the man out of the waiting room and delivered him to the Orthopedic resident who had several people lined up waiting for the results of their x-rays. The Orthopedist glanced at the broken arm, spoke a few words to the man in a low voice, reassuring him, and sent him off to x-ray. Ed started to walk away. He was stopped by the sound of an unfamiliar voice, deep, rich, and resonant.

"Thank you, Doc."

Ed turned and smiled. The tall man smiled back and Ed realized that he had not heard the man's voice before that moment despite their involvement. And he knew that although he would probably not hear his voice again, they would probably remember each other for a very long time.

As Ed returned to the Pediatric area of the Emergency Room, he was greeted by the loud screams of a child. He walked quickly over and entered the area casually separated from the general trauma and death by a flimsy curtain. A light-skinned Negro boy was writhing on one of the tables, shouting uncontrollably. His arm was taped down and the all too familiar tubing was attached to a vein. A brief glance suggested to Ed that the boy was about nine or ten years old. His mother stood at the head of the bed, wringing her hands in anxiety as she looked helplessly around for some means to satisfy her child's need without harming him. She caught sight of Ed standing in the doorway and he could detect her eyebrows lift as if asking him if he had come at her unspoken request.

The boy stopped shouting and it was then that Ed could see why he had been hospitalized. His breathing was labored with the audible wheezing that marks the asthmatic as decidedly as needle punctures brand the addict. The spaces between his ribs sucked in desperately as he attempted each breath and the notch above his sternum stayed sunken during each phase of his measured respirations. His face was punctuated by his wide eyes which shone with the too obvious white sclera of fear. After a few moments during which his terrified eyes moved fleetingly over the equipment around him and tubing leading into him, he opened his mouth as wide as his state of suffocation would allow and let out a piercing scream followed by another and then another. His mother jumped imperceptibly with the first scream and continued to stir restlessly as the violent noise continued as before.

At that moment, the nurse whom Ed had confronted in the hallway walked briskly into the room. She picked up a white pledget and vigorously rubbed the taped arm of the youngster. The boy didn't seem to feel anything since Ed could detect no change in the rhythm of his outburst. She then inspected a loaded syringe, holding it upright in the overhead illumination and proceeded to insert it into his arm and inject the contents quickly and steadily. The boy's mother averted her head slightly during this act looking toward Ed standing quietly in the curtained opening while the boy stopped his hollering and stared at the white face of the nurse with an expression of surprise which quickly changed to hate.

"Bitch." His gasp was barely audible.

"Donald, please." His mother stared down at him and the hoarse sound of her voice was more of a soft wail than a whisper. "I'm sorry. He gets so scared. After it's over, he tells me he thinks he's going to die each time."

The nurse nodded, not giving or transmitting more than an acknowledgment of speech. She checked the bottle hanging over the boy's bed noting the fluid level on a chart and counted the boy's breathing as she spoke. "I just gave him something to quiet him down. Dr. Thomas said to tell you he will be here in a minute. He said he's sorry he has been so busy with that other baby but it's sick too."

The mother smiled with false acceptance and nodded. She had been here before with the boy. She knew the routine—the shots, the waiting, the continued wheezing, the anxious dilated eyes, more shots, the fluid bottles and eventually the quieter breathing, the boy's sleep, her relief, her sleep, and the waiting for the next time—the continuous, numbing waiting for the next long night. But this time the child's panic had frightened her. She had never seen him so afraid, so violent. Despite what they told her, she felt instinctively that he was sicker than usual and maybe he knew something about what was happening inside his chest that none of these outsiders were aware of. And so she too had a feeling of panic.

Just then the tall broad figure of Lem Thomas moved smoothly into the room. The contrast of the dark face against the white uniform stood out in sharp relief under the glaring lights surrounding the boy's bed. His black hair was cut close to the skull and contrasted strikingly with the bushy black eyebrows and pencil thin black mustache. The deep brown of his face was lined with fatigue and there were black circles under his eyes. He placed his large bony hand on the woman's shoulder as he looked down at the boy. He spoke in a voice unexpectedly gentle, considering the giant size of the man from which it came.

"Don't worry, sister. He's just afraid. The medicine's gonna work soon."

"Dear God, I hope so." She stood quietly, seeming to rest more easily with the firm hand on her shoulder.

The boy continued to cry out and thrash around on the bed. The big man watched him for a while and then lowered his body so that he was resting on one knee. He leaned over the edge of the bed, his big frame obscuring the boy from Ed's view. The cries slowed and diminished.

"Man, I'm here. Look, man, take it slow. I promise you're going to make it. You ain't gonna die, man. I won't let you. Look at me. Look at me, I said." Suddenly there was a complete cessation of noise. The room seemed dangerously quiet.

The only sound was the high sibilant wheezes that rose from behind the huge kneeling figure in front of the bed.

"I'm not kiddin'. You gotta sleep. You're gonna wake up fine." The voice continued in the now otherwise silent room. The mother stood swaying in the bright light, staring down at the man talking to her child.

Suddenly Ed saw a small arm rise from behind the shoulder of the kneeling doctor, reach around him, and clasp the big man tightly. The coffee-colored fingers attached themselves to the white coat and hung. The still audible breathing slowed; the sibilant noises diminished. The black man remained fixed in his position as did the mother. The drops cascading down from the overhead bottle into the cone-shaped container and tubing seemed to be the only active participants in the tableaux. The muted voice continued droning on, cajoling, reassuring. Time passed slowly, lulled into passive movement as the monotonous soft voice talked to the now quiet child. Then a large, darker hand reached back and slowly removed the fingers one by one from the wrinkled coat. As the boy's hand slipped back, the massive frame slowly unwound itself and delicately rose from its kneeling position.

At that moment Lem noticed Ed standing in the doorway. He raised his finger to his lips in a gesture of silence and pointed toward the table. The boy was asleep. His mother pulled a chair to the edge of the bed and sat down, the tilt of her back suggesting a combination of relief and exhaustion.

Lem looked directly into Ed's eyes and his features changed completely into a smile which commandeered his whole face. Lem never smiled or laughed partially. Everything he did was total. His laughter was loud, ricocheting off all those around him, tickling them, forcing them at the least to smile but more often to join him. His scorn was also terrible. Ed remembered the time that Lem discovered that a student had poured a urine specimen down the laboratory sink and had reported a

55

negative result on the sheet. Lem had been suspicious of the results because they disagreed violently from what he would have expected from his clinical findings, so he did another himself. Afterward he marched down the hall from the laboratory and stormed into the nurse's station where the student was sitting, chatting and laughing with a classmate and Lem had thrust the sheet in front of the boy's face and had pointed to his own results. The boy had stood up quickly, immediately aware that Lem knew what he had done. Lem had taken one tentative step toward the student who retreated quickly into the corner of the small area where he stood tensely waiting. Lem had stared at him, not speaking, not moving, just staring —a look of such fierce disdain that the student didn't blink or turn away. A crowd gathered. Finally Lem had thrown down the sheet on the table and spit out:

"Get your ass off this ward and don't come back. I don't give a damn where you go to learn Pediatrics but get off my ward." He had moved his massive body to one side and allowed the youth to slide carefully past him, pick up his new equipment, and move out of sight. No one tried to get Lem to reconsider. Lem never reconsidered. He reached decisions slowly but totally, and he rarely looked back. Because of his decisions, it was natural that he made enemies. There were teachers in the medical school who could not accept his total approach to life; that combined with several instructors' instinctive intolerance toward his color had made his four years of school, ones of precarious continuity. He had polarized the faculty but had had the good fortune of having some younger members recognize his unusual talents. One of the reasons he had gone into Pediatrics was because the professor under whom he now worked was one of these perceptive young men.

Both Ed and Lem looked toward the sleeping boy.

"He finally responded. Did you hear him hollering upstairs?"

Ed smiled, shook his head in affirmation and asked, "Do

56

you have any more gems down here like that kid with meningitis Cliff sent up this morning?"

"So you came down to spy." Lem chuckled. "That was a sick kid. How's he doing?"

"Still alive. No change at last check."

"Let me know how he does. His folks were real people, shook up awful. It sure can get shitty down here." Lem's voice took on a hard edge.

"Okay. You're gonna talk serious, I'm leavin'."

Lem laughed and grabbed him by the shoulder and squeezed. Ed winced. Lem didn't seem to realize his strength and Ed had become accustomed to occasional bruises. Lem's wife, Althea, had playfully warned Ed last week at dinner that the friendlier he got with Lem, the more dangerous it might be for him. Ed smiled as he recalled Althea telling him of the time that Lem had squeezed her father's hand at their wedding and had broken two of his fingers. He could still hear her gasping laughter as she leaned over the strawberry shortcake and barely missed it, "The old man didn't tell us until we came back from Niagara. He went through the whole wedding reception afraid that the rest of the guests would find out. From then on, he kept about ten feet from Lem and kept asking me if I felt all right." Through all of this Lem had sat staring sheepishly at the plastic tablecloth with the pressed flowers. It was only when Ed and Althea noted the absence of his usual booming laugh that they became aware of the extent of his embarrassment.

"My God, honey, I didn't know you were ashamed of that." Althea probed directly into Lem as no one else dared for it was only with Althea that Lem tried to modify his reactions. She seemed an extension of his personality that permitted a softening of intent, widening of tolerance.

"I am." Lem said nothing more. Nor did Althea need more to be said. She had stood up, the laughter finished and firmly directed both men out of her kitchen into the living room so she could do the dishes and muse in private at the never-ending unknown threads that made up the tapestry of the big man that she had married.

Ed rubbed his shoulder quickly, looked at the dusty curtains hanging limply around the Pediatric area and started toward the elevator.

"How about coming over for dinner this Saturday?" Lem called after him. Ed quickly noted that Lem had taken for granted that he would be available. He hadn't questioned whether Ed had a date that night; he had simply asked him over. There was the silent knowledge that Ed did not go out often, rarely on dates. No one asked for explanations. It was accepted without comment.

"I'd love to come," he called back over his shoulder. "When are you going to let me pay you back?"

"The day after you get married, we'll be over," Lem shouted back.

Ed didn't answer, but as he pressed the button marked "Up" he gave such a painful sigh that the elderly lady carrying the sheets of Accident Room charges looked over at him concerned that something was wrong. He caught her glance and burrowed into the back of the elevator as it rose, afraid that she had seen what he had been thinking.

Later that afternoon, as he lowered himself fatigued to the point of numbness onto the creaking bedsprings, the phone rang and sent Ed hurrying to the delivery room. There, cradled in the small warming bed, lay a gasping infant, tiny, premature, pale with blue feet and hands, struggling as if begging for help to pull the oxygen into itself.

"Glad to see you, Erikson," said the man hunched over the delivery room table in a strained voice. "Baby's probably about seven months at best. Spontaneous labor. No known complications. Not much prenatal care."

Ed grunted and began the ritual designed to prolong the infant's life—the resuscitation, fluids, suctioning, artificial breathing, stimulants, antibiotics, looking at the clock, trying oxygen a second time, watching the lungs expand more fully, counting the pulse, suctioning more mucous, recording the change in color from blue to pink, listening, waiting, hearing the feeble cry, counting the now even respirations. Then came the process of moving the baby downstairs to the nursery, waiting, watching for complications, writing orders, noting the return of breathing problems, more ordering and more watching. Finally, several hours later, he was ready to see the child's mother.

As he entered the room, the girl was lying facing the wall opposite the door. She did not stir and Ed wondered if she was awake. He coughed and waited. Slowly the girl's head turned toward him. Her face was small and heart-shaped with large round eyes, so big that the whites of the sclera framed the flecked green of her pupils. Her brown hair was loosely plaited into a single braid, tightly tied at the bottom with wool yarn of several different colors. Her hairline glistened with perspiration. She seemed to sense Ed's discomfort and smiled weakly at him.

"Hello."

Ed's voice was shaky, wary of her reaction to his news about her child.

"Mrs. Yarborough?"

Her voice from the inner recesses of the pillow blended hurt and fear.

"Miss Yarborough."

Ed swallowed and started again.

"Miss Yarborough. I'm the baby's doctor . . . one of the people that has been working on your baby since he was born several hours ago."

"Has my baby died yet? It came so early. I tried to hold it in but it wouldn't stay." She started to cry, turning her face into the pillow. She sobbed pitifully like a child. Ed stood, miserably shifting his feet in the doorway of the room, wanting to touch her but afraid of moving at that moment. He waited until she had stopped crying and was lying with her face turned toward him.

"No. The baby is still alive. He only weighs two pounds and he's starting to have serious trouble breathing. We call it hyaline membrane disease. He's very small, Miss Yarborough. I'm sorry but his chances are only fair at best."

There was a pause. The young girl sighed and raised her head slightly.

"Please come closer so I can see you. You're standing in the shadow. Please let me see you."

Ed moved further into the room.

"Sit here." The girl patted the sheet.

Ed sat uncomfortably on the edge of her bed.

"Would you just stay with me for a little while? You don't have to talk or do anything. Just sit with me like you belong."

Ed didn't move. He sat gazing at the small girl whose face had eased into unlined tranquility and whose eyelids were fluttering closed. Her hands that had been clutching tightly onto the sheets unfolded into open, still fingers. Ed felt himself sagging into sleep. Suddenly her small, frightened voice aroused him and he jumped slightly.

"Please help me. I don't know what to do. I tried not to think about making decisions yet. I thought I had so much time. But the baby's here. And it might live . . . and I want it to live . . . but I don't know what to do." The words rushed out, tumbling over each other in breathless sequence.

"I don't understand." Ed frowned, studying the tear-streaked face.

"When I found out I was pregnant, or knew I was, anyway, I was happy. I wanted a baby, something to love and to love me back. . . . To have done something right for once . . . to have finally seen something through to the end. But at the same time, I also knew that I can't take care of the baby, not yet, anyway. I live alone. I go to school here." She took a deep breath. "And I won't go back to Chicago and let my mother destroy this baby like she did me." Her last words contained a bitterness that was in sharp contrast to the gentle inexperience of her face.

Ed cleared his throat and waited a few seconds. A feeling of helplessness overwhelmed him.

"May I send our social worker in to see you?" he said at last. "She'll have better answers for you than I have. Meanwhile, I'm going to work with the baby. He's my responsibility." Ed paused. The room was still. Finally the girl sat up so that he could see her full face. My God, she's so young, he thought, and so pretty.

"Send someone . . . please . . . and soon . . . I feel so lost all of a sudden. Why do I feel like I'm being punished for something I couldn't help? Do you think I am?"

Ed shook his head slowly, watching her, and felt a sudden overwhelming attraction for this girl. He wanted to hold her quietly in his arms and calm her down, cradle her, reassure her. He quickly slipped off the edge of the bed and turned to leave. Her voice stopped him.

"Do you have to go?"

He swallowed hard and nodded.

"You're very sweet." He looked down at the floor. She continued softly, "He needs a father. Do a good job."

She turned away from him and started crying softly, her voice encircling him and lingering in his memory long after he had slipped out of the hospital room.

VII

MIKE put down the phone wondering what to do next. He had phoned Allison's private doctor who wouldn't be in for an hour or more; and he had contacted the lab technician to do the blood tests but she was at lunch. Now he leaned against the firm rim of the desk, his feet stretched out in front of him and rested there. He amused himself briefly by pushing up on his heels and sliding dangerously backward. He caught himself just short of falling over.

Shaking off his mood, he went to look in on his most recent patient. Her bed was empty; books and toys were strewn over the covers, many with the wrappings still intact. He shifted his gaze and saw the two girls sprawled over the other bed, giggling and coloring on pieces of large tinted paper. Allison was holding up her sheet and pointing to the figure in the center.

"Allison, that's silly," Reggie squealed.

"No, it's not. That's what I'm going to look like."

"When, Allison, when?"

"When I'm grownup. See all those bumps, I'll have all those bumps."

Mike cleared his throat to be recognized, but they were laughing too hard to hear him. He waited a minute, then called out, "Hey, isn't anybody going to let me in on the joke?"

63

Allison looked up quickly and continued smiling. She picked up the paper and showed him a grotesque human caricature. The breasts hung crazily around the navel while the eyes and lips were so darkened and overdrawn that they occupied at least one third of the bizarre figure.

"Boy, she's pretty." Mike looked quizzically at the figure.

"Is she sexy?" Allison croaked out the last word, causing him suddenly to explode with his own laughter.

"Sexy? She's the sexiest lady I know except for you two girls."

The two girls looked at each other, obviously pleased. They remained this way waiting for Mike to continue. But he was watching the slim, graceful body that Allison took for granted but which he knew was in serious danger. The room remained still. The girls suddenly became quiet as if they realized that Mike was there for reasons other than to see Allison's drawings.

"Just came in to see if everything's okay." It sounded foolish. He wasn't sure why he had come into the room. He picked up the paper lying on the bed and looked at it seriously again making a face and whistling softly.

"Sure is sexy." He smiled at the two girls who sat looking at his face with blank expressions. Allison seemed to sense his discomfort. "If you'll help me down, I'll walk you to the door."

Mike stared for a minute. "You don't have to do that."

"But I want to."

Very gently, as if holding a piece of delicate crystal, he lifted her to the floor. She wedged her feet into slippers and as they walked toward the door he felt a warm, small hand insinuate itself into his open palm.

"Thank you for coming in to see if I was all right." Her expression didn't change, still serious and gentle. "From the first time I saw you today, I liked you, too."

All Mike could manage was a vigorous shake of his head and a soft, "Right, see you later."

"Hello, Mike."

A rippling female voice startled him as he was stepping into the elevator. A short, dark, attractive nurse looked up, smiling at him. He felt the air in the elevator tingle with the electricity of her message. He knew the signal; he had received it before from her and had responded. Remembering the nights at her apartment, he quickly undressed her and mentally repeated their previous sexual contact. His hands began sweating and he unconsciously moistened his lips.

"Hi, Marion. How've you been?"

"Great. Long time no see, Mike. I've missed you."

"I'll call you, Marion. You look great, as usual."

She chuckled in a low voice, catching his meaning. She glided off the elevator, her small hips thrusting backward toward him as she clicked across the floor. He made a mental note to call her soon. She was a great lay. No brains, but a great lay. No recriminations, no demands. All she wanted was his body and all he wanted was hers. He wasn't sure whether she even liked him. He knew damn well he barely liked her. But that never mattered to Mike. The minute after his body had satisfied its pent-up hunger he felt nothing, only emptiness. He tried to tell himself now that it didn't matter. What the hell. He had no trouble finding partners, so that those that seemed to expect too much of him were easy to eliminate. Don't eliminate Marion, he mused. She just wants that moment in bed. Nothing more.

The elevator deposited him in front of the mailboxes in the basement. He pulled out the voluminous colored brochures wondering how much money he was discarding into the large gray wastecan. He knew the mail slots were all stuffed with these brochures and so was the trashcan as he lifted the lid.

As he deposited the last one into the wastecan, he realized that his hands were empty. There were no letters. He experienced that same inner sense of disappointment that recurred each time he realized he had received no communication from his family. And yet this happened every day of his life. Why couldn't he accept the reality? There were no letters from his family, there would not be any, there had not been any for weeks, for months, he was certain, for years.

Mike knew that life was made up of moments of contact, only moments, no more; and that all the time in between must be periods of waiting, periods of preparation, of getting ready so that those moments of contact wouldn't be lost. Even these momentary contacts had dissolved, with his family, he feared, with everyone. But first with his family. . . . When had it begun? How long ago? As he stood in the basement of the hospital with the dull walls illuminated by dim lights and the floors echoing the sounds of activity from the nearby Emergency Room, he remembered the small Illinois hospital where he had first heard those now familiar sounds as a boy of ten.

He had fallen off his bike. Everything at that time had revolved around his bike. He could picture the tall, blond, tearful boy being rushed into the hospital, bleeding, frightened, and as the fear and pain ebbed a fascination with the hospital scenes took its place. He had looked on as families fought, women fainted, and fathers died, and he had never forgotten —the fascination still motivated him. He had waited for his own parents to come and comfort him. Mike took a deep breath in the silence of the hospital basement as he remembered his father walking down the long hall in the gray basement of that Illinois hospital, looking at him as he lay on the stretcher, and shaking his head as his voice boomed out over the entire room.

"You and that Goddamn bike. I knew you'd both end up broken one day."

"I'm sorry, Dad." Mike remembered hating having to be sorry that he was lying there with a broken leg. He wanted to be consoled, to see his father's elderly face soften with concern. It had remained impassive and the boy had repeated several times that he was sorry as the older man lowered himself into a chair next to the stretcher and began to drum his fingers on the side of the metal casing waiting for the night to pass and his son to be declared well enough to take home. They sat not speaking throughout the long night, Mike huddled in the corner of the bed trying to involve himself in the hospital scenes being played out around him.

His father still lived unemotionally accepting the very infrequent attentions Mike would offer. His mother had eased so imperceptibly into old age that he had difficulty remembering the year of her birth when filling out a recent form on his own life. She existed only to serve his father and now was simply less agile at running her husband's errands. Mike had once screamed at her, "Don't you give a damn about what I am or what I'm doing or about me?" She stopped folding the weekly laundry and looked up at Mike towering over her with his hands clenched and his face contorted so that he wouldn't cry. After a moment she had risen from the worn sofa on which she had been sitting, stood up to her full height which was barely up to Mike's shoulder, and struck him hard across the mouth. "That's how much I care, Mike. Almost as much as that." He had been stunned. That was the first real physical contact that they had had for months. His face stung from the force of her blow. She returned to her sofa and quietly resumed folding the clothes. "Now what is it that you are wanting?" she asked. What Mike had wanted had been minor, insignificant. What he had needed he had received. A pause hung uncomfortably in the room. Finally he cleared his throat. "Nothing. But thanks for the crack across the mouth. It's better than nothing." She had looked up with an expression of pain in her eyes that he had never seen before. He remembered feeling elation.

Mike's face stung as he relived the moment, the moment of rending, of tearing away from these old people who, even then, had irrevocably imprinted on their lined faces their early years together in the fields of their first farm. They had moved into the nearest big city years before Mike was born; several years

67

after that his two older sisters had married and moved away. His parents had talked little when they were young together and seemed to have exhausted their sparse words during the years before Mike knew them. He had often wondered how long he would retain the sound of their voices after they were gone. He knew they would leave no echoes.

Mike glanced down at his empty hands, shrugged his shoulders sadly, and moved toward the elevator doors.

As he rode upstairs he thought about Allison, smiling as he remembered the way she had walked him to the door, as if she were showing him graciously out of her home. He began to worry that he might not be able to do the bone marrow satisfactorily. As he pictured the child's face contorted with pain, he felt a strange tingling in his skin. Maybe I should ask Ed to do this marrow, he thought. Shit, what's the matter with me? How many chances am I going to have to do this procedure? But he couldn't get the image of that lovely blonde face screwed up in agony out of his mind. When he reached the Treatment Room the nurse took one look at him and said,

"You sick?"

"Why?"

"You're pale as a ghost."

"No. Probably something I didn't get to eat."

"That's a good one. Me, too. I'm always starved to death. Can't you tell just by looking at me?" She chuckled good-naturedly at her considerable overweight. "What are you looking for?" She slipped quickly around the treatment table, moving with a speed and lightness so often seen and found surprising in heavy people.

"Bone marrow tray." She nodded and brought out a towel covered metal tray and some gloves from which Mike selected the right size.

"Thanks. That's it." Mike picked up the equipment, bottles of antiseptic solution and gauze, and smiled as the nurse called after him, "Don't forget to eat."

Allison was sitting in the bed comfortably resting on two pillows which were propped up behind her. She was staring intently at an open book, her forehead wrinkled, her eyes filled with tears. He quietly called her name so as not to frighten her. She looked up slowly and smiled. He had the uneasy feeling that she had been waiting for him. He placed the metal tray on the bed and the paper envelope with the sterile gloves inside on the ledge above the sink. Her voice reached out to him.

"Have you ever read *The Wind in the Willows?*"

Mike stood still, watching the hot water run in rivulets over his hands, beginning to feel the heat as it increased.

"No. I've never read that one."

"You should. It's so beautiful, it makes you cry."

"Why is that so good?"

"What?" Her voice sounded surprised and he could feel her eyes driving into his back as he carefully put on the sterile rubber gloves. As he pulled them over his fingers, he turned just enough to catch the wondering look on her tilted face.

"Why is it good to feel like crying?"

"Crying because something's beautiful is different from crying because something hurts."

Here it comes, Mike thought. She is going to ask me what I have to do. He steeled himself, knowing the pain of anticipation can far exceed the pain of the procedure. His gloves on, he began pouring the cleansing solution onto the raw cotton.

Allison regarded him and leaned forward. "Do you ever cry because you're happy or someone else has made you happy?"

Mike automatically shook his head, no, without pausing to think, knowing instinctively that she would detect a lie. "No, I don't."

"I'm sorry." She said this soberly and kindly staring at his face and not his hands which held the dripping raw cotton.

"I am too," Mike answered honestly. They stood sharing

69

this moment of revelation, refusing to avert their eyes at Mike's inner exposure. Mike cleared his throat.

"Please take off your top, Allison. I have to clean you up and then perform a test on you."

"With a needle?"

"Yes, a needle. It looks worse than it is. I'll put something there to keep it from hurting too much."

"You won't hurt me. I know that. Please don't worry about hurting me."

Mike felt his hand tremble slightly as she spoke. She signaled him to pull the curtains around the bed, shielding herself with the front of her robe until they were closed. Then she modestly, and with eyes averted, dropped her robe, her pajama top hanging open revealing a child's chest with the flat small nipples and smooth pale skin. There was a moderate bluish-yellow bruise over the left ribcage near the armpit which stood out glaringly in contrast to the creamy skin around it. Allison noticed Mike looking at the bruise and her eyes slipped to the mark, regarding it with somewhat wry amusement.

"That's what everyone got so excited about. That's why I'm here. That one and a bunch more on my leg." She looked carefully at him. Then she shook her head as he stood quietly not answering. "Oh, I forgot, you saw all of me before in that other room." She lowered her pajama pants at his signal.

He nodded and motioned her to lie down. He lifted the tray and placed it on the night table which he had cleared, being careful not to allow the clean white cover to disassemble. Allison slid down on the sheet and laid her head on the pillow, all of the time staring intently at Mike's face which had not changed expression at all.

"I thought you might like me to do this here rather than the Treatment Room."

"You think I will like it better here?"

"Yes." Mike watched her solemn eyes, puzzled at the level

of the conversation they were holding. He tried to imagine if he was being condescending or patronizing, but as he listened to both the sound and texture of his questions and responses, he realized that what was disturbing him was that he was not used to such a free flow of understanding. It was a feeling of infinite acceptance and empathy that frightened him because he couldn't explain it and that meant that he probably couldn't control the results. But no matter how he tried to tighten his defenses, the girl refused to allow him to hide.

"Then let's go. I'm ready. Are you?"

He nodded and began to gently wipe the area over her right hip with various sterilizing solutions. She giggled with the first few applications because of the sensation of chilled rubbing.

"I'm sorry. I don't mean to laugh, but it tickles. I know this is serious and I'll try harder not to laugh."

"You can laugh. If you feel like it, please laugh." Mike heard himself encouraging her.

He pulled off the rubber gloves which now had many colored streaks running down the empty fingers and carefully inserted his hands into a fresh pair. Then he gingerly opened the tray, picked up a small syringe and needle, connected them, and began drawing up a clear fluid from a tiny vial into the syringe.

"This is to take the pain away. I'm going to put it in the place where I'm going to do the test, wait a minute, and then you won't feel a thing."

Allison nodded.

"While you're doing that, can I tell you the story of *The Wind in the Willows*?"

"Yes."

"If my talking bothers you, let me know."

Mike smiled and indicated that he was about to stick her with the small needle. She averted her face and began to speak, pausing only as the needle entered and the solution was injected. Then she picked up her conversation as if the inci-

71

dent had not occurred. Her voice was steady and clear. Occasionally as the story of the animals became exciting or meaningful to her, her voice would rise and become slightly breathless. Mike stood by the bed, waiting for the anesthetic to take effect, listening carefully to her words. Just before she reached a part of the story that held danger for the animals whom she obviously equated with humans, her hands would clench. Mike almost forgot why he was standing next to her bed. He interrupted her for a moment explaining what he was about to do. When he was finished, she continued her story as if the interruption had been for his sake rather than hers.

As he pushed the trochar into the bone and aspirated the marrow contents into the large syringe, he could feel her body tensing against the large bore of the needle. But her story continued with no change in tempo or enthusiasm. He squirted the bloody contents on plates, slides, and into bottles. His other hand pressed firmly onto the bone immediately above her hip trying to stop the flow of blood which seemed to erupt in unnaturally large amounts. Her face was turned away still chattering on. He wanted to tell her that he was finished but he was enchanted by her descriptions. So he stood by her side pressing firmly with the special impregnated gauze, waiting for her words to turn to silence.

When the blood finally clotted, Mike interrupted to say that he was done. He placed several pads over the puncture site, taping them firmly in place, and indicated that she could pull up her pajamas. He collected all of the materials on the tray and turned back to Allison who was now fully dressed.

"Don't leave me in suspense. How does it end?"

She smiled broadly and grabbed his hands in hers and started talking rapidly, apparently aware that he had very little time left to spend with her. She brought the story to a close with a great deal of feeling and Mike noted that her eyes were beginning to fill. When she was all finished one tear slid precariously down her cheek. Mike leaned over and wiped it gently away.

"What a fine story, Allison. Now it'll be one of my favorites too."

"I knew you'd like it. You want to know why?"

"Why?"

"Because I think you're just like me."

"In what way, Allison?"

"Always looking for people who really love you."

Mike stood transfixed. She couldn't have said that, he thought. I imagined it. She couldn't have discovered that. My dreams are beginning to interfere with my reason. He suddenly felt very cold. All he could manage was a choked, "What?"

"When I told you I liked you this morning, you got all funny. And you stare at me a lot when I tell you not to worry. That's like me. And that's because I'm never really sure the people I love really love me back. I bet you're the same."

Mike bent down and lifted up the tray and balanced it in his arm, watching carefully to be sure the slides and bottles were in no danger of falling off. He paused by the bedside and looked down at the girl. She stared up at him, waiting for some sign that she had not hurt him with her remarks. He stood, tray in hand, puzzled by what was happening to him. They remained still for a long moment and then unexpectedly for both of them, Mike leaned down and softly touched his lips to her forehead. The next second he hurried out of the room, forgetting to draw back the curtains.

Allison jumped down from the bed and pulled them back.

"You all right, Alli?" The thin voice rose out of the pillows across the room as the birdlike head bobbed around the edge of the sheets to peer out at her roommate. "Did it hurt?"

"No, it didn't hurt, Reggie. You know why? He kissed it," Allison said, not looking directly at the girl in the other bed

73

but staring at the door as if watching the shadow of the already departed figure.

Reggie crooked her head to the side and gazed bewildered at Allison. Her voice was barely audible as she repeated to herself, "He kissed it?"

Mike removed the slides from the last bottle of staining liquid and carefully washed them off. He placed them on the rack to dry and began to adjust the microscope so that he could study the results before the hematologist came back from the clinic.

He picked one up and placed it in the gripping springlike arms of the microscope. Then he placed a drop of oil on the surface and slowly lowered the tubular apparatus downward, peering into the upper windows and adjusting the handles on the sides of the scope until the cells on the slide swam into view. He waited until he could acclimate his eyes to the sight and then began to study the red and blue circular filled figures which stood out in sharp relief in front of him. For a minute, he was able to detach what he saw from the child he had just left. There were too many big cells, young cells, cells with much intricate material contained in the widened envelopes. He picked his head up from the microscope and stared down at the table top murmuring, "All those blasts. All those blasts." He looked again trying to convince himself that he was wrong. He tried so hard to abrogate his former opinion that he found himself desperately moving the slide, searching for a view that would deny what he already knew to be a fact. Allison had acute leukemia. All those lymphoblasts announced her condition with frightening clarity. Suddenly the child's face stood out against the black tabletop and Mike looked down at the large eyes and wistful smile so intently that he didn't hear the arrival of the woman who stood impatiently in the doorway. Her gravelly voice startled him and he stood up so abruptly that he knocked over the stool.

74

"Did you do the marrow, Hillman?"

"Yes, Dr. Gilberg. It's on the scope."

Hands pushed firmly into the pockets of a long white lab coat, far too long for her short, plump stature, she waited in front of the microscope. Mike looked at her for a time wondering when she was going to look at the slide and confirm his diagnosis.

"Pick up the damn stool, Hillman." The command sounded natural coming from this truncated, masculine woman. Mike's head snapped around and noted the overturned stool for the first time. He bent over quickly and righted it. The woman sat, spilling over in layers on either side of the stool, and her pudgy, unadorned fingers moved the dials on the sides of the microscope with amazing alacrity. She continued her inspection, grunting slightly as she moved the slide from place to place. After a minute she motioned for Mike to get her a pencil and paper and then began to note how many of each item she was seeing. Finally she was finished. She sighed loudly, looked carefully at the paper lying on the table, and then lifted her eyes to stare impassively at Mike.

"Did you look at the slide, Hillman?"

"Yes, Ma'am."

"Yes, Doctor." The words were spit out, emphasizing the last word so that it lingered in the corners of the room.

"Yes, Dr. Gilberg."

"Well?"

"Acute lymphoblastic leukemia."

"Right, Hillman. Good. By the way, Hillman, a good slide also. What's the child's name?"

Mike told her the name of the girl in the room upstairs and as he repeated the name to this woman, the enormity of what lay on the microscope hit him. And he quietly repeated Allison's name.

"Do you think I can't hear, Hillman?" The woman turned in the doorway and stared at the young intern. Mike merely

75

smiled and stood very still until she stopped staring at him and walked out of the room. He knew where he could reach her when he had spoken to Allison's private doctor. He would certainly want Gilberg to look after Allison.

Mike became aware of the fact that he was feeling pain. Then he realized he had bitten into his lower lip so firmly that he could taste blood.

He heard his name bleating out of the overhead speaker in the hall outside. He could recall his excitement as a medical student when he had first heard himself being paged. Now the loud speaker had become an annoyance, rather than a sign of personal achievement. "Dr. Hillman, Dr. Hillman" the voice repeated. He went to the phone, dialed a number and picked up his page. Then he dialed another number, waited a minute and heard Dr. Rudolph's deep voice erupt through the receiver.

"Mike, where are you? I'll come there. Have you done the marrow? What does it look like? Where are you, Mike?"

The questions followed each other so rapidly that he couldn't reply. He could picture Rudolph walking agitatedly around the desk in the nurse's station, talking heatedly into the phone without waiting for any response. Mike smiled. He truly liked this older man. He felt that, more than any of the other doctors that sent their patients into this hospital, Dr. Rudolph really wanted these children to love him and leave the hospital whole and well. Because of this, Rudolph found the diagnosis of serious or fatal disease beyond his emotional capabilities. He suffered and mourned with each of the parents and searched diligently for someone else to take over the responsibility of caring for his children during their last months of pain and withering.

Mike suggested that Rudolph come down to the lab so that he could show him the slide.

"Christ, that sounds bad, Mike." Rudolph's voice assumed the edge of grief. "I'm coming right down. Christ, Mike."

Soon the short, squat figure with the deep voice virtually burst into the small room.

"Well, let's see it, Mike. Let's see it. I know it can't be good from the way you sounded."

Rudolph looked quickly through the microscope and stood up. Mike wondered if he could possibly have seen anything. He walked around the room muttering to himself and then he returned to the instrument, sat down again, and moved the field several times, murmuring indistinguishably all the time.

When he looked up again, Mike found himself staring inquisitively into the older doctor's eyes for some message that would help him over this episode. But all he saw was the furtive look of a man wanting to find a way out of a situation too painful to abide.

"That's it." Rudolph stood up and walked briskly to the door. "Call Dr. Gilberg, please, to consult. She's handled my leukemics before. I'll call the parents and speak to them in my office. They'll call her after I've spoken to them. Nice people. A little selfish, perhaps, but nice people." He paused for a moment and looked at Mike carefully.

"Have you spoken to the girl?"

Mike knew what he was asking. Somehow, he understood this man's complexities better than anyone else and Rudolph sensed it. Rudolph was childless and daily he worked in a children's world. Mike had met his wife at a faculty mixer. She was a small, empty woman of indeterminate years who seemed perpetually distracted. He had subsequently learned that Rudolph had lived many years alone as his wife had passed through various institutions throughout the state, depressed, speechless, withdrawn. The day of the mixer, Mike had mustered his always available charm, only to find himself talking to a vacant stare and a fleeting smile. Rudolph had come up and rescued both of them, chatting lightly, repeatedly asking for his wife's confirmation, not waiting for a response, talking on as the woman sat looking aimlessly around, arousing herself sufficiently to utter the few banal amenities that would get her through the afternoon. Because of this encounter Mike always tried to understand the direction that Rudolph's thinking was taking though the rapid change of topic and failure to wait for responses often required some mental gymnastics on Mike's part.

"Yes, I have. I feel as if I know her pretty well already."

Rudolph wrinkled his forehead, not speaking. Finally he said, his voice almost a whisper, as if he was sharing a secret with Mike that he could never bear to reveal to anyone else, "Makes you wonder sometimes, doesn't it, if life is worth living."

Mike wanted to walk over to this magnificent older man and put his arm around his shoulder and clasp him tightly and reassure him. But he couldn't. Even if Rudolph would permit such a gesture Mike hadn't learned how to make it. All he could do was stand next to the stool and murmur, "It does."

"Mike, how about if I get you two tickets to this weekend's football game?"

"Thank you, Dr. Rudolph, but I'm on. Maybe next game. Thanks anyway."

"I'll remember. You'll see."

The older man walked quickly out of the room. Mike turned off the lamp underneath the microscope, and went upstairs, promising himself that he wouldn't go back into Allison's room before he left the hospital for the night. But as soon as the elevator stopped at the fifth floor, he instinctively moved in that direction. He walked past it slowly, glancing inside. She peered out at him with a tentative smile flickering across her face. He continued on to the nurse's station, pulled her chart from the rack, opened it to a clean page and entered the fatal words. Then he looked at what he had written and firmly closed the metal cover, pushing the clipboard angrily back into its slot. As he walked toward the room where Allison was waiting he saw Sandy pull the chart out again. She had seen his face and had waited silently to read herself what she suspected was written down.

Mike walked into the room with his eyebrows slightly raised and his lips widened into what he hoped was a genuine smile.

"Hi." Her voice was expectant.

"It's me again. Just wanted to tell you that you make pretty slides."

"Oh good." She still wasn't sure what she was expected to think.

"Yeah, nothing serious. Just something that a week or two of medicine in here will correct." I'm lying, he thought. I'm lying purposely, doing what I had been taught never to do with a sick child. I'm lying, and I'm sick with remorse and I hope she believes every word and every lie that I will continue to tell her. He stopped and watched for her reaction. She smiled warmly and picked up a new book off the covers.

"Then I'll be here long enough to read this and tell you another story. That's what I'll be looking forward to and so it won't seem long and I won't get lonely."

She believes me, he thought. Thank God. Still smiling with his lips frozen and stinging, he turned and walked out of the room, fearing that he might not be able to continue the charade much longer if he stayed.

VIII

SANDY turned the key in the lock of her apartment and pushed on the door with her shoulder, knowing that it stuck routinely. The door eased open and slid across the pile of the thick green rug on the living-room floor. She stood for a second contemplating the calculated simplicity of the room. It was uncluttered and functional without the specific signature of a feminine approach anywhere. Her eyes scanned the low modern furniture with pleasure, before she picked up her evening paper and walked in.

She slipped out of her coat and casually tossed it onto a round white leather chair. Then she walked over to a glass tea-cart with brass wheels and sides standing against the wall, and picked up a bottle, estimating its contents. After removing the top, she poured about two shots of the clear brown liquid and adding nothing else drank down the entire contents in three gulps. She kicked off her shoes and leaned back on her heels, feeling the invisible bands of tension that she had wound around herself during the day begin to loosen. She licked her lips unconsciously and glanced again at the bottles lined up carefully on the top of the cart. I'd better not have another, she thought. I'm going out tonight and we'll probably go somewhere to drink. She put her glass back down on the tea-cart and methodically poured out about half as much of the liquor again. I'll just leave it there, she thought, just in case I get a little tense before he arrives.

She moved silently around the room surveying everything and placing any item seemingly out of place into a position of order. Reaching the stereo set she flipped on a switch. She waited in front of the set for a moment, curious to know what record she had left on the turntable. Listening for a recognizable phrase, she quickly identified the pianist and then the piece. Fleisher playing Beethoven. The composer and pianist were her favorites; their combination was one of the few things that worked better than the alcohol to help her push aside the hundred defenses that protected her during the day. She sat there, barely moving her body, eyes closed, until she realized that the record was finished and she had not put on another.

She rose and smiled. I know I'm loose, I'm hungry as hell, she thought. In the tiny kitchen she opened the refrigerator and came face to face with almost empty racks.

"Damn." The sound of her own voice startled her for a second. She had forgotten to stop by the market on the way home. She opened the small freezer compartment and smiled appreciatively when she saw a prepared television dinner in an aluminum tray tucked away to one side. She took it out, scraped away the ice, and slipped it into the oven.

The same Goddamn ritual, she thought. Home, drink, music, usually another drink, simple dinner. Why can't I be more original? She knew, however, that it was the ritual at that time of day that sustained her. The repeated routine combined with the unchanging surroundings provided the roots that Sandy felt were essential to her life. The men changed often; the daily tasks varied depending on the illness of the child or the whim of the resident. She saw her family too infrequently to gain meaning from her involvement within their structure. Thus the comfort of her apartment and the privilege of establishing her own routine reassured her that she had an identity that was unchangeable by anyone other than herself.

82

Later, as she sat at the table eating the warm, stringy roast beef, she thought about the girl that Mike had admitted that morning. Despite an air of self-sufficiency, there was something oddly defenseless about the child that demanded attention and care. Sandy had felt somewhat uncomfortable facing this obvious desire for affection, not because of the inappropriateness of the tacit request but because of her own strong inclination to submit to it. For years she had been able to remain distant enough to give good care without inflicting upon herself the pain of emotional attachment. Possibly, she cared for one child slightly more than another; and watched others leave the ward with regret, as if a friend had left after a particularly pleasant visit. But she had never permitted herself the luxury of caring so deeply that a sense of loss had reentered her life with the discharge or death of any of her patients. But this child was different. Her reaction when Mike had morosely jotted his note into the chart had been one of fleeting panic. The dizziness that she had experienced upon reading his terse and foreboding comment frightened her. The last time had been many years ago and the chart had been that of her lover. She had slipped it out of the rack the day after he was admitted for removal of the black mole that had appeared on his back months before. There had been an equally short note: "David Harmon has a malignant melanoma with multiple lung metastasis. May God have mercy on his soul." It had been signed by a fellow house officer, one of their dearest friends, and she realized later how distorted and trembling the handwriting had been. She had felt dizzy then too. She had swayed holding the chart, remembering the horrible noise as it slipped from her hand and fell to the floor. The dizziness had increased and she had silently slipped to the floor. Her next recollection was that of a student nurse washing her forehead with a wet, cold towel and helplessly chattering about hope and drugs and words irrelevant to reality.

Sandy returned to the present and found that her dinner

had become cold and the sauce had congealed as she sat holding her fork in her hand daydreaming. She pushed the dish
away with finality, stood up, walked over to the teacart, and
finished her second drink. As she started getting ready for her
date, she resolved not to ever allow herself to be drawn into a
relationship with that girl or anyone else which would expose
her to the same involuntary agony.

Half an hour later, as she settled comfortably onto the front
seat of Mike's Chevrolet, she studied him carefully with a side
glance. How self-assured he seems, she thought, how naturally
he handles himself. Is it because he is young and rather good-
looking, or is it an inner sense of future accomplishment, she
wondered. He moved the steering wheel smoothly, looking
over at her occasionally and smiling, all the time maintaining
an easy flow of words. He mentioned a cocktail lounge toward
the center of town which had a pianist that had become a favorite with many of the young people at the hospital. She
smiled and agreed. She had become a fixture at that bar. It
seemed that every one of the interns took her there. She found
it characteristic that the young men at the hospital relied so
thoroughly upon each other for their stores, restaurants and
bars—almost all of the activities that would take them outside
of the four walls that proved so confining during the day.
Sandy had heard a young physician bitterly describe the hospital as a monastery which cloistered its young men with the
suffocating arms of sickness. There was truth in that analogy,
Sandy realized, though the young man who had made the accusation had problems far beyond those of the hospital as she
learned later that night. She wondered how and where that
boy was, and if he had solved any of the problems that had
forced him to leave the hospital after only six months of his internship.

Now she searched Mike's relaxed face, wondering what his
imperfections were. God knows, they were well hidden behind

that blond, natural exterior, if they indeed existed at all. Inside the lounge, he removed her coat, checked it, and selected a table in the far right corner a distance from the pianist and the vocal crowd surrounding him hollering requests and voicing approval. They sat down, ordered drinks and found the silence separating them could no longer be filled with the insignificant talk of strangers.

"I needed a few drinks tonight," said Mike. "It's been a tough day." His voice lost its previous urbanity.

"You started out well. Your presentation was quite good."

"Thanks. That was the last good thing that happened."

She paused for a moment, thinking how to phrase the next question so as to get an honest response.

"You're really upset about the new kid with leukemia, aren't you?"

To Sandy's surprise, he acted as if he expected and needed the question to be asked. However, she noticed his expression which had been pleasantly bland take on the resigned look of anguish she had seen earlier when he had written hurriedly into the girl's chart.

"Yes."

The waiter reached across their line of vision, placing a basket of packaged cocktail snacks in the center of the table. He stopped for a second trying to recollect which drink went to whom, then put them down. They glanced down, smiled and waited until he had left before exchanging glasses.

"It was a natural mistake. How many gals drink bourbon straight-up while their men order whiskey sours?"

"You're right," Mike returned. "We're a matched set, but in reverse."

They both laughed easily and picked up their drinks. Sandy welcomed the familiar taste which she knew would help her reach this attractive man opposite her.

"You didn't completely answer my question." She waited but no reply. "Why are you so upset?"

"I'm not sure. But she seems so ready to give of herself—she seems so vulnerable." Mike paused and took a deep breath. "I've gotten so hung up on finding emptiness wherever I looked that I stopped looking for a while. But that didn't work. I knew that I was missing too much. I haven't been able to find my way out. But this kid—it's like she's trying to teach me how."

Sandy picked up her fork and began to draw lines on the tablecloth. She felt uneasy. This man was uncovering too many old wounds.

"What makes you think Allison can show you—she's only a child." Sandy spoke her name purposefully to bring the girl more completely into the conversation.

"She's still in the searching stage. Everywhere she looks she sees beauty but she seems to have difficulty in grabbing hold of it. But she's still trying, rather desperately as a matter of fact. I find her compelling. Frankly, I have trouble getting her out of my mind."

Sandy said nothing about her own affinity for the child, nothing about her unexpected and unwanted reaction to the diagnosis. She became conscious of the music from the piano on the other side of the room. The melody persisted as if trying to crowd out the revelations she feared lay too close to the surface. Her voice became louder without her knowing it.

"Isn't it odd, though, to get so involved in so short a period of time?"

"Is it, really? How long does it take to recognize something special in someone?"

"If it's so painful, why not trade cases?"

"It's crazy, but I think she needs me, or maybe I need her." He was no longer looking at her but staring straight ahead unseeing. After a moment he turned toward her and smiled the type of smile that asks for tolerance of a noticeable but charming defect.

"It's not crazy. It's not." She reached over and placed her

hand on his briefly but firmly. When she had taken it away, he put out his arm and grabbed it back.

"Don't take it away. Not yet." They sat that way, clasping hands for several long minutes and then he released her fingers and picked up his glass and drained it.

"Another?" She nodded. He signaled to the waiter who was leaning up against the wall next to the bar.

"You want to know how tight I am?" He leaned over toward her. She simply sat very still knowing that he had decided to say these things aloud tonight and she had been selected to listen. "Do you know that I haven't cried, I mean really cried, since I was seven years old?"

All she said was a gentle "Why?"

"Damn it, I'm not sure. I think because I've always known deep down that nobody cared whether I cried or not. I never saw my parents cry . . . not laugh much either . . . they merely lived . . . existed. At first I thought crying was wrong to do in public. I can remember my mother telling me that. Then my father reminded me that crying was a sign of weakness, internal weakness. Are you getting a candid picture of my folks? Anyway, other than when I broke a leg or did something pretty dramatic, I wasn't allowed to cry. And I didn't, even though I can still taste the feeling of wanting to and holding tight—that bitter, dry taste . . . Now I don't think I could if I tried." He paused, having said all of this in a rush without breathing. The music continued to float around them without getting in their way. He lowered his head and looked down at the floor so that his next words were barely audible. "I couldn't cry if I wanted to."

Sandy examined the distress that this seemingly well put together young man was revealing and she wanted to help. She wasn't sure what was required.

"Is that so serious, Mike? Most men don't cry. It's not supposed to be healthy not to cry but it's so common." That sounded like crap, she thought.

87

"Sure, if that were all. But it's only a symptom. I don't feel anything very deeply." He paused, took a deep breath and plunged on. "I have no real attachment when making love, no aftertaste of friendship, no feelings for family. I feel at times like an attractive mannequin who's been motorized to perform like a man."

"Don't you think it will all burst open one day? Don't you think the right set of circumstances will open it up for you?"

"I've been thinking that for years. I've been trying for years to do as you say, open it up. But nothing. I'm getting scared that there's nothing in there to open up." He let his hands slap listlessly against his chest and fall into his lap.

Sandy wondered for a moment whether he was sincere or whether this could be the damnedest approach to her bedroom yet. She watched his body move as if warding off an unseen blow as he talked about himself and she knew that he meant it, it was his imperfection, the crack in the perfect façade that he presented to the outside world. Somehow she seemed to find these cracks more easily than most women, usually the first time that she was with a man. Probably because I work so closely with the sick, with pain, the aura of death and its finality—these boys feel that they can give to me some of their pain, and I will share it without accusation.

She adroitly changed the subject, mentioning her familiarity with the lounge and the piano player. They listened to the music for a while. He asked her some probing questions about her family and her background which she answered without revealing much of herself.

Sensing that she wasn't ready to really speak to him, Mike asked her if she wanted to take their drinks and sit around the piano with the crowd. Sandy appreciated his tactfulness. The piano crowd was not new to her. She had spent many evenings there allowing the musical noise to drown out the endless inconsequential conversation to which her partner was subjecting her. Tonight she hadn't felt the need to recommend it; but the drift of the discussion had found her unwilling to expose herself as easily as Mike had.

They picked up their drinks and walked slowly across the floor. Several people sitting at the small round tables called to Sandy. She smiled and waved back. Mike, who was leading the way, slowed down until she was directly behind him. He turned his head around, tilted it back and whispered,

"Do you own this damn place?"

"No," she giggled. "I've been here a lot lately."

"Wow, I thought you were the mayor of the cocktail lounges."

"I probably could be." She smiled but the sentence was disturbing as she allowed the thought behind it to take hold.

The piano player was olive-complexioned with jet black wavy hair which was carefully combed and cut. His concentration upon the keys was often intense and monastic. The crowd around him knew each other, waved their hands, and slid off the stools to embrace and talk excitedly in whispered confidences.

Mike and Sandy talked and drank. Time passed quickly until Mike checked his watch and suggested that they leave.

"Come up, Mike," Sandy said when they parked outside her apartment.

He didn't answer, simply got out of the car and walked around to help her out. Waiting for the elevator button, he smiled and Sandy wondered if she should offer him something to drink; it seemed foolish since they had just come from a bar. But she knew that she would because she contemplated the very same problem each time she stood waiting for the elevator with a man standing impatiently beside her. This time, however, Sandy realized that she was unusually tense. Ordinarily she was patiently resolved to what she felt certain was about to happen. Somehow tonight she felt a peculiar nervousness. She doubted that it had anything to do with his looks; though, indeed, he was unusually good-looking, but she felt an urge to touch and know Mike that transcended the usual reasons that she had for going to bed with a man. This urge frightened her; and yet she knew that she would not stop the process she had already begun.

"Nice," Mike said when they stepped into her living room. "Compared to our pad, this is a mansion."

"Thanks. Get comfortable."

Mike took off his jacket and placed it over the back of one of the chairs in the dining area. He reached down and slipped off his moccasins.

"Can I make you a drink?" Sandy smiled hearing herself ask the question.

"No, thanks. I'm full of booze now. No more." He untied his tie and Sandy stood still as he walked across the rug. He came up to her and bent over. She felt his lips in the nape of her neck, working their way slowly up toward her face. As he gently pressed her lips, she slipped her arms around his shoulders. He kissed her repeatedly, taking his time, pausing to stroke and kiss her neck. She knew his fingers were rubbing her back but she only became aware of what he was doing when her zipper slid open to the waist. His hands moved to the back of her bra easily unsnapping the hooks and eyes which strained against the forward force of her breasts. They stood in that position for a minute, his hands moving casually over her exposed back and his face burrowed in the hollow of her neck. She held him closely, acutely conscious of his whole body pressing into hers separated by their layers of clothing.

He stepped back smiling a sleepy, sensual smile that barely moved his lips already red with lipstick and excitement. When he reached across toward her, she knew that she must remain motionless. There was something in his manner that insisted that she be as passive and receiving as possible. Slowly he moved her dress and brassiere straps across her shoulders and pulled them down. Her breasts erupted from their casing and settled as her dress hung around her waist, her bra falling to the floor. Mike lifted her breasts, each separately, touching, feeling, massaging the erect nipples as she leaned toward him. She felt her knees weakening and she wanted desperately to lie down but he had not given her the sign so she stood quietly, her eyes now closed, her lips moistened frequently by her tongue, swaying slightly as he expertly aroused her first with his hands and then with his lips.

Perspiration appeared on her upper lip and she lifted her arm to wipe it away. He paused until she leaned toward him again and then resumed caressing her. Now she realized that his hands were touching her thighs, moving slowly upward. She glanced down, seeing his tousled blond hair begin a downward descent from her breasts. Her dress was now lying on the floor and she felt his hands moving over her whole body. She lifted her legs as he hurriedly took off her underpants and tossed them aside. He was on his knees as if worshiping before her except that his hands were probing and his lips exploring. Her mouth opened and she moaned loudly as her knees began to sag.

"Oh, God, Mike, please. Not here."

"Go into your room onto the bed. I'll be right in." His voice was warm but controlled. She lay down on her bed watching him undress. He was not a muscular man but he was well proportioned and had the compact, contained look of youth. He walked toward the door of the bedroom and stood briefly framed in the doorway with the light behind him emphasizing his masculine outlines.

Then he was lying beside her concentrating on her arousal. She longed to touch him, to show her own ability at making love. She reached down but suddenly felt his body stiffen and his movements slow.

"Not yet, Sandy. Wait."

She removed her hands and lay back puzzled. She knew she was very close and she sensed that he was aware of this also. He lifted his body and moved over her gently, positioning himself within her legs. She accepted his rejection of her caresses and concentrated on herself. She felt him enter her and her legs grabbed his body in a vise-like grip. As he began moving rhythmically within her she felt herself slipping back into a dream. She was lying on a musty cot in an attic room which smelled of tobacco and moist, slowly rotting wood. A boy was asking if he was hurting her for it was her first time. And she was crying, crying because she wanted him to stop talking and to join her in the unbelievable sensations coursing through her body. Stop talking, David, she heard herself saying, and she felt herself attain the peak for which she had been so carefully prepared. Her head moved to the side and she sighed loudly and lay still. The man above continued moving his firm body within her and she suddenly sensed him stop, draw in his breath, and whisper breathlessly, "I'm coming." He shuddered as he released himself within her and she pulled him toward her so she could help prolong his moment. But he lingered only a second before rolling over onto his back.

"Who's David?"

The question was a soft entreaty, not an accusation. Sandy raised herself on her elbow and stared at him. She shook her head gently back and forth as if she wanted to deny him the right to discuss this now.

"How do you know about David?"

"You mentioned his name before. You said for me to stop talking and called me David."

"I'm sorry."

"That's okay. I didn't mind. Who is he?"

"A boy I loved. A dead boy I loved."

"Jesus." He looked away. Nothing was said. Sandy lay back down. She thought that she might cry. And that wasn't part of the agreement. No tears, no obligations. She knew the rules of this particular game. She had created them herself. Why had she done such a stupid thing? As if reading her mind, Mike turned toward her so that she felt his knee resting lightly against the back of her calf.

"Did I remind you of him?"

"In a way." Stop, she cried inside. Stop. I don't want to tell you how you were unlike him. Oh, God, stop.

"How?"

"You were so anxious for me to be satisfied."

"But I wasn't the same, was I?"

Why does he want to be punished, Sandy thought. Why has he selected me to hurt him? She couldn't help shaking her head so forcefully that he felt her whole body vibrate with her negative response.

"Why?"

"Don't." Her voice was muffled and pleading. "Don't, Mike."

"Why?" He waited.

"You didn't want me to touch you. You retreated from me. My David shared himself with me."

"Thank you." His response surprised her. His voice was steady and clear. His eyes returned to the ceiling and then closed slowly.

"Thank you?" She wasn't sure how to react.

"You're honest . . . and you're right."

"I'm sorry if you weren't satisfied. You satisfied me."

Mike turned and stared at her. For a fleeting moment his eyes widened with anger and then cooled into shadowy beacons.

"Christ, Sandy, don't you understand? That's what I call satisfied. That's all I can allow myself." He laughed a short, bitter laugh that erased the distance she had established at the mention of David's name. She wanted to cradle him in her arms and force him to let her teach him, but when she reached out to touch his thigh, he got off the bed and stood up.

"Thanks, Sandy. If it's any comfort, despite the afterthoughts, it was good . . . and needed."

93

She watched quietly, not moving, as he silently dressed in the living room and let himself out of the front door. When she heard the latch click, she buried her head in the pillow and tried to cry. But nothing came. Finally she sat up, stretched her arms and looked around the room, her eyes eventually returning to the crumpled bed.

"Oh God, I can barely tell he's actually been here." She walked into the living room and reached for the whiskey bottle to help her go to sleep.

IX

ALLISON looked at the little hand mirror inside of her pocketbook. I'm getting fat, she thought. I've only been in here for one week and that medicine is already making me fat. A puffiness around her eyes and a fullness of the cheeks was becoming evident for the first time. She stared at her face in the mirror for a long time and then in a fit of pique stuck her tongue out.

"What are you doing?" Reggie's reedy voice wafted out of the thick coverings pulled up tightly around her neck.

"Seeing how fat I'm getting."

"You're getting fatter and I'm getting thinner."

Allison looked at Reggie huddled in the tall iron bed surrounded by high metal poles holding dripping fluids and hanging plastic bags. Tubes protruded from the covers leading to the plastic bags filled with urine. These past two days since Reggie had come from the operating room, Allison often stared at the clear liquid dripping from the overhead bottle, and at the golden yellow liquid that was slowly inching its way along the plastic tubing from Reggie into the swinging transparent bag below. To her, it seemed almost like magic.

"As soon as they give you something good to eat you'll get fat like me. They're just waiting until you're ready to be better."

"Allison," the voice was weary and far away, "I've been ready a long time."

"You sound grouchy today. I'm coming over to read to you."

"Do you think you should?"

Allison picked up the book and jumped agilely off the edge of her bed onto the floor. She walked over to the door and stuck her head out. Sandy was talking to another girl who was fully dressed and looking down at a torn suitcase. The girl's mother was smoothing the collar of the child's coat, stroking it long after it had settled into place as if the sight of the outdoor garment on the child held a special joy for her. No one else moved anywhere in the long hallway.

"Sandy's busy. Penny, the girl who had the burn, is going home." She hurried over to the bed, suddenly realizing how long Reggie had been in the hospital without hearing those words "going home" said about her. And she did not seem to be getting stronger. In the last few days Allison had noticed that she had stopped lifting her head off the pillow as much as before. And Reggie herself was becoming alarmed at the hourly attention she was receiving; doctors in long white coats arriving at all times of the day to examine her and stare pensively at her metal chart. The children never discussed these unexplained visits but Allison could sense the terror that permeated the room immediately after the strange doctors had retreated.

Now, sitting on Reggie's bed, she hoped the story would distract them both. She was about four pages from the end of the book when a slight sound made her pause. Allison looked up and saw a shadow standing in the doorway. The newcomer advanced slowly into the room, eyes darting from side to side avoiding all of the equipment surrounding the bed on which Allison was precariously perched. The woman was of an indeterminate age, probably older than Allison's parents but not very old. Her face was caked with makeup so that the wrinkles cracked the powdered façade and heaped little mounds of powder in the creases. She wore no rouge but her lips were painted a bright red and her eyes were heavily mascaraed. She carried a worn beaver coat, clutching it tightly in the crook of her arm as if afraid it might fall apart or disappear. She was small and very thin.

"Mother." Allison heard Reggie's surprise.

"Hello, Regina. How are you feeling?"

"Mother, I didn't know you were home."

"Just got home, love. Wanted to see my little girl. Are they treating you okay?"

"Yes, Mother. I was operated on this past week. My kidneys again, I think."

"Yeah, they told me at the Institute. The worker told me."

"Will you be staying home, Mother, or just for a visit like before?"

"No, they tell me I can stay home if I'm a good girl."

There was a long silence in the room. Allison slipped back to her own bed. Reggie's mother had not moved from the center of the room. She stared at the wasting figure in the bed without any emotion evident on her face.

"Are you living at the old place, Mother?"

"Yeah. Still had the same room for me."

"Just the one room?"

"Yeah."

Again a deep, painful pause. Allison did not follow the drift of the conversation. Something was not being said and she could not discern what it was.

"Are you well now, Mother?"

"Think so, love. Wish you felt as well as I did."

"I've been staying with Uncle Tom, you know, when I'm not in here."

"Uh huh. He told me. He's a great guy. You're lucky."

Again nothing was said. Allison saw the small woman sway slightly on her high heels and grab for the door. Reggie had seen this movement also and with a violent effort had turned herself half way around to face her mother.

"Will you take me home with you now, Mother, when I get out?"

The woman threw her fur coat over her shoulders as if she had suddenly experienced a chill.

"Regina, you know very well the psychiatrist doesn't think I can take on that much responsibility yet. Not yet, love. Maybe later, when you're better."

"Mother, please try to take me home with you if I can get out of here. I'll look after myself. I won't be a bother."

The woman shifted from one foot to the other. She stared momentarily at Reggie and rubbed her cheeks unconsciously. Then her attention fell upon some of Allison's cards.

"My, what dear cards." Again a restless silence with the shuffling feet and wandering eyes. "Well, love, I must be going. Got to look for a job. We have no daddy to look after us, do we?" She smiled ruefully. Before Allison realized what had happened, the woman had fled from the room.

"Mother, take me home with you when I can go. Please. Please." Reggie kept chanting as if unaware that her mother had left. Allison leaned against the cold iron railing and bent her head.

She was still in the same position when Ed came into the room and calculated the yellow liquid quivering inside the distended container under Reggie's bed.

"Hi, girls." Allison smiled. He was so serious. And he talked to them like she always imagined a doctor would talk. He was different from Mike. Mike was like he belonged to her. Ed didn't seem to belong to anyone. It was as if he were trying to impress and love the children at the same time but not able to keep his feelings under control.

"Reggie, you keep this up and we'll need a bag bigger than you."

"Is that good?" The words were whispered anxiously.

98

"Good? It's great. We're happy with you."

Allison looked at him suddenly. She knew that tone. She had heard it so often from her parents. He was lying. He was smiling at Reggie and lying to her. But Reggie believed him. She wasn't hearing the tone. She was only listening to the words she wanted desperately to hear. And she accepted the lie as truth, truth which she had to have if she was to continue facing her crippled body and the bottles and tubes that violated it.

"I think we'll change those tubes today. Would you like some fancy new ones?"

No answer. Just a smile and a look of faith and anticipation. Allison wondered if she would only hear the words if she was lied to in the same way. What would they say? What words would they use? For the first time since she had entered the hospital, Allison felt truly afraid.

Ed was pushing Reggie's bed slowly through the door, talking steadily to her. Allison wondered why he didn't call for an orderly or aide to help him, why he had to push the bed himself. But as she watched, he bent over and Allison caught his expression and suddenly understood. He had to work hard for Reggie; he had to feel something of the efforts of living that she was feeling; he needed her to need him or he would suffer more than she.

The room was dark before her parents arrived that evening.

"Why isn't the light on, darling?" Her mother's words were partially swallowed as she looked about her. "Where's your little roommate, what's her name?"

"Her name is Reggie, Mother. She's in the Treatment Room with Dr. Erikson and the light was off because I was thinking and I think much better in the dark." Her mother glided over to the doorway and flipped up the switch that returned the room to its bright metallic luster. She wore a short print dress with much jewelry and very carefully applied makeup and seemed to Allison so attractive that she forgot her anger.

"Now there's some light on the situation. Were you depressed, darling? Is that why the lights were off?"

Allison watched her parents moving restlessly around the room straightening up the sheet on her bed, checking her cupboard for dirty clothes, doing the very things that they would never have done within their own home. Her mother rarely even entered Allison's room, its tidiness was the maid's concern, the clothes Allison wore were Allison's decision. New clothes were bought with help from other friends of the family with the excuse that Allison's mother had no expertise in buying children's clothes, despite the fact that she dressed so well herself. And now, Allison was amused as the pair of them busied themselves in the room, obviously unused to caring for a child but feeling the need to express their concern in some tangible fashion.

"Are you feeling all right, dear? Were the lights out because you aren't well?"

"No, Mother, the lights were out because I wanted them out. That's all. And please stand still for one moment." There was an embarrassed pause. Her father who had yet to utter a word walked over to a chair and slowly dragged it across the floor until it stood at the foot of her bed.

"Hi, Dad. You tired?"

His head raised slowly and his eyes looked into hers with an intensity that seared her with pity. The lines in his face had deepened since she had last noticed and his eyes seemed older, more settled. He sat staring at her for a long time before he said,

"Yes, Allison, I'm beat. I think I need a vacation. Need to get away."

Take me with you this time, please, Allison thought quickly. Please, this time let it be different. I'll be no trouble. No questions like I always ask, no requests for special things. Just take me. Suddenly she raised her head sharply. Where had she heard those words? The pain of the moment returned; she again heard Reggie pleading to the departing figure of her mother. Allison gritted her teeth so she wouldn't cry. They're not the same, she thought. How can they be the same? Anyway, I'm sick so they probably won't want to go.

Her mother walked to the edge of the bed where Allison sat looking over the railing at her father's upturned face. She quickly took in the situation and smiled blandly at Allison.

"The doctors are very pleased with you, dear. They tell us you will be ready to go home in several days. Isn't that fine?"

"I'm getting fat."

"I thought we would pick you up and Daddy would take off a few days to be with you."

Allison didn't answer because she knew that her mother hadn't finished. Her mother had to make herself feel that whatever followed had been compensated for by what she had promised Allison before. So Allison waited for the rest of the proposal.

"Well, dear, isn't that good?" Allison had to nod so that she could hear the rest.

"Then dear, Daddy and I are going for a short trip to the Islands. I asked the doctors and they felt that it would be perfectly all right. So you see, you really are getting better."

Well, it's been said, Allison thought. Okay. I'll take my medicine and get fat all by myself at home.

"I hope you have a good time," she made herself say. "Who's staying this time?"

Her mother sighed deeply and placed her hands calmly on Allison's shoulders while her father looked away.

"Mrs. Lawson. You don't know her, dear, but she comes very well recommended. She stayed with Babs Chester last Christmas. Babs loved her."

Babs Chester is an idiot, Allison thought. She would like King Kong. Well, another new face to educate into the running of the house. Allison almost had a perverse pleasure in looking forward to the indoctrination of this new custodian. She and her brother had broken in so many elderly ladies to the proper functioning of her home and each time the two of them stressed different things so that each babysitter left thinking she had been to a home quite different from the ones who had been there before and those who would certainly follow.

"By the way, Allison, Dr. Hillman, that nice young intern, asked if he could take you out one afternoon while we were away. You must have made quite an impression. What shall we tell him, dear? Do you want to go?"

Allison didn't know why but she started to cry. Her eyes filled with tears and she could feel them trickling down her cheeks. Her mother arched her eyebrows and looked over at her husband who was peering out of the window and had missed the whole exchange. She turned back to Allison and started to speak but Allison shook her head vigorously as if asking her to wait. Her mother closed her mouth and continued to watch Allison carefully.

"Yes, please, tell him yes. Mother, go out now and tell him yes."

Her mother said nothing but nodded that she would. She beckoned to her husband and began to gather her coat and the bag of dirty clothes. Mr. Reddy grinned awkwardly at his daughter.

"Night, Allison. We're looking forward to your coming home."

"Night, Dad."

He seemed so uncomfortable in this hospital room that Allison felt sorry for him. She wasn't sure why he was so restless now but whatever the reason she didn't want him to have to suffer because of it. But if she asked him not to come any more, he might not understand, so she remained quiet.

"Mother, don't forget to tell Mike I can go. Tell him tonight."

"I will, Allison, I will. My goodness, you make it sound like a date or something."

Allison frowned and cocked her head to one side. The gesture was not lost on the older woman. She pursed her lips and nodded.

"Allison, I said I would and I will."

She turned and walked away from the bed toward the doorway.

Reggie had not returned by the time dinner was served. Allison had been down the hall to the playroom searching for her and asking the nurses if they knew where she was. Everyone answered vaguely either that they did not know or that they were waiting for her to come back from the treatment area. When Sandy came in with the medicine tray Allison said,

"Where is she, Sandy? Please tell me. Don't lie. Please."

Sandy stood with the paper cup in her hand unconsciously crushing it in her fist. Then realizing what she had done, she filled another cup with water and handed it to Allison with two white tablets.

"Sandy, I asked you a question. Where's Reggie? Ed took her to the Treatment Room this morning and she's not back yet."

Allison put the pills into her mouth and swallowed.

"She's not doing so well today, Allison. She's been moved into Intensive Care."

"How sick is she?"

"Very sick, Allison."

Allison didn't answer or move. She merely sat in the chair next to the empty space where her friend had been and looked out the door. She knew that she couldn't go and see her. But she would sit by her bed space and wait until they brought her back.

"I'm leaving now, Allison. My shift is over. Anything you want before I go?"

Allison shook her head. Sandy knelt down and leaned on the leather covering of the seat of Allison's chair.

"I wish I could take you to see her. It would do you both good. But she has a few more tubes in her today and they think girls like you and me are sissies and can't take that."

Allison reached out toward the blonde hair that hung limply around Sandy's worried face and began to stroke it. The woman put her arms about the slim shoulders of the huddled child pulling her toward her. Silently they hugged each other. Then Sandy stood up and walked out of the room, leaving Allison seated in the leather chair, waiting.

Her dinner came and was taken away without much of it being eaten. She remained sitting in the chair despite requests by the night nurse that she go to her bed and get ready for lights out. She remained unmoving, listening for the squeal of the wheels on the large bed that would tell her that her friend was being rolled back down the hall to her room.

It was much, much later when Mike came slowly into the room.

"I hear you don't want to get into bed tonight."

"I'm waiting for Reggie, Mike. I'm waiting for someone to bring her back."

"Can I wait with you?"

Allison scanned his handsome face to try to detect a meaning behind his words but he merely smiled warmly and found another chair. He placed it directly opposite Allison and sat down.

"You tired?" His manner was casual but friendly, as if he were sitting with someone with whom he had shared many such moments repeatedly in the past. "It's getting late."

"I am a little tired, but I'm going to try and stay up."

"Do you think that will make a difference?"

"With Reggie?" He nodded. "I hope so."

"You're a good friend to have, you know. I hope if I'm ever in some trouble you'll stick by me like this."

Allison didn't reply. She slid forward and laid her head on his lap. In a moment, she felt his hand softly patting the back of her head.

"Mike, why can't she get better?"

"Allison, you ask hard questions. Some people have a tougher time getting better and some people don't get better at all."

"Which kind is Reggie, Mike?"

Mike didn't answer her. Instead he sat opposite her, very still with his hand upon her head and her head cushioned in his lap.

"Your mother tells me you'll let me take you out next week or the week after while they're out of town. How would you like to go to a ball game? The baseball season starts this week."

She looked up and grinned. For a moment, the heavy pall lifted and was replaced by enthusiasm for her own tomorrow.

"Oh, Mike, that sounds great."

"Then I'll get us tickets and we have a date."

They sat peacefully for a long time until Allison remembered where she was and why they were sitting as they were. She clenched her fists and rubbed her tired eyes.

"Mike, take me to Reggie. Let me see for myself that she's all right."

"I can't, Allison." His voice was low and controlled.

"Why, Mike, more rules? You think I would cry or something?"

"No, Allison, that's not why."

Allison listened to the sadness in his voice and grabbed his forearm firmly.

"Why, Mike?"

"Reggie won't be coming back here to stay in this room ever again, Allison."

"Mike?" Allison squeezed harder on his arm but he gave no indication that he felt anything.

"She turned out to be the kind that doesn't get better, Allison. She left us today."

Allison sat squeezing his arm, allowing the finality of what he said seep into her. She laid her head back into his lap and began to cry softly but without pain. The sound of her sadness hung in the room as she rocked back and forth in his lap, her tears spilling onto the clean wrinkled white pants beneath her head. His arms were around her but he said nothing and he didn't move.

Minutes drifted slowly into an hour and finally the sobs ebbed and her body relaxed. She was asleep. He reached down and lifted her gently into his arms and carried her over to her bed.

X

"DR. ERIKSON, Dr. Erikson."

The shrill voice stopped Ed halfway down the ward. He walked over to a phone, dialed "one," and waited. Finally the same high-pitched voice answered.

"Yes?"

"Dr. Erikson here."

"Oh, thank God. Where have you been? Call Dr. Rosensweig's office."

"Right."

"And next time, please, let me know where you are if you move out of the sound of my voice."

Oh, Lord, for only one day let me move out of the range of that inquisitive shriek, thought Ed. All he said was, "Yes, Ma'am. Right, I will," and put the receiver carefully into the cradle. What does Rosensweig want, he wondered. Did I do something wrong? Rosensweig is not the type just to call me in to chat. Ed had had his first interview with the chief last year when he had applied for his internship and then was so concerned about the impression that he was making that he had hardly noticed the man interviewing him. Since then, he had been at Grand Rounds and other medical gatherings with Rosensweig but had never spent any time alone with him and had no idea what the other man was really like.

Ed dialed the number of the departmental office.

"Mrs. Gilmore. This is Dr. Erikson. Dr. Rosensweig called before?"

"Yes. Can you come in to see him in a short while?"

"Yes, I can. Anything in particular the matter?" Ed tried to hide the tinge of fear that had crept into his voice.

"I really couldn't say. Now don't be late. You know Dr. Rosensweig's schedule."

"I'll be there in a few minutes."

He turned away from the phone and bumped into Sandy.

"Sorry to hear about the kid last night," she said. "She was going downhill so slowly that I almost forgot how bad her kidneys were."

"Christ, you're so right. I always hoped I would be off one night and would come back in the next morning and it would have happened and I wouldn't have been there. Maybe then it wouldn't linger with me so long."

Sandy crossed her arms in front of her breasts as if unconsciously protecting herself. "Wasn't she a candidate for more dialysis?"

"That's when it happened. I took her up for another dialysis and soon after we went into the peritoneum she became pale, cold, and you know the picture. Anyway she went into shock and we couldn't bring her out. We tried. Christ, did I try. She must have bled . . ." His voice trailed off as he remembered the futile activity in the Treatment Room culminating in helplessness . . . and a dead child. He glanced up to see Sandy watching his face carefully.

"Ed, take it easy. It was going to happen. You just happened to be there. There is only so much you can do."

He knew that she was right, but wondered if he would go through his training—indeed through the rest of his life—replacing pictures of desperately ill and dead children with those of their successors. He couldn't tolerate that prospect. For a moment, he felt himself grow cold.

"Have to go in and see the Chief."

"When you're through, come back. I have something good to show you."

"Hey, I'm curious. What is it?"

"It'll wait. Go see the boss and behave."

When Ed opened the door to Rosensweig's office the woman sitting behind the desk motioned to a large walnut armchair in the corner of the room.

"Sit there, please. He's on the phone. He'll be with you in a minute."

Her references to the man for whom she worked suggested that to her the word "he" should be permanently capitalized.

Ed sat hunched in the chair, his arms swinging irreverently back and forth.

"Please stop that swinging. You're distracting me. I must go over these plans for the new Intensive Care unit before he sees them or he'll be very angry at the mistakes."

"I'm sorry." Ed hated her. He hated having to apologize to the white-haired bitch. Who in the hell does she think she is?

Suddenly the door to the inner office opened and a voice shouted,

"Where's the Goddamn budget for the nursery? I can't make any decisions without the figures. Every time I look for them, they're gone. Goddamn it."

Ed saw the woman stand up quickly and walk over to the dark green metal cabinet standing against the wall. She opened a drawer, flipped through several files, and carried it to the unseen figure standing in the doorway. The folder disappeared from her hands with a grunting approval. The door did not close but remained ajar.

A moment later the voice boomed again. "I knew it. I knew it. Those bastards tell me that I can't build that extra room 'cause I overspent my budget. They're a bunch of liars. A bunch of Goddamn liars. It's right here. Gilly, come here. It's right here." The woman jumped at the sound of her name and scurried into the room.

"Gilly, you're too much. What would I do without you? Hell, Gilly, you're more devious than I am and that's going some. Imagine their faces when I show them the money you line-itemed under miscellaneous expenses and overhead that will pay for my nursery changes." He laughed again, and was joined by a thin, wispy giggle.

"Okay. That's settled. Good. What's next?" Ed heard whispered words, surely about him. He tensed as the door swung open all the way and Rosensweig appeared in the anteroom. He was over six-foot-tall with unusually broad shoulders and a big-boned frame. There was the air of a retired football player about him that most people mistook for camaraderie until they faced him in competitive situations. He dressed in the latest style and never had the careless look that large men unwittingly possess when they are too casual about their clothes. Ed thought that he appeared less like a Professor of Pediatrics than the Vice President of a bank.

"What the hell are you doing sitting in the corner?"

Ed shrugged his shoulders and smiled.

"Miss Gilmore put me here."

"I can believe it. She's been putting me in the corner ever since I got here. Great woman, though. Only reason she gets away with bossing me around is that she's smarter than me."

Miss Gilmore had returned to her desk in full view of both men and sat quietly through this interchange, coloring slightly. Over the years her relationship with Rosensweig had developed into a protective co-existence based on mutual self-respect. What an unusual combination and how well it seemed to work, Ed thought.

"Get off your ass and come in. I have a job for you."

Ed got up and walked into the inner office. On the wall were pictures of young men and women looking seriously uncomfortable. Ed recognized a few of the faces and realized that they had all been in charge of the house staff under Rosensweig's reign. And reign he did, with a firm but evident hand. Little happened in the department that he didn't know. He asked questions endlessly, watched people working in all situations, dogged behind nurses and interns and talked to patients. He was his own quality control. He complimented his staff rarely as if he expected only the best or at least their best, but he berated easily. His booming voice could often be heard echoing down the long halls hurling expletives at a hapless intern who had overlooked a test on a child or failed to give the parents the attention that Rosensweig demanded. Ed had heard the man shouting at Sheila Plotkin one night when she had been rude to a parent out of exhaustion and despair. "It's easy to be a good doctor," he had screamed, "but it's an art to be a good human being." And yet the young men and women clamored to join his service, and once there stayed if permitted and drew the bonds of loyalty even tighter around themselves and this difficult man every year that they were near him.

Rosensweig turned in his swivel chair for a second to stare out of the window. "Spring's coming, Ed. That's something to look forward to."

Ed nodded. Small talk had never been one of his best features and easy conversation with this aggressive man was out of the question.

"I have a job for you, Ed. That kid that died last night. What's her name, damn it, I can't remember her first name. The kid with the kidneys who was here so long." He looked straight at Ed as if expecting help.

"Regina Carmichael."

"Right, Carmichael. Well, anyway, Phil Casper, the Pediatric Urologist, my old boss, is coming through town this week and I thought that a special presentation of this case in front of the house staff and attendings would fit in great. What do you think?"

Ed knew what he was expected to answer. There were only

a few people in the department whom Rosensweig allowed to disagree.

"Good idea. When is he coming?"

"Today at four." Rosensweig was aware of what he was asking. Four o'clock was less than an hour away. Ed recalled the bulk of the child's chart. Good God, she was in the hospital for over two months this time. And he wants me to get up in less than one hour and summarize the case in front of the staff.

"You sure know how to test a guy."

"Well, Ed, can you do it?" said Rosensweig.

"I think so." There was no response. Ed knew what was expected next. "Yes, I can do it. I'll be ready."

"Thank you, Ed. By the way, you handled that case very well, both medically and as a person."

Ed reddened. It was strange to hear praise from the chief.

"Thank you, sir."

"Ed, you're planning to stay with us next year, aren't you? I hope so."

He's telling me that I have the residency next year. I think he's offering me one of the jobs. Ed looked down at his folded hands and rubbed them together, feeling the moisture beginning to accumulate there.

"Yes. If you want me as one of your residents, I'd like to stay."

"The matter's settled then. Damn it, Ed, smile. I don't see you smile enough. Life's only a pain in the ass if you make it that way. Smile, boy."

Ed forced himself to smile. He never realized how hard it was. His face felt painfully creased and he was suddenly aware of his teeth.

"Christ, stop smiling, Ed. You look like somebody's pulling on your balls."

Ed laughed. He sensed the older man's humanity and remembered his mammoth hands as they gently lifted a newborn in the nursery.

He has something else to tell me, Ed thought. I can sense it. In the silence Ed wished he had the nerve to excuse himself and leave.

"There's something bothering you, isn't there?" Rosensweig said finally. "Something that won't leave you alone. What is it? Can I help?"

Ed sat stunned. He knew he had to answer, but what in the hell could he say?

"You're right, sir. I don't know what it is. Maybe it's just fatigue and getting used to constantly being around sick children."

"That's part of it, I'm sure, Ed. And that's something that even conscious training may not solve completely. But there's more." Ed felt his chief's probing eyes. Without changing his expression, Rosensweig suddenly said, "Have you been getting laid much?"

There was an embarrassed pause. Then Ed said, "No, I haven't."

"Christ, that'll curdle any man's work."

"It's been this year, sir. Just this year. I don't know whether it's the work, or if I'm just tired all of the time or what. I am shy, sir—very shy—but I've overcome that before now."

"Sorry if I'm probing but you're so uptight at times. And the thing that makes most young men uptight is sex. I know. I'm still young enough to feel the strain myself. Shy, shit. Go out and settle it, Ed. How you do it is your business. But when I see you smile, boy, I'll know you're getting laid . . . regularly."

Ed didn't answer, not wanting to seem disrespectful but also not wanting to hear any more.

The older man sensed his discomfort and thought how much the boy resembled himself at that age. Would the solution that had worked for him work here also? He wondered. What an inexact science we practice, he thought. We recommend for the next what worked for us before and so often their

113

problems vary as do their bodies. Well, I'll keep my eye on him. He's clever and hard-working but too Goddamn tense. Rosensweig got out of his chair and placed a hand very briefly on Ed's shoulder before walking to the door.

Ed knew the interview was over. As he left he turned to look at Rosensweig who was already back at his desk, muttering obscenities at something which displeased him. He looked up for a second.

"I'll see you in about forty minutes, friend. And remember —I'll be looking for that smile." He laughed. "And until then, get your ass up off the floor."

Ed walked back to the floor in a daze until a hand reached out and grabbed his arm. He looked up startled, and found himself gazing into the moist eyes of Sheila Plotkin.

"Ed, come out of it." She looked very small in her gleaming white coat. Ed remembered that Rosensweig had talked to her twice in his office recently and it was rumored he had received copious tears in reply.

"You okay?" she asked.

"Yeah. I just left Rosensweig . . . and was lost in thought."

"He does that to me too and makes me cry. I'm scared to death of that man." She made the statement as if her fears weren't common knowledge.

"He didn't frighten me, just startled me. I didn't realize that he knew each of us so well."

Plotkin's eyes widened and a new layer of fright rimmed her pupils. God, now I've scared her even more, Ed thought. Finally Sheila stretched out her hand holding a small piece of white paper.

"Sandy left this for you. That's why I stopped you." She added the latter almost apologetically not wanting him to expect that kind of familiarity so soon again.

"Thanks." Ed took the paper and read the message. "I've got a head nurses' conference till five. Meet me back at the ward if you can. I promised you a pick-up, remember." Ed crumpled the note and tossed it into the wastecan. He had to finish studying Reggie's chart by four. He glanced at his watch and saw it was three-thirty. Damn, a half hour. I'll never make it. Fortunately he found the just completed chart on Sandy's desk ready to be sent down to Medical Records. That's a break, he thought. It would have been fifteen minutes at best for them to find it.

He quickly turned the pages, reading entries by consultants, nurses, interns, and medical students; constructing from these scribbled notes a portrait of the dying child. The family emerged: psychotic mother, deserting father, alcoholic grandmother, suffering and loving bachelor uncle all seen through the eyes of different observers and recorded within these pages for strangers to peruse. There was nothing in this voluminous chart that told of Reggie's wistful sweetness; her love of bright colors; her thin, whispered laughter; her seeming lack of anger. So much was missing that was of importance to those who cared for the child. But Ed took down only the facts that appeared before him, the numbers that were written almost illegibly on the laboratory slips, the operative reports, the medical events of her life and death.

Soon he was finished. He gathered his notes together, roughing out his speech in his mind. As he walked down the hall he saw Allison standing at the open door of her room, her face swollen from crying. She motioned for him to come over to her. He looked at his watch. Almost time. What the hell. I can be a minute late. He bent over just far enough so that they could speak quietly.

"Hi. You going to the conference room?"

"Yeah. How you doing?"

"I'm done crying."

"Good, Allison. You know Reggie didn't like anyone to cry."

The girl nodded. "Mike just told me that you were going to talk about Reggie in there."

"That's right."

"You're going to tell them all about her?"

"Yes."

There was a moment's pause. She whispered the next words so that Ed had to strain to hear what she was saying.

"Say only nice things about her . . . please . . ." Ed stood transfixed as a tear coursed down her cheek. After a period of mutual mourning, he turned away from her, and walked toward the waiting adults in the room beyond.

When Ed went back to the floor he found Sandy gesturing happily to Mrs. Mazetti, the mother of the child with meningitis that he had worked on the previous week. She wore the same worn coat but had on more makeup, suggesting that several years before she had been an attractive if not a beautiful woman. Her cheeks were flushed and she smiled easily. Ed had not seen her since the hectic day of admission because the boy had been transferred to a different ward. Sandy grabbed his hand.

"Mrs. Mazetti wants to talk to you. She's been looking for you all week, she tells me, and hasn't been able to catch up with you."

Ed smiled and looked at the obviously excited woman. He stood quietly watching her advance toward him and place both of her arms on his shoulders. She placed a moist kiss on his cheek.

"Thank you. Thank you so much for my little boy."

Ed nodded and looked into the boy's room. Sitting up in bed and laughing at his father was the same child that Ed had seen lying moribund in the Treatment Room just days before. The man playing with him was also totally different; involved, and seemingly recovered from his own immobilizing melancholia.

"You're welcome. I am so glad he is better." He was slightly embarrassed by the woman's effusiveness. Sandy just smiled.

"Ed, Mrs. Mazetti baked you some special cookies. She says they're Italian though people who don't know any better call them Greek." The older woman chuckled, reached into a large shopping bag next to her feet and brought out a round tin packed tightly and wrapped around with several rubber bands.

"Come," she said, pulling gently at him. "Come and say good-bye to the boy." Ed went with her toward the bed where the boy sat playing with a set of blocks. His clothes were laid out at the bottom of the bed in anticipation. The boy's father stood up as they approached, took Ed's hand in his and squeezed tightly. Ed turned toward the child. The lifeless arms were now moving quickly among the blocks; the flushed, immobile face was now creased with smiles.

"Anthony, look who's here. It's Dr. Erikson. Say good-bye to him. He's a special friend." Ed smiled at the boy but the boy looked back without any sign of recognition.

"I said, say good-bye to your friend." The mother's voice took on an edge of insistence.

Ed turned toward her and patted her arm.

"He doesn't know me, Mrs. Mazetti. He doesn't remember me. He was too sick that first day. And I haven't seen him since he regained consciousness. This is not my ward."

She searched the young doctor's face with puzzlement, shaking her head.

"You mean, after all you done for him, he'll never know it was you?"

Ed shook his head.

"No, he doesn't know me, Mrs. Mazetti. And please, don't pressure him, it's all right. It's enough that I know him. . . . And thank you for the cookies." Ed bent down, kissed the woman slightly on the cheek, and walked quickly out of the room.

117

XI

IN the nursery Ed eased his way into the anteroom filled with stacks of folded white gowns in tilted piles crammed into metal cabinets. He pulled off his wrinkled white coat and searched hopelessly for a hanger. He finally settled on an empty metal hook which had the strict instructions that it was "for nurses only." Ed always had the feeling that the nursery was hallowed ground, run by the nursing staff which only allowed the doctors to enter on sufferance.

He slipped on a fresh white gown which smelled of detergent and bleach and went into the nursery hallway. A large, well-girdled woman walked resolutely toward him, glancing up at the clock immediately above their heads. She carried a blanketed infant cradled in the crook of her right arm, shaking it gently even as she walked. She pointed her chubby hand up toward the clock.

"You're late today."

Ed smiled easily. "Yes, I know. I'm sorry." There was a brief pause when nothing was said. Then Ed added uneasily, "You didn't feed him, did you?"

"No. We didn't feed him. But how would you like to wait over forty-five minutes for your supper."

Ed nodded. "You're right, Mrs. Lorbin, but I was delayed."

The woman frowned. "It's none of my business, I know, but

119

would you please tell me why, after you've been out of this nursery for over a week, that you insist on coming back here every day at this time to feed that premature baby? Would you please tell me that."

Ed shifted his weight slightly from foot to foot. "I was there when he was born, Mrs. Lorbin."

She shrugged. "So are a lot of you there when they are born . . . and you had other premies—why this one? And why every day? You're the first intern in my ten years in this particular nursery that's done that. The nurses feed; the doctors treat."

Ed said nothing. He knew that she wasn't finished.

"It's not easy for us in here waiting for you each day, not knowing when and if you're going to come."

Ed answered quietly. "Have I ever not come, Mrs. Lorbin?"

She shook her head. "No. That's right. You always come. That's it, Dr. Erikson, you always come."

Ed looked at the large woman gently rocking the sleeping infant. She demanded some kind of answer, he knew.

"Mrs. Lorbin, it's very hard to explain. Certain things are a challenge to all of us, and well, I guess Henry represents that challenge to me."

"Henry. My God, what a name for a two and a half pound premature who was less than that when you started. The crazy thing is that all of the other nurses around here are calling him Henry now too."

Ed smiled and asked quietly, "Do you, Mrs. Lorbin?"

"Yes, I do!" she said, putting the baby back in his basinette. "That's almost as crazy to me as your coming here every day. I do call that tiny thing Henry."

"Good for you, Mrs. Lorbin."

"You know," the nurse said, handing him a bottle, "his mother has been coming in every day to see him." She paused and watched Ed's reaction. "Are you surprised?"

Ed raised his eyebrows slightly. "Yes. Yes, I'm surprised. I thought she was putting him up for adoption or foster care or whatever he qualifies for. . . ."

The nurse sighed heavily. "My God, I'll never understand people. She comes in every day, stares at him through the glass and wants to give Henry to other people to bring him up." There was a pause during which both gowned figures stared at each other and then recognizing her easy use of the infant's nickname, they began to laugh. When the sound of their laughter stilled, Mrs. Lorbin rubbed her hands quickly over her eyes, caught herself in the act, and quickly went over to the faucet and ceremoniously washed her hands.

"If you have any trouble, Dr. Erikson, just holler. I'll be in the room across the hall." She dried her hands, avoided his direct stare, and heavily made her way back into the sequestered nursery.

Ed approached the isolette slowly and peered into the plastic box that housed his friend. The infant lay on his back, his eyes open gazing blankly in front of him, his pupils wandering aimlessly at times as if the outside world were invisible to him.

As Ed touched the glass top of the isolette, the infant detected a sensation and both arms fluttered up over his chest with jerky, tentative movements and, just as tremulously, settled back into place.

Ed placed his left hand under the almost weightless head of the tiny child and lifted it gently. He then began to thread the rubber tube down the right nostril of the infant, and checked its position carefully.

"Well, here it comes Henry," said Ed. "Steak and potatoes." He connected the tubing to the open syringe at the top of the isolette.

The infant's stirring ceased as if he was enjoying the liquid meal. Ed watched the abdomen bulge slightly as the special formula flowed slowly into it.

He placed his right elbow on the top of the isolette and laid the baby's head in his hand, oblivious of the rules that prevent such familiarity with the infant's home. He peered down at the small figure lying passively on the covered mattress.

"Henry, you are going to make it, aren't you?"

Silence resounded from the walls.

"Henry, you've got to make it, do you hear me? You've got to. I'm so tired of things dying."

The baby stirred automatically, a slight tremor disturbing the fragile tranquility inside the box.

"Will I make it, my friend? Henry, I'm afraid I won't make it so please, do your job. Don't let me down, get fat and we'll get you out. Tell you the truth, I don't know where you're going, but we'll get you out. Is it a deal?"

The syringe was empty. The baby's abdomen was full but the breathing was steady. Ed slipped both hands into the isolette and turned the tiny body onto its right side after removing the rubber tubing from the nostril.

As he stood up, he noticed a young woman outside the nursery window staring at them. Her nose was pressed so firmly into the glass that Ed could not make out the shape but remembered how small it had been their first meeting. Her lips were without makeup and were smiling at him, softly, but with wonder. She was short because her face just cleared the lower rim of the viewing glass. Ed knew this girl, remembered her from the visit to her room on that first night after Henry's birth when his survival was in grave doubt.

Now, over two weeks later, she stood facing him, looking down at the tiny baby who had survived the respiratory disease, the low blood sugar, the calcium abnormalities, to have reached this moment without the instruments attached to his body, announcing his partial independence from science.

Ed suddenly realized how ridiculous he must have looked, talking intently to the infant. He smiled at the girl who signaled for him to meet her at the nursery door. He picked up the equipment and looked once more at the infant lying peacefully on his side. The young woman was gone from the window.

"Well, Henry, now I'm going to get acquainted with the rest of your family, for better or worse. Don't worry, I'll behave myself. She'll never know we're a pair of nuts. I'll even put in a good word for you."

Ed went into the hallway between the nurseries. Mrs. Lorbin was charting some notes.

"All finished?"

"Yes Ma'am. He gobbled it all down."

She smiled tolerantly. "Dr. Erikson, that's what I'm waiting for, the day he goes onto the nipple and you want to feed him."

Ed made a face. "Don't underestimate me, Mrs. Lorbin. I might talk him into going directly to the cup." He winked and walked into the anteroom where he shed his gown. He glanced down at his wrinkled uniform and took several seconds to tuck in the shirt and smooth down the creases in the trousers.

She was waiting outside.

"Hi." Her voice was clear and steady.

Ed nodded. "Hi. I'm really glad you're coming here."

She ran her fingers over her large silver belt buckle which caught the sunlight from the window next to her and intermittently glinted in Ed's eyes.

"I haven't had a chance to thank you for that first night."

Ed folded his hands and let them hang awkwardly in front of him. "You're welcome. It was touch and go with him the first days."

She shook her head. "No, I mean thanks for helping me. That night was a very bad scene, but you helped."

Ed nodded and felt his face begin to flush. Damn it, I'm blushing, he thought. I can't even talk to her without acting like an adolescent. He wiped his forehead very slowly trying to divert attention from his reddened face, and relaxed as he felt the heat subside.

123

"He's starting to grow. You can see his arms and legs filling out now. Did you notice?"

"He's still awfully small to me, but I must admit the little peanut is beginning to appeal to me. Last week, when I first saw him, he frightened me, but now . . ." She paused painfully. "Now I'm beginning to care about him."

"He's really not a peanut. For his age, he's doing fine, though I must admit he's a little underdeveloped compared to his roommates across the hall."

"I probably don't know him well enough to call him names yet, but you're right, he does look like the 'before' pictures in the muscle-building ads."

Ed laughed. "Actually I think he's turning into a pretty nice kid. I told him today that he might be handsome if he tries hard enough."

She reached over and quietly touched his sleeve. He didn't move. They stood in this position for a long minute until she spoke. "I saw you talking to Henry like he could hear you."

Ed leaned against the wall as her hand fell from his arm. "So you know that I gave him the name 'Henry.' Somehow I felt that he should be called something besides 'Boy Yarborough.' When I looked at him, he looked to me like a Henry. I apologize if it makes you angry. But he still looks like a Henry . . . to me, at least."

She laughed. "You know, I'm afraid to ask what a Henry looks like because that's going to be his name."

Ed waited and finally asked in a constricted voice, "Are you taking him home with you?"

Her eyes clouded slightly. Her answer was delivered to the floor. "Oh, God, I'd love to. I want to, but I don't know. My mother is supporting me through art school. She doesn't even know I was pregnant. She's three hundred miles away and very busy. Always has been very busy and very righteous and very right, and how in the hell can I explain that tiny baby to that woman with her pearls and her little black dresses?" She stopped and took a deep breath. Ed sensed that she wanted to say more. He waited. "I could never take the baby home and I know her solution would be for me to put it into a home or some place like that. And, Jesus Christ, do you know the irony, that's just what I may have to do. . . ." Her face was contorted and she was trying desperately not to cry.

"Your father?" asked Ed.

"California, even farther away, with his twenty-seven-year-old wife and three children. It's been years and years, so damned many years since he's even written to me. He's out."

Ed looked at her, scanning her small, delicate features. His palms were moist and he ran his tongue over his front teeth. "How about marrying Henry's father? That might be the answer."

She reached up to push her loose hair back over her shoulder, and in doing this, turned her face away from Ed. But her words were clear and distinct and sad.

"Oh, yes, that would be a very good answer, except that he's married and very happy with his wife or so he told me a hundred times. You see, to him I was like instant therapy to remind him that he wasn't really forty-four years old. At least not to me, but that's the crazy part." She ceased speaking and began chewing on her fingernails.

"What do you mean that's the crazy part?" Ed asked.

"I knew he was forty-four. I wanted him to be forty-four. When I was in bed with him, just knowing that he was older, steadier, and could protect me even for that brief hour or so and that he knew the answers that I didn't know, because he was gentle, older and kinder, and I could hold onto him for a second and pretend that he didn't need me more than I needed him, that's why I think I liked him." She paused and pursed her lips. "And the only way a girl my age, a girl of eighteen can go with a man that age is to sleep with him. So I did. And the dumb part is that he got to feel younger and I got pregnant."

"Does he know?"

"Of course not. It was over long before I knew. And anyway, he has four kids already. What does he want with another one?"

Ed smiled at her answer. "I hope you don't mind all of the questions."

"No, I don't mind. I feel very comfortable talking to you, like you might understand."

"I do understand, but I don't see how to help."

"Then you're in the same boat as me . . . stuck. . . ."

"It's just that the idea of you taking him home makes it all seem worth while," Ed said gently. He was conscious of the girl throughout his entire body. "Maybe you'll come again. I feed him this time every day."

"I cut class to see you. I mean, him, this time. I'll try. I only went back to school yesterday."

Before Ed could answer, reach out to touch her, she turned on her heel and disappeared down the short corridor leading to the outside.

Ed shook his head slowly as he remembered her presence and her youth and he quickly recognized his desire. Great, he thought, just like you to fuck up a good relationship with a fine, upstanding premie by getting the hots for his mother. He pushed himself away from the wall and started out of the nursery.

Before going back to the ward where he had signed out to Mike he decided to stop by the cafeteria for a cup of coffee. He walked down the stairs slowly, thinking over the last hour, the infant in the isolette and the appealing girl staring at him through the glass window. He pushed open the doorway to the basement floor and walked to the cafeteria.

Lem was sitting alone at a table in the center of the room. Only a few of the other tables were occupied, mainly with chattering nurses taking a late afternoon break before the long evening of patients, visitors, and endless medications. Lem was holding his empty coffee cup and staring at the discolored bottom as he moved it in tiny circles on the table in front of him.

Ed walked over and said in a low voice, "Can a white boy sit at this table? Or is reserved only for brothers of special renown?"

"Well, it is a table for the black elite, but I think it's about time we had a token white man, so park your ass, boy, and play the part."

Ed slid into the empty chair directly opposite, picked up his coffee cup and drank.

"How come they let you out of the Emergency Room, Lem? I must tell Rosensweig he's getting awful permissive with the help these days."

"Wash your mouth, boy. I ain't help. I am one of *you* these days . . ."

Ed laughed, spilling some of the hot coffee onto his already soiled white pants. "How is the pit today? You've had your share of problems these last few days."

Lem made a face and shrugged his shoulders. "No worse than usual. Just a lot of sick kids dragging in."

Ed put down his coffee cup and sat staring at the contents.

"What's eating you, Ed? You look like hell, all tired out, worse than I've ever seen you look."

Ed looked up at the calm, dark face of his friend. "Doesn't it ever get to you, Lem, the sickness, the kids crying in pain . . . the kids." There was a long pause. "The kids dying. Jesus, Lem, doesn't it ever make you wonder?"

The black man laid his palms flat on the table top. "No, Ed, I never wonder. Oh, sometimes I get tired of the pain I see, but I grew up in the middle of a lot of pain and sickness and hangin' around Accident Rooms, and kids found knifed and dead from overdoses, so I don't wonder too much. But every once in a while I get mad at the people that bring the suffering in to me, 'cause they're the ones. They are responsible, not the kids, and that's when I wonder."

127

Ed pressed his lips together. He didn't want to talk but this was the only person who might understand. He said so softly that Lem had to lean over the table to hear, "Lem . . . I'm seriously thinking . . ." He paused. "I'm seriously thinking of quitting Pediatrics." Lem didn't speak. "I can't sleep well at nights worrying about the kids. And the sickness and the dying are getting to me. I love them, Lem, the children, but maybe I'm in the wrong specialty. Am I really doing more than somebody else who wouldn't bruise so easily? Maybe there's another field in Medicine where I can work without constant sadness."

Ed moistened his lips and moved uncomfortably in his seat.

"Lem, it's been building, this doubt. It's been getting stronger and stronger. I was almost ready to tell Rosensweig this afternoon but I couldn't. All I could do was accept his offer for a job next year. Like a fool I accepted when I'm still not sure where I'll be."

There was no response from the huge, dark figure sitting opposite him. Ed clenched his fists and softly banged the table.

"Lem, don't you ever think you're in the wrong place, ever?"

"No."

Ed stared at Lem's impassive face. "How come?"

Lem shifted his weight around in the chair and let his long legs slide out into the aisle.

"First, 'cause I'm making it. I'm really making it. All those years in medical school I wondered were they going to let me get through? You must remember I sure didn't shuffle and scrape my way through our medical school. If anything I sorta bullied my way through, but they kept moving me on and now, man, I'm making it.

"And then it's the kids," Lem continued. "They don't ask no questions. Who you are. Where you're from. Man, I can remember walking into a black sister's room when I was a senior student on Medicine." He paused to swallow. "I can remember her look when I pulled out my stethoscope and told her I was her doctor. And I'll never forget what she said to me. 'Boy, go out and get one of those white boys and stop puttin' on airs.' No child will ever hurt me like that, Ed."

Ed was embarrassed and wanted Lem to stop but he knew that the black man never stopped until he was finished.

"Third, well, Althea and I can't seem to have our own. She wants to adopt. That's hard for me, Ed, it's hard. For several years I kept telling her that I couldn't care for another person's child, but I'm learning how to, Ed, and one of these days Althea will be able to adopt her a baby. And even if it's not mine, I'll have learned to accept it." He paused. "Do you think that's a crazy reason for being where I am today?"

Ed shook his head. "No, Lem, for you, all of those reasons are right, but they're not right for me."

Lem stared at him for a long moment. "I can't give you any great reasons for not quitting today, Ed. But give it some more time. Hang in for me. I believe in you. Have faith, man."

"I'll try, Lem." Ed rose from the seat, flushed and tired. "And thanks, Lem. . . ." Ed left the cafeteria.

XII

THE next morning Mike got off the elevator on the fifth floor and immediately saw the rows of children in wheelchairs and portable cribs lined up outside the Treatment Room waiting for the morning blood drawing. From inside, the sound of crying could be heard. As the door opened to admit the next patient or to discharge the last one, the noise increased in the hall outside; and the older children seated next to the door glanced at each other with discomfort.

Mike smiled at several of the patients that he knew and hurried to the ward where Allison was dressing to go home. He stopped at the nurse's station, flipped open the order book, and solemnly wrote her discharge. After signing his name, he stood up and rubbed his hands together. The blunt figure of Dr. Gilberg came heavily out of Allison's door. When she saw Mike she strode over to him.

"Did you write her discharge?"

Mike nodded. He respected Dr. Gilberg but she made him uncomfortable. She accentuated the difference in their levels of training more than any other doctor on the staff. It was as if her status depended on her position rather than her ability. And what a shame. Because her talent itself was enormously impressive.

"That kid did very well so far," she said. "Don't know how

long the remission will last, though. She had so many stem cells in that marrow when she came in."

She reached into her pocket and pulled out a pack of cigarettes. Mike made no attempt to light her a match.

"She's getting Cushingoid from the steroids. Keeps telling me how fat she's getting. Seems more upset than most of the kids about it. Well, that's the least of my worries now. She's in remission. That's what counts. Don't you agree, Hillman?"

Mike decided to speak. He usually nodded and waited until the woman moved away before he would pound the table or hurl an expletive at her departing bulk. But this time she was talking about a kid that meant more to him than just another remission.

"Dr. Gilberg, if the child is worried about getting fat, don't you think she deserves some explanation of why and for how long she'll be fat."

The woman stared at him, then crushed her cigarette out in the ashtray on the desk.

"If you feel so strongly about it, Hillman, and it's pretty obvious that you do, then you go in and tell her that she has leukemia and will stay fat like this until she gets sick again and either dies or takes another medication. Be my guest." She spit the last few words out at him and then thrust her hands deep into the pockets of the long white coat and walked down the hall.

"Bitch!" The word was whispered at her back as she moved out of sight. One day I'll say it loud enough for her to hear. That castrating bitch. The increasing gaiety of the sounds emanating from Allison's room distracted him from his anger. Inside was Allison, fully dressed in a full-skirted organdy dress, pink and feminine. Sandy stood near the bed trying to close her overstuffed suitcase. Allison watched her with a mixture of supervisory concern and poorly concealed delight. Her books were stacked on the bed and wrapped several times around with heavy cord. The stuffed animals that she had accumu-

132

lated were sticking out of a shopping bag that barely could stand under the weight of its bulky contents.

"Looks to me like you need some help." He walked over to the bed and took the suitcase and pressed it firmly together. Nothing happened. He opened the suitcase and looked inside. A large metal frame wrapped in several layers of underwear was keeping it from closing. He pulled it out and held it up. "What's this?"

Allison jumped slightly.

"It's a picture of Reggie. Her uncle came in to see me and gave it to me and Sandy bought me the frame. Please. It has to fit in."

Mike unwrapped a few layers of cloth from the metal frame and saw the thin, smiling face of the dead child staring up at him.

"Great picture of her. Sure you'll take it with you but maybe better in the shopping bag. Okay?" He put the metal frame into the shopping bag, pushing several of the furry animals toward the bottom. The suitcase now closed easily. "See. It works."

Allison clapped her hands. Her full face was flushed with excitement and her eyes danced. She *is* becoming more Cushingoid, Mike thought. I hadn't noticed how full her face had become the last few days.

Mike turned to Sandy. "The orders are written. Gilberg has given her signature. So everything's set." Sandy nodded. "Allison, don't forget our date. Would you mind if Sandy came along?" Allison shook her head and ran over and grabbed Sandy's hand in hers. Sandy looked over at Mike.

"Where are we going and when? Allison, you got asked before me so I'm completely in the dark."

"We're going to a baseball game."

Mike signaled to Sandy that he would speak to her later. He heard his name being repeated over the loudspeaker and excused himself to pick up the phone.

"Hello. Lem Thomas here."

"Lem, Mike. Did you call?"

"Yeah, Mike. I got a badly beat up kid down here. Old man's drunk and raisin' hell and the kid's comatose and looks bad. Can you come down? I need a hand."

"Be right there."

The phone clicked. Mike held it for a second and then replaced it. He walked over to Allison's door and looked in.

"I've got to go down to the pit on an emergency. I don't know how long I'll be, so I'd better say good-bye now, Allison."

The child stood for a moment and then ran toward him with her arms outstretched. He lifted her into his arms and held her very tightly. When she buried her head in the curve of his neck, he knew that she was crying.

"Hey, most people laugh to get out of here." He held her close and waited. Her head came up and she leaned toward him and kissed him full upon the mouth. When she pulled away, she dropped her head so that she rested on his shoulder. They stood in this position for a time and then he gently placed her down on the floor.

"See you in about ten days for that date. I'll call you a couple of days before. Be a good girl while I'm not around to keep you honest."

As he walked down the narrow corridor to the Emergency Pediatric section, he saw two figures struggling silently against the pale yellow wall. As he came closer, he realized that they were a man and a woman. The woman was pressing the man toward the wall, struggling to keep him from moving. She had pinned him with her shoulder and held him, whispering all the time that they rocked back and forth. She wore a faded print housedress, tied around the waist only once because of the protruding abdomen announcing the far advanced state of her pregnancy. The arm pushing firmly against the man hung in folds of fat. The other arm grabbed him tightly around his ample abdomen squeezing as tightly as she could. The man was equally obese. He snarled at the woman with mouth open revealing several missing teeth.

"Billy, please. You're drunk. Oh, Billy, quiet down. Haven't you done enough already? Billy, listen to me. Stop! Oh, God, Billy, the baby's in there, don't you remember? You beat on the baby, Billy. He didn't do no harm to you. You was drunk."

The woman saw Mike who was now level with her and she eased the struggle slightly without removing her shoulder from the man's chest. Releasing one hand from around the man's middle she reached out to Mike. The man didn't move, conscious of Mike's presence.

"Oh, Doc, they got my baby in there. You goin' to look at him? He's only hurt a little. We was playin' with him and he fell off the bed. See to him, Doc, please."

"Shit." The man belched and turned his face toward the wall, repeating the word several more times.

"Shut up, Billy. Please, ain't it bad enough, Billy, I'm beggin' you."

The man slumped, sliding slowly down the wall until he was sitting on the floor. He leaned his head against his knees and his voice bounced off against the worn linoleum floor. "Fuck it." The woman turned away from him and placed both hands over her face. Mike started walking more rapidly.

He found Lem leaning over the prostrate body of a small white baby. He would look up and talk occasionally to the nurse standing at the foot of the bed. The rest of the time he peered into the child's eyes with a pinpoint light. The baby didn't move at all. Mike moved over to stand beside Lem, waiting for him to finish checking the retina. The child was approximately a year old, very pale and undernourished, the arms and legs thin and flabby from the absence of fat and subcutaneous tissue. Mike ran his hand over the right leg and thigh and felt two large abnormal prominences. Both were

135

firm and bony and caused no stirring from the child as Mike pressed and tried to move them. As Lem stood up, Mike could see the child's face and chest. The face was covered with fresh bruises and there were several more marks under each arm as if the child had been severely squeezed or thrown. The abdomen contained several surface bruises particularly over the liver area. Lem turned and looked at Mike, his eyes a mixture of pain and anger.

"Kid's bad, Mike. He's been beaten up badly. I've put in a call for the neurosurgeon. I think he's bleeding in his head. He's deep as you can see and has been going down slightly since he came in. I've alerted the O.R."

"Anything in his fundi?"

"I think I can see some hemorrhages and some venous engorgement. It's too early for much else."

"He's been beat before."

"I haven't checked him out by x-ray but I felt those healing fractures in his legs too. I'm sure you're right."

The nurse grabbed Lem's arm as he stood looking at Mike.

"He's stopped. Quick, he's stopped breathing."

Lem jumped slightly, leaned over the child, and called out to the nurse for the emergency tray. Then he signaled to Mike to start artificial respiration. Before Mike could begin, Lem was back with an endotracheal tube in one hand and a metal laryngoscope in the other.

"Hold him, Mike, I'm going down."

Mike pulled the child's head back and tilted his chin. The nurse had a stethoscope over the child's chest marking the slowing heart beat with her moving finger.

"Damn it, I can't see your finger. Call it out." Mike had not seen Lem so rattled before. Neither he nor the nurse said anything. She began calling out the heart beat in slow cadence. Lem inserted the metal blade into the inert child's mouth looking intently through the tunneled end. He picked up the plastic endotracheal tube and slipped it down. It disappeared

136

part of the way leaving an open tube at the entrance of the child's mouth. The nurse's eyes were riveted to the child's chest.

"Mike, get an Ambu bag while I breathe the child. And ask the other nurse to call the anesthesiologist."

He put his lips to the end of the plastic tube and blew gently into the open exposed end of the endotracheal tube. The child's chest rose perceptibly. Lem pointed to the child's lateral chest wall and signaled to the nurse to listen. When he breathed in the second time, she nodded vigorously indicating that he was in the trachea and inflating the child's lungs. He pointed to the oxygen tank against the wall with the rubber tube attached. She understood, dropped the stethoscope onto the child's chest and pulled the heavy tank over to Lem's side handing him the mask, which he promptly pulled off, leaving only the rubber tubing attached. She turned the metal handle and the insistent hissing sound of the escaping oxygen began. In steady rhythm Lem would breathe in a mouthful of oxygen and then blow it slowly but steadily into the open end of the endotracheal tube. The child's color had become mottled and dusky. His pulse beats were slowing.

Lem looked up to see the nurse motioning to the doorway. A heavy, short man was peering into the room. Lem turned back to the nurse who whispered to him that the man was the child's father. There was nothing they could do.

"Please close the door. Things are serious and we would like you to wait outside." The nurse's voice was shaky but pleasant. She was obviously trying not to alarm nor antagonize the man.

"What's that nigger doin' with my kid?" The slurred words broke into the room like a firecracker. The nurse glanced at Lem who didn't move or even acknowledge the man's presence. He continued to breathe in the hissing oxygen and blow it into the tube sustaining the infant's life.

137

"Get that fuckin' nigger away from my kid. I'd rather have him dead than have a nigger blowin' into his mouth."

The nurse looked frantically around for Mike hoping that he would come back and close the door. She saw a woman's arms on the man's shoulders pulling at him. Soon the sounds of her pleading rose into a whining, sibilant wail.

"Billy. Oh, God, please come away. The baby's bad. Ain't you done enough? Can't you see the baby's bad. . . ."

"Get off o' me, damn it. There's a nigger workin' on my baby. Can't you see that, you stupid shit? A black nigger . . ."

Lem continued to work on the child, but the nurse noticed that beads of perspiration were forming around his hairline and his neck muscles had tightened into taut ropes. The infant's heart beat was slowing even more. Mike rushed back into the room saying,

"Can't find the damn Ambu bag. They must have taken it up to the clinic or the nursery. Nobody down here knows where it is. I told the anesthesiologist to bring one, he's on his way down."

Lem stopped for a second to move his head in the direction of the door. "Look who we got for a visitor."

Mike immediately recognized the man leaning against the door with the hate pouring out of his eyes and the saliva dribbling down his chin. He started toward him. In between breaths, Lem shook his head and as he came up to get more oxygen, he said,

"Don't send him away. Let the bastard watch. He did it. Let him watch."

Mike stood rooted to the spot. Lem's anger was new to him and he didn't want to push it further.

"Hey, you, Doc, you, the white one, get that nigger off my kid before I got to come in there and do it myself."

The nurse looked panic stricken. The baby lay limp and blue on the table.

"No pulse, the baby's got no pulse."

Lem continued working for several more puffs but she shook her head. Mike had heard the nurse's words and was drawing adrenalin up in a syringe.

"Take over, Mike." Lem stood up. His body was sagging under the efforts to keep his anger underneath the surface.

"What's a matter, black bastard, after you killed my kid, you give up?"

Mike had placed a long needle into the child's chest, drawn blood, injected the adrenalin and waited briefly for a response. None came. Lem stood, looking at the child lying motionless on the table. His fists were clenched and he was rocking back and forth on the balls of his feet. Mike looked up and gave a hopeless shrug of his shoulders. He began pressing intermittently on the child's chest in an attempt at closed chest heart massage.

The woman outside started to weep. "Billy, come away. They're doin' their best. It's no use, I warned you. Oh, Sweet Jesus, my baby. Billy, that was my baby."

The man beat his fist against the door jamb. "That baby jes' fell offn' the bed. If that nigger hadn't laid his han's on him, the baby'd be all right."

Mike heard a low growl and saw Lem facing the man in the doorway and realized that the ominous sound was coming from his associate.

"Lem, don't," Mike called. He reached his free arm out and knew it was hopeless. Lem took three steps toward the man who seemed oblivious to his impending danger. He kept staring at the floor and repeating the word "nigger" over and over, until he felt the full impact of the black doctor's body. Lem crashed into him, his face contorted in anger, his mouth twisted with hate. The man, at first startled, fell down upon his back. Lem reached down and picked him up off the floor. The woman covered her mouth but her cries, though muffled, pierced the room. Lem lifted the stunned body easily and held it poised in the air.

"Oh, God. Oh, God." The woman's words surrounded the two men.

The man in the air hung slackly, too stunned and drunk to fully comprehend.

Lem's face glistened with perspiration. Mike left the child, instructing the nurse to take over, knowing the child could not be saved. As he moved toward the two men Lem hurled the drunken father violently against the yellow tile wall of the corridor, the sound of the impact reverberating down the hall. The man's head struck the wall, fell forward, and blood began running down his right temple. His head slid down on his chest which sagged into the distended, relaxed abdomen. He was still. The only sound was the woman's sobbing. Mike was paralyzed. Then Lem's deep, strained voice erupted.

"Now you white trash, now you know what that little kid felt like. If you're what it's like to be white, you bastard, I'm glad I'm a nigger. God damn you. You murderer. God damn you." Lem started to run. Mike tried to follow him but Lem was too fast and Mike was left in front of the hospital, watching his friend racing down the street, his white uniform the only thing now visible between the darkness of his body and the glare of the afternoon sun.

XIII

AFTER helping Allison dress and pack to go home, Sandy decided to call her mother. She listened to the ringing on the other end of the phone, suspecting that her mother was outside planting the early spring seedlings. She pictured her looking frantically around as the ringing started for one of her children to answer it, forgetting that they all were in school or working, fully grown, no longer squatting by her side digging in the fresh, rich soil. She would drop her gloves onto the ground after hastily peeling them off, rush to the front door, discover that she had locked herself out from that entrance, scurry around the side of the house, push open the screen door which had not been taken down during the winter, and hurry inside. The phone continued to ring several more times. Sandy stood patiently holding the black plastic instrument against her ear. Suddenly the repetitive ringing was interrupted by an occupied silence punctuated by rapid, heavy breathing. Sandy smiled.

"Mother?"

"Yes."

"This is Sandy. How are you?"

"Well, right now, I'm out of wind. Ran all around the house to the side door. Locked myself out again." There was a short pause. Then the voice returned somewhat bewildered.

"Why do I do that so often, do you think, Sandy? It's a darned nuisance."

"I don't know, Mother. I guess you just forget when you're out in the garden."

"You're right, dear, but how did you know I was out in the garden? That's very clever."

"I guessed, Mother. It's that time of year, isn't it?"

"Yes it is, my dear." Again a brief pause. "Well, now I feel better. Got my breath back. How are you, Sandy? Is everything all right?" The question was carefully phrased not to show too much concern, not to suggest prying. Since the day, years before, when Sandy had moved out of her mother's home to live alone and have her baby in solitary emptiness, her mother had ceased questioning her about her actions. She had come home to recuperate after the birth, alone, without the child that her mother knew that she had been carrying, and announced only once to the woman standing in the shadow of her bedroom that she had given the baby up for adoption. There had been no further discussion of the matter. She had lain around for slightly more than ten days when her mother quietly suggested that she get up and help in the house if she intended to stay. She remembered her initial anger at what she thought was her mother's obtuse lack of sensitivity and her eventual admiration at the older woman's gentle refusal to watch her daughter destroy herself.

"Oh, yes, I'm fine Mother. Still single with not too much change in sight."

"I wasn't referring to that. I'll let you worry about that. I'll save myself to wonder about your health."

"Mother, how about inviting me over for dinner this evening?"

"Sandy, you've never needed an invitation. I'm thrilled. I'll just take out a couple more lamb chops from the freezer and I'm set."

"Usual time?"

"A little earlier now, dear. Sam started evening classes this semester."

"Five, then?"

"That's fine, Sandy. See you then. Good-bye."

Sandy hung up the phone and reflected on what her mother had said. Her younger brother had begun night school months before and she had not known. She felt restless and ambivalent, guilty about the wasted days that followed her rejection of family ties and uncomfortable at the thought of attaching herself again to the concrete existence of a family.

She drove down the shaded street lined on each side with large weatherbeaten frame houses surrounded by well-kept lawns. The tall trees with the thick trunks announced the substantial age of the street. There was an inbred smugness about it; a middle-class complacent satisfaction that Sandy had found so frightening during her years of nurse's training and especially after David's death. This unalterable calm now seemed no less unrealistic to her but had acquired a new quality of permanence that was insidiously becoming important to her.

She parked the car along the pavement next to the mailbox and sat for a moment contemplating the outside of the house. The gray paint on the shingles was peeling just enough to be noticeable at that distance; the rainspouts had rusted at the corners and one was hanging loose; the trellis holding the rosebush at a corner of the house had sagged badly under the weight of a winter snow and had not been repaired. Sandy noted these things with some inner pain. Before he died, her father had never allowed the house to show its age. He treated it as if it were his mistress. He pampered each shingle. Paint went on everything at the first sign that the winter onslaught had ceased. Nails were beaten into creaking wood. Screendoors came on and off each season. The lawn was seeded and regularly mowed. Flowers were planted by both husband and wife with an edge of competition existing between the two of them in anticipation of whose flower bed would have the most colorful and exuberant yield. She recalled sitting on the cement walk that led from the front door down to the mailbox watching him standing on a stepladder, hammer in hand and pounding upon the wood until every shingle fell into place. She had loved him totally; but when she had needed him most, when she was sixteen, he was gone. She had lost him. The pain of that loss had been dulled by David's death, but had not been abandoned. For as she gazed at her home, at its gradual deterioration, she remembered her first loss; and for those moments that she sat in her car, she grieved anew. She recalled the terrible restlessness that followed her father's death, her own terror, her anger at her mother, unexplained, unwarranted, flaring, remorseful anger that only deepened the older woman's feelings of unexpected responsibility and climaxed in scenes where the two women held each other as if drowning. Even as she sat in the front seat of her car looking at a withering home that had once bulged with the vitality of the man within, she wondered again at the resilience of her younger brother and sister whose ability to mourn seemed circumscribed to an appropriate time period while hers was boundless. Was that why she came home today? Did she have to end the first stage of her mourning here, in this house, among her family?

As she walked up the winding cement pathway to the front door, she could see her mother's face peering out of the kitchen window. Then the door opened and her mother stood there, apron over her skirt, arms extended, waiting. Sandy slipped her own arms around the older woman's waist. They stood silently holding each other for a long period of time, and then they quietly parted. She glanced at her mother's face and was somewhat alarmed to see how much the woman had aged in the months that had elapsed since their last visit together. Her usually slender frame seemed strangely smaller. The apron strings folded twice around the small waist; and the legs had slimmed down even more, losing some of the curves that had made them her most attractive feature. Her hair was the only thing that Sandy knew would not change. As long as she could remember, her mother had gone once a month to have her hair dyed a bright red. Once Sandy had gone with her mother, and pulling on her sleeve while walking home, she had asked her mother why she chose such a vibrant color. "Because he likes it." That was all she had said. The "he" was understood. After his death, the red hair persisted. No one asked why.

"You were outside in the car a long time."

"Looking at the house. Going back a few years. I can't help but think of so many things when I see the house."

"It's not what it was. The street's as nice but the house isn't. I don't have the knack or the money so the seasons have their way with it, the snow in the winter especially."

"It's developed a certain charm." Sandy lied and linked arms with her mother and walked into the kitchen where the smells of food cooking engulfed her. She sat down as her mother lifted the lids on the pots on the stove and automatically stirred each, using the heavy wooden ladle that Sandy could remember licking as a child.

"I used to worry about the house, about how he would be upset if he could see it developing this 'charm' that you call it; but I don't any longer. The other two children don't give me time to worry about the house. It takes all my energy trying to keep up with them." She sat down and placed her elbows on the table and leaned her lined face in the palms of her open hands. "You know, they are so different from you, when you were growing up. It's frightening."

"How are they different?" Sandy slipped her suit coat off and draped it over the plastic back of the kitchen chair.

"Well, first it's the dress, then the hair, then the language. Sam doesn't dress. It's that simple. And the barbers would starve if they depended on his head for their living. Half the time I can't understand a thing he says. He keeps talking, I keep nodding as if I understood; and that's how we spend our evenings together. And Amy is catching up to him. Although she still likes to look nice, thank God."

"Mom, all seventeen-year-old boys are like that these days, don't you think?"

"You're right, I guess. Actually, dear, I'm not complaining. I've been doing some reading lately on how to act with teen-agers; and I think I'm coming across."

Sandy smiled. Her mother always went to the library and took out armfuls of books whenever she came up against a problem that confused her. She would sit for hours, her head propped up on a pillow in bed, her glasses perched on the middle of her nose, the books lying in wild disarray over the bed-covers, reading long into the night, doing what Sandy's father had called her "research."

"Yes, dear, I've been reading," her mother said. "Particularly about drugs and dope and pot and things like that. Maybe if I can talk about what's happening and recognize what's going on with the children, I can prevent their getting caught up in it."

Her naïve insight suddenly stopped Sandy cold. She was certain that no one would fully realize the scope of this woman after she was gone; her mother sent up waves of helplessness that hid the resilient strength underneath. Sandy had been trying to convince herself that this was just a visit, but now admitted that she was here to draw something from her mother that would help her solve her continuing preoccupation with the past.

"Mother, anything new with you?"

"No, dear. Let's stop talking about me and tell me about you. What's new for you? I hope life has been good to you."

"The same, Mother. The same. I go to the hospital every day and take care of other people's sick children and some-times I fall in love with one of them, and they either die or I send them home to their parents and I start over again. My life is the same as it was last year this time."

"It's never the same, my dear. You're a year older."

"Yes, that too."

Her mother looked up. "Are you feeling sorry for yourself, Sandy? Because if you are, please don't ask me to join in."

Sandy turned her face away and looked out of the window, staring at the fresh leaves fluttering in the tentative April wind. "Mother, I am feeling sorry for myself. I don't quite know what to do. I feel lost." She felt her mother's hand lying on her own on the table. There was a brief moment between the two of them that meant more than any words. It was as if that physical act was a beginning, a renewal, a returning.

"Sandy, there's no one?"

"Oh, God, Mother, there's everyone, that's the trouble. Please don't be shocked but I'm very easy to have."

Her mother's expression didn't change. "I understand the need, Sandy. I've often thought about the same thing for myself. At first, at least. One gets so lonely."

Sandy sat feeling as if she was walking naked and not experiencing any shame. For the first time in her life, guilt and grief had evaporated from the restless tides of her body. "Yes, it is loneliness, at least part of it. A need to find something or someone. Oh, Christ, Mother, I feel so damn incomplete."

"Isn't that Gordon boy still interested?"

"Yes."

No other mention, no explanations, merely the name inserted at this moment. Sandy turned toward her mother, smiled and took her hand in hers and squeezed gently.

At that moment, her brother dashed through the front door, his long hair flying behind him. His blue dungarees were streaked with white and his moccasins torn and thready. The beginnings of a mustache looked like unwashed dirt on his upper lip but gave signs of filling in. He was tall and rangy, his smile open, his manner fluctuating between diffidence and defiance. He threw his gloves and long scarf on the table in the hall and stuck his head into the kitchen.

"Hi, Mom. Hey, hi, Sis."

The two women released their hands somewhat embarrassed.

"What's for dinner, Mom?"

"Lamb chops."

"Great. You know, early dinner tonight. I've got school." His mother nodded and rose. Sandy surveyed her brother and saw so much of the man she had adored in his face. He resembled her father far more than did the girls in the family.

"Sam, how's work?"

"How can construction work be, Sis? Pays good. And lets me go to night school."

"It seems to agree with you."

"Anywhere I can do my thing, rap around with some real guys, and make bread agrees with me. You're looking great, too."

"Thanks."

"Good to see you holding hands. Let it all hang out. That's what I'm trying to teach Mom."

He swung around, jumped high into the air as if landing a basketball shot and careened into the table in the foyer. He laughed and fled down the hall into his room. Sandy turned toward her mother who was wearing a tolerant, amused expression.

"Sandy, you just met my teacher. The man in my life who is going to drag me screaming into the next generation."

Sandy laughed. She felt so relaxed and at home.

"Doesn't he mind having to work like that so he can go to school?"

"Mind? My God, he picked it. I got him offers for offices. No, not my Paul Bunyan, he told me he wanted fresh air and the outside. So it's dragging lumber and you name it. But Sandy, he's very happy. Isn't that what counts? And he is doing well in his night classes."

"Amy?"

Her mother chuckled, stirred the stewed tomatoes, and spoke. "I'm getting ready for her. She may have to drag me back into my own generation so that she too can teach me how to hang it all out all over again."

They both laughed.

"I was glad to know that you are planting again, Mother. You had stopped for a while. But these last few years the garden has looked like it was before."

"But it's different." Her mother sounded suddenly more serious.

"How different? It seemed the same to me."

Her mother didn't speak as she bent over and slipped the lamb chops into the oven. Then she walked over to the table and sat down opposite Sandy.

"I'm planting all new kinds of flowers. None of the old ones."

Sandy lifted her eyebrows.

"Why, Mother? That was the thing Daddy loved the most, his flowers. Those particular flowers."

"That's why, my dear. Your father's dead. When someone dies, they're gone. We must accept it and start fresh, do new things, not hold tightly onto the past. And we have to show ourselves that we survived, made it, are going on. I didn't move or go out with a lot of men. My hair stayed red. I had come to like it. But I stopped planting those same flowers. I planted new ones so each year I could see my new life begin again as the flowers bloomed."

Sandy sat very still. She knew what was being said. They didn't touch. Her mother's next words were a whisper meant only for her.

149

"Plant your own garden differently, Sandy. Pull up those old flowers."

Her mother walked into the dining room, leaving Sandy sitting very still, staring blindly out of the window.

XIV

Mike strode across the lobby, his duffel bag slung over his shoulder. He smiled at a nurse, his face animated and his arm shrugging slightly under the weight of his bag. Ed, who was already waiting, saw the girl unconsciously smoothing down her uniform stretched tightly across her buttocks and shifting her weight from one leg to another. Mike stood talking for a moment, then spotted Ed standing up against the information desk.

"Hi, been waiting long?"

Ed shook his head. "No. A few minutes. Watching the passing parade."

"Where we goin' first?"

"I thought we should stop by the store and pick up a couple of steaks and maybe a small bottle of wine. We might have a party. I feel like I've earned one."

Mike smiled and lifted his duffel bag higher. "I'm for that. Sounds great."

Ed watched the persistent juggling. "Can I help you? You look weighed down. What the hell's in the duffel anyway?"

"Journals. Rosensweig wants me to discuss Rocky Mountain Spotted Fever next week at Journal Club, and all the good articles are in the fattest damn journals in the library. But I can manage."

The two men moved toward the glass doors and walked out into the clean April evening.

Ed's Volkswagen sat in the doctors' parking lot dwarfed by the heavy, shiny American cars lined up in rows around it. As he pulled into the heavy urban traffic, Ed asked,

"Did Lem come back today?"

"Yeah, about an hour ago. It was gruesome. I knew that something was about to blow when the drunk wouldn't let up. But you know, I don't think it was the black bit with Lem as much as it was that dead kid lying on that table. When he couldn't bring him back, I sensed him change. And Jesus, when he blew."

"What happened to the kid's father?"

"Actually he was so damn drunk that he landed like a sack of potatoes and didn't break anything. He's bruised but nothing serious."

"Thank God for Lem. Mike, where did Lem go?"

"You know where he ran. I was so sure I could have called ahead."

"Althea?"

"Of course. I can picture just what happened. He hollered and cried and she sat quietly and listened and then went to the closet, handed him his coat and told him that he had to go back and see what he had done. And after some ineffectual refusals while Althea stood at the door with his coat over her arm, he grabbed his coat, cursed, and came back."

"I think you're probably right except that I've never heard Lem curse in his own home in front of Althea."

"Ed, today was a special day for Lem. He couldn't turn such fury off that quickly."

"What do you think is going to happen?"

Mike cupped his fingers around one of his knees. "I'm not sure. But rumor has it that when Todd told Rosensweig what had happened, he looked at Todd and said that the bastard was lucky that it hadn't been him, that he would have broken his ass. I'm told those were his exact words. If I read Rosensweig right, I think he was saying that he'll go to bat for Lem in a big way."

Ed thought of his own interview with the Chief. "I think so. Rosensweig will probably love the crusade. I hope he doesn't crucify Lem in the process."

When they finally reached their apartment, Ed laden with the groceries, they found a telegram wedged in the door. Ed scanned the envelope.

"Mike, it's for you."

Mike ripped it open, unfolded the message and read it as the envelope sailed unnoticed down to the ground. He read the message twice, trying not to miss any nuance. The words were terse and direct as he would have expected. It simply said, "Father ill. Call. Do not come. Mother." He handed the telegram to Ed who read it and handed it back.

"Call now and I'll start dinner. Don't try to eat until you know."

Mike dialed the number. As he waited he pictured the old man lying in bed ordering his arthritic wife around the house and telling the doctor, a personal friend, how ridiculous his instructions were. Mike's pain at the thought of his father's illness was not caused by the danger of a relationship ending but by the fact that one had never begun. He heard the phone ring several times and then a cracked voice spoke into his ear.

"Yes?"

"Mother, this is Mike. I just opened your telegram. What's the matter with Father?"

"According to the doctor, he's had a stroke. He is conscious but his left side is paralyzed and his speech is not so good."

"Is there any danger?"

"Dr. Cochran says that there is always the threat of pneumonia at his age. Your father refuses to go to the hospital so I am taking care of him at home."

"Are you okay?"

The voice was irritated and sharp. "Of course, I'm fine. I've taken care of him all these years. Why should I have trouble now?"

"Any of the other children there with him?"

"Your sisters drove in yesterday and saw him. They've been here today and expect to leave tomorrow."

"When did this happen, Mother?"

"Let me see, four days ago. That's right, today is Thursday. It happened Monday."

Mike didn't ask why he was just being notified. The answer was implicit in the action. He marveled at how insignificant was the hurt he felt at realizing that delay had occurred.

"Mother, would you like me to fly out for the day to see him. I'd be happy to."

There was a brief pause, time enough for both parties to prepare themselves for the answer.

"That won't be necessary, Mike. Your father hasn't asked for you. If he does, I'll call or send another wire."

"Right. Well, call me if you want me. . . ." There was a short pause. Mike was angry now, just angry enough to want to remind his mother that she had traded her son for her husband years ago and now was in danger of losing both. "By the way, Mother, I'm well, even though you didn't ask."

There was no response on the other end of the phone, merely a slight wheezing. Suddenly the phone clicked in Mike's ear and the dial tone resumed. He replaced the receiver and walked away from the desk. Ed was setting the table and Mike could hear a spitting sound as the steaks grilled in the small rotisserie that they used for most of their meals.

"What's up?"

"My father's had a stroke but he still is conscious. Taciturn as ever, I'm sure. . . ." And he didn't speak for a second as Ed looked up, plate in hand, to study his face. "They don't think I should come 'cause he hasn't asked for me. Christ, if they waited for him to ask for me, we'd have lost contact completely."

Ed watched him carefully. "You shook up about his being ill?"

Mike stripped off his jacket and placed it on the shabby living-room chair.

"It's crazy, Ed, but I guess I've always thought about him being sick. I always pictured him as old and slightly sick. I think that's what kept me from hating him more than I did. Thinking that he was too sick to notice me or care about what I cared about or show any affection made his behavior seem reasonable on the very bad days. Of course he wasn't sick. It was my fantasy. Now it's a reality. So I don't think that phone call changed very much in my own mind."

They sat down to eat, Mike paying more attention to the wine than to the food.

"Ed, have you ever given any thought to what you're going to end up doing? You know, five years or even ten years from now?"

Ed cleared his throat of an imaginary obstruction. His voice was louder than he imagined it would be. "Mike, at this minute I'm not even sure whether I'm going to end up a Pediatrician."

Mike frowned. "You'd rather not discuss it?"

"Not about me, if you don't mind. I'm getting like somebody under analysis. Everybody I meet gets a dose of my problems."

"Well, I'll talk about myself then. I never find that very hard. You know what I dream about? It's crazy." Mike stopped for a minute and flushed slightly. "I picture myself returning to that goddamn town in Illinois and getting so well known, so famous, that everybody who's important uses me for their kids . . . and that even my father will ask me to come when he's sick . . . and my mother will tell the corner-store man that I'm her boy . . . with pride, goddamn it . . . with a little bit of pride." He stopped and grinned rather foolishly. "I'm pretty hung up, aren't I? I feel wedged in, wedged in between my anger and my hope for payment, some kind of payment for old pain."

After a long silence, Ed said, "The telegram started it and then the wine. It's better out."

Mike shook his head violently. "No . . . it started years ago, years ago when I rode through the streets of a small town on my bicycle staring into the windows of families that I vaguely knew, imagining myself sitting at their tables, sleeping in their beds, feeling their arms holding me, riding from dinnertime until it was dark . . . that's when it really began . . . but the problem always is when will it end. . . ." He abruptly stood up, reaching across the table, picking up Ed's plate and his own and walking into the kitchen without uttering another word. Ed heard the water start in the sink.

"Mike, how about going to a movie tonight? I think we both need it."

Mike looked up, flipped the plate onto the drying rack, and shook his head.

"No, thanks, Ed. I'm all right now, a small explosion that only hurt the man in the immediate vicinity. Besides, I have to start work on the damn presentation for Rosensweig. He asked me to stay next year, so if I'm lousy, I'll hear about it for the next fifteen months or longer. You know him."

Ed smiled. "Yes, I know him and I can also hear him if you fuck up. Well, I think I'm going to go anyway, if you don't mind."

Mike grabbed a streaked, dirty towel off the drying rack. "Mind? Hell no, go and see one of those Danish sex jobs and then tell me all about it."

156

Ed checked his pockets for his car keys and waved to Mike who was vigorously rubbing the inside of a dry glass.

He left his car in the parking lot and walked to the movie theater which was only up the block. The line at the ticket window moved slowly as the doors to the movie house opened at intervals discharging squinting, hesitant adults into the warm evening air. Ed debated whether to wait.

"Hello, Henry's friend."

Ed looked up and saw a pair of large green eyes staring at him. The girl stood with one arm fondling the strap of a large stuffed purse which was draped over her small shoulder. Her head was tilted to the side; her lips were parted in the beginnings of a tentative smile.

"Hello, Henry's mother," said Ed.

She frowned for a moment, looked around at the milling crowd which seemed totally oblivious to the two of them standing there and shook her head. "I've never been referred to as anybody's mother before in public. That sounds middle-aged."

Ed smiled. "Nobody in their right mind would think of you as middle-aged."

"God, I hope not."

"In fact, each time I see you I have trouble remembering that you're grown-up."

Her face darkened and she brushed away a strand of loose hair that had fallen over her forehead. "I'm not. That's what my problem is, at least according to the two psychiatrists my mother dragged me to—that was three years ago. 'She's not mature yet.' That cost her close to a thousand dollars. And look, you've met me just twice, not counting tonight, and you made the same diagnosis for nothing."

"I didn't mean to upset you. It wasn't meant as an insult."

"You would have trouble insulting me. I like you too much.

157

People I like try but don't insult me easily. Now my mother insults me by just opening her mouth."

Ed looked around for something that would help him change the subject. There was an unsteady silence between them. "How's school?"

She shrugged. "It's okay, when I go, which isn't too often."

"Why?"

"Why what?"

"Why don't you go more often?"

She raised her eyebrows. "Well, I tell you, Doctor, it's like this." She paused and he quickly interrupted.

"Listen, I wasn't trying to get too personal, it was just curiosity."

She nodded. "I've told you half my life already. I don't go often because I don't think I paint or design very well and even though the teachers all tell me that I do, I have the feeling that they're putting me on. They may not be but that's how I feel. Anyway, that's been the story wherever I've gone, so don't get uptight about it. Mother will pay for something else just as soon as they kick me out, but something out of Chicago, you can be sure. I'm her only investment, and her only failure."

"You know, you really do underrate yourself. Why?"

"And you don't think I should?"

"No."

"Who knows me better, me or you?"

"You, but maybe you can't see for being so close."

"Maybe, and now, how are you?"

Ed smiled. "I'm fine." He stopped and stared at her for a second. "You know I don't know your first name."

She laughed. "That's right. It's Jill, like fell down and broke her crown. Mother had foresight."

Ed tightened his lips. "That's enough of that, while you're with me, cut out the low esteem bit."

"Am I with you? I like the idea very much but now I don't

know your first name. All I know is that you're Henry's doctor."

"My name's Ed. Ed Erikson."

"And you want me to be with you, Ed?"

Ed nodded and felt slightly foolish. "Yes. How about coming in to see the movie?"

"I just came out. I see all the movies, that's how I spend all of the spare time I have, seeing movies about other people's problems and smoking pot. Both things make me forget better than anything else what I should be doing but I'm not. Someday they're going to legalize pot and I'll go to the movies and sit there turning-on and watching and forgetting about myself for good."

"Damn it, Jill, stop the melodramatics for a minute."

She looked at his disturbed features and smiled after a while.

"You win. I was feeling angry at myself tonight and you happened to overhear me. Forgive me, please."

"Jill, let's do something tonight to change your mood. Go somewhere or do something where you can be yourself. I'm not sure I know who you are yet. You've shown me so many different faces."

She squeezed his arm and started walking. Her strides increased and he felt his legs accelerating to keep step with her. Her hair swung recklessly around her head as they breezed down the street.

"Where are we going?" Ed asked, slightly breathless.

"To my apartment. It's only two blocks away, and we're going to have coffee, espresso. I just bought the apparatus yesterday and I've been drinking espresso all day long. We're going to drink espresso all night and we're going to talk and well, we'll see."

Ed blinked and stuttered out the next few words. "But my car is parked here," pointing to the garage that they were passing.

She looked at him and smiled warmly. "They're open all night. See the sign. You can pick it up later."

They walked briskly for a short distance arm in arm, Ed beginning to feel streams of perspiration trickling down his back when Jill stopped and pointed. "Here we are. Second floor."

They climbed the old wooden stairs breathing in the moldy corners of the dimly lit hallway. Ed walked behind Jill because of the narrow stairway. Her small, taut buttocks swayed before him and he felt a heightening excitement. Jill unlocked the door and walked inside, flipping the switch that lit up the small room. The sheets were rumpled and hung precariously over the edge of the single bed. A wash basin jutted out from the far wall and a small two-burner stove faced Ed as he walked in. Three unpainted straight-back chairs were scattered at random around the room. A folded card table leaned against the chair nearest the door. The room was dramatically highlighted, however, by the brilliantly colored oil paintings and watercolors that studded all four walls. They injected a sense of vibrant life that was at once vivid and abstract. Ed stopped and stared. Jill followed his eyes.

"I told you I paint."

"Jesus, you really *do* paint."

"This is my year for Art school, last year it was ballet. Next year, who knows, perhaps Henry." Ed listened for but did not hear any strains of bitterness in her voice.

She moved quickly around the room pointing to the card table for him to set up and busying herself at the stove with the coffee and the shiny new silver pots already streaked with today's unwashed coffee grounds. Ed threw his sport coat on the closest chair and opened the table.

"Take off your shoes. Get comfortable."

Ed obeyed, kicking his shoes under the bed. He pulled up the two remaining chairs and sat down on one as she came to the table with coffee cups filled with the steaming jet black

160

mixture. She slid into her seat and pushed one cup toward him.

"Aren't you impressed?"

Ed raised his eyebrows. "By what?"

"By the fact that I could make espresso so fast, you nut."

Ed nodded as he raised the cup. "Impressive." He took his first swallow of the thick, bitter liquid and he tried desperately not to choke. His tongue burned and his eyes filled with tears that threatened to betray him but he placed his cup down and slowly finished swallowing what was left in his mouth. He smiled.

"Not bad."

Jill put her cup down and studied the coffee. "It's better than that. It's damn good."

Ed didn't answer. He sat watching the changing expressions on the face of this strange, quixotic girl facing him. She caught him staring and he turned quickly away.

Her voice was hard for the first time that night. "Do you find me shocking?"

"Not really."

"Goddamn it, you should. I try hard enough."

"Hey, don't get mad. If you want, I'll be shocked. I'll be any damn thing you want me to be."

Her expression changed and she closed her eyes momentarily. The lines around her eyes softened and her features relaxed. "Do you mean that?"

"Yes."

"Anything?"

"I'll try."

"Will you treat me like you're going to stay around for a long time, not forever, that's too long, but tonight, please talk to me and touch me and make love to me and pretend. But make me believe it, that you're going to stay with me . . . and be kind to me for a long time."

"So soon . . . after the baby, I mean?"

"Don't worry, I'll be fine."

Ed leaned over the table and picked up both of her hands and placed them over his mouth. He pressed his lips gently into her palms. When he removed her hands, he spoke in a barely audible whisper.

"I'll try. It's been a very long time, but I'll try."

Jill picked up the cups quickly and placed them back on the stove while Ed folded up the table and leaned it against the wall. As he turned around toward her she was unbuttoning her blouse and tossing it onto the floor. She stepped out of her skirt as he stared at the slender contours of her thighs.

"Put the rest of your stuff on the same chair." Her voice sounded like a child's.

Ed unbuttoned his shirt and took it off. He dropped it on the chair and followed quickly with his undershirt. He unfastened his belt and stepped out of his pants, turned and draped them over the chair. He pulled off his socks and turned around. She was standing directly across the room, naked, her small breasts rising with each breath, the nipples starting to tighten. The boyish contours of her hips and thighs led his eyes to the mound of recently shaved brown hair resting flat against the soft bulge beneath her waist. Her long, flowing hair rippled down around her face quietly framing her arms and breasts.

Jill walked toward him and stopped in front of him as he stood staring at her. Her hands dropped slowly until they were gently rubbing the bulge in the front of his jockey shorts.

"Take them off."

Ed felt himself swelling inside of the tightening shorts. He hooked his hands in the waistband of the shorts and pulled them down. His breathing was short and rapid. His mouth was dry and his hands trembled slightly. His penis was hard and throbbing. He touched the girl on her shoulder and they came together into a deep kiss. He felt her firm body pressing against his own and his knees felt like water. His hands began exploring her body as hers lingered carefully over his. Slowly they sank onto the bed and the covers fell silently to the floor.

XV

SANDY walked out into the bright sunlight. She felt her eyes fill as the sudden stunning light blinded her. Placing his arm around her shoulder, Mike lifted her face toward his. Slowly his features came into perspective as her vision adjusted to the unexpected brilliance. They began walking toward his car. There was a tantalizing hint of summer warmth in the fresh spring air.

About five feet from the car, Sandy saw a beaming face pressed obliquely against the glass of the back window. A hand waved furiously. Mike opened the door and Sandy bent to get in. Two arms immediately circled her neck and she felt the girl's warm lips against her right cheek. Flushed with anticipation, Allison licked her lips as if delighting in something that tasted unusually good. She wore a starched blue cotton dress with puffed sleeves. A blue satin belt tied into a large bow in front and along the hem a thin blue satin ribbon twined through the stiff blue cotton. Her blonde hair was closely brushed and tied in back with a blue ribbon exposing the full face with the distended cheeks and the vivid eyes. This was not the type of outfit suited to a baseball stadium. Sandy suspected that the woman caring for the girl as well as the girl herself had never been to a baseball game so that Allison had dressed herself as if going to a party. Since starting the drugs in the hospital, her body as well as her face had lost the early pubertal contours and had developed undifferentiated plumpness. But the medicines had not dulled her acute perceptions of how she would best be seen by others. Even in moments of uninhibited delight, she unconsciously seemed to appear in control of herself and her body.

At the stadium, they inched themselves into the slowly accumulating crowds. Mike stood in line for tickets while Sandy and Allison stood off to the side and waited. A young black boy shouted about the starting baseball line-up as he passed, shoving a newspaper defiantly upward into the air above his head in an effort to attract buyers. Allison could feel her heart racing slightly as she held Sandy's hand and searched for Mike at the box-office window. A moment later he came loping back, looking very vulnerable, his blond hair carelessly tousled by the wind and his tall body gracefully in motion. They walked into the stadium. The aroma of cooking hot dogs and burning grease curled around the inner smells of dust and spilled beer that increased, the closer they walked to the stands. A small man with an ill-fitting red jacket hanging loosely over his shiny gabardine pants showed them to their seats, carefully dusting off some imaginary dirt. Reaching into his pocket, Mike handed him a quarter.

When Allison settled into her seat and Sandy unstrapped her binoculars, Mike, who was between them, asked,

"Now . . . who knows about baseball?"

There was no response. Allison shook her head slowly and Mike watched her start to slide over toward him. He turned and stared at Sandy. Laughing helplessly, she threw up her arms.

"Do you mean to tell me that I brought two girls here who don't know anything about the greatest sport of all time?" Both Allison and Sandy sat quietly waiting. "Well, it looks like I had better start explaining or else I'm going to have two confused ladies on my hands today."

166

Sandy watched him as he described the field and the names of the players and their positions. As his voice rambled on, she paid attention only to his ebullience, his pleasure at teaching Allison about his favorite sport. Every once in a while he would turn to Sandy who smiled, showing she understood why he was ignoring her. He had pulled out a program and was moving his fingers down the page where the players' names were listed, describing each one and what he did. Allison put her hand on the program, her small index finger moving down the page with him. Pausing, he thought for a minute, and then asked her a question on a point which he had described before. She bit her lip, waited for a minute, and then blurted out an answer which was apparently correct because Mike laughed, grabbing her hands and holding them tightly. Sandy froze them in that position in her mind. She gazed at Allison's sparkling eyes and full red cheeks and ached to hold her and know that when she opened her eyes the child would not be gone. She stared at the profile of the handsome, blond man sitting next to her, his head thrown back, his expression completely free and unguarded. When Sandy had lain next to him she had longed to see that look in his eyes even for a moment. She would have accepted it as a pinnacle of lust if nothing else but she had not been able to unloosen him. As she studied him now, she thought, how ironic. He claimed not to be able to feel, but what does he think is happening to him at this moment?

She was abruptly awakened by a roar from the crowd as the players rushed onto the field, dressed in identical uniforms, distinguished by different numbers on their backs. The booming voice of the loudspeaker announced their names and positions. The sun was quite strong, the rays slanting down over the field so that the ballplayers appeared to gyrate sinuously although actually standing quietly in place. Rummaging through her purse, Sandy found her sunglasses and slipped them on.

She watched the first innings with interest, but as the game wore on her attention wandered. Leaning back against the wooden slats of the seat, she closed her eyes for a moment aware of the sun's warmth as it stroked her forehead. She felt comfortable but alone. Her life was slowing down; she felt at peace with herself. She opened her eyes and scanned the scoreboard directly across the field to bring herself up to date. On the first row, five zeros rested monotonously next to each other representing the fruitless sum total of the visiting team's accomplishments while directly below four more zeros indicated the home team's score. She was aware of a restlessness in the crowd, a growing urgency for action.

She watched the ball sail swiftly from the pitcher's hand into the heavy glove of the masked man kneeling behind the plate. Swinging fiercely, the batter stirred only air. A soft groan lifted from the stands. Again the ball moved toward the plate. This time there was a sharp crack and the ball flew into the air. Sandy could feel Mike half rising in his seat. Continuing aloft, the ball cleared the short fence and fell into the stands across the field from where they were seated. The crowd went wild. Mike jumped up and shoved both hands upwards in delight, then turned to Allison who was standing and clapping excitedly. Grabbing her around the waist, he lifted her high enough into the air so that her face was directly parallel to his and kissed her hard upon the cheek.

Sandy watched them silently; and after they had settled back into their seats she rose, excused herself, climbed over the peanut shells and lifted feet and walked down the steps, into the dim passageway underneath the stands. She looked around the walls for a phone and saw only booths of frying meat, popping corn and flowing beer. Finally she found the phone—hidden behind a man selling programs. The phone book hanging from a rusty iron chain was torn and had numbers scribbled haphazardly across most of the first few pages. Whole pages were ripped in half. She thumbed through the book hoping the page she wanted was still intact. At last she saw the name Gordon, Bertram, and noted the number. Repeating it several times to herself, she walked into the empty booth and closed the door. After a few rings Bert said "Hello" and waited.

Suddenly Sandy pictured the gentle expectant man at the other end of the line and she knew that the solution to her aching needs could never be found there. She listened as the soft voice said "Hello" several more times, heard no response, and then hung up.

"Good-bye, Bert. I'm sorry . . . for both of us," she whispered to the dial tone. She stood for several deep breaths inside the humid booth and then painfully opened the door and edged out. She climbed the steps and made her way across the row to her seat. Turning toward her, Mike smiled.

"Hi. Everything okay?"

"Fine, Mike. Anything happen in the game?"

"No . . . still one to nothing after eight innings. We're ahead." He swung his head around and stared at Allison and turned back to Sandy. "Allison is having a ball. I think she really understands the game. She asks the most intelligent questions." He paused. "She's quite a remarkable child, don't you think?"

"Yes, Mike, she's really a remarkable and wonderful little girl."

He turned again to the game. Sandy watched the parade of players move to the plate. Hurling instructions to the home team pitcher, the crowd tried desperately to instill strength into his tiring arm. The last inning began and the crowd developed an unsettling silence. Mike leaned forward in his chair, his elbows on his knees, his chin cupped in his hands. Allison clung to his side. The first batter did nothing and the silence grew in waves. The second batter struck the ball and scampered safely to first base. Allison whispered a question to which Mike nodded affirmatively without turning his head.

169

The next man at the plate let several balls go by and then connected hard. The people in the stands rose and watched the pirouetting grace of the third baseman as he scooped up the ball and twirled around on the balls of his feet to toss it to the waiting second baseman who fondled it briefly and then fired it to first. The crowd held its collective breath as the first base umpire paused and then thrust up his right arm. A double play and the game was over. A surge of happiness swelled upward from the stands.

Mike took a deep breath and stroked Allison's back several times.

"Allison, you were good luck. They must have known this was your first game. They've never played better."

Laughing, Allison tossed her hair back. "It was great, Mike. I had a wonderful time. Thanks so much."

When they had reached the parking lot, Sandy touched Mike's arm and he turned toward her.

"Drop me off first, Mike. Then take Allison home."

"Sandy, I thought we'd go out to dinner."

"I have a headache from the sun, Mike. Please take Allison instead. It will be a big treat."

Smiling at Sandy, Mike took her hand in his and directed his eyes toward Allison for a second.

"Thanks for the suggestion, Sandy. And if I'm acting like a fool, please don't tell me."

They returned to Allison who stood caught up in the excitement of the rushing crowds.

XVI

VIEWING his lathered face in the mirror, Ed blew the foamy substance from his lips. The steam from the hot water rose and clouded the mirror. He cursed softly, laid down his razor and wiped off the center of the mirror. Despite an increasing tendency to go to bed earlier each night, Ed experienced overwhelming fatigue, not symptomatic of the muscle aching of overwork but the cloudy atmosphere of anxiety. Mornings and the hospital were becoming harder to face. He stared at himself, wondering what he was going to do.

The sound of off-key singing reached him from the bedroom. Leaning over the edge of the bed, Mike was pulling on a pair of socks. He stuck his head into the bathroom and bellowed the last notes of an indistinguishable song. Picking up his razor, Ed said,

"You're mighty happy this morning. That Goddamn good humor so early sets my teeth on edge."

"I've been sleeping great. I feel fantastic." He walked into the bathroom and stood behind Ed, looking into the mirror while Ed finished shaving.

"Mike, please save me the sight of your self-adoration. I'm cutting the shit out of my face."

Mike danced out of the bathroom. He called back over his shoulder.

"Lem's car is in the shop. He wants us to pick him up today."

"You'd better take your Chevy then. Lem'll never fit in the back of my Volks and you know what happens to your legs there."

"Right. Anyway, Lem is taking me on a home-care visit today so I have to take my wreck."

When they drove up, Lem was sitting on the steps of the cement staircase leading to his apartment. His back rested against the metal railing which glittered in the sunlight. His head was thrown back, and as the car approached they could tell that his lips were puckered as if he were whistling. A large brown bag rested on the step below and a worn brown imitation leather overnight case sat like a sentinel at his feet.

"You cats were ten minutes late," he said. "Man, you white boys are lazy. Never on time."

Mike laughed and drove off. Ed turned around and said, "How's Althea?"

"She's cool, but mad as hell at you 'cause we haven't seen you lately. We gave up on your friend Mike here. He's always so busy running around looking for ass that he forgot about his black brother. . . ."

"Now wait a minute," said Mike. "You know it's only been a month."

There was a brief silence before Ed spoke hesitantly, "Anything else new, Lem?"

"Well," said Lem. "Did you know how near I came to being kicked out last week? It was only Rosensweig who saved my neck. By the time I dragged myself back into that hospital the Chief had heard all about the incident. He personally checked the cracker I tossed around and then informed him that any action on his part would only intensify our prosecution. The wife thanked him and Rosensweig parked himself next to that white bastard until the police came. The fucker only said that

I got . . ." Lem paused for a moment as if thinking. "What did that prick call it? Oh, yeah, he said, 'That nigger doctor pushed me against the wall he got so upset when my little boy died.' Rosensweig accompanied the man out of the hospital making sure that the cops had his story. Afterward he dragged me up to his office and said, 'Lem, I often wanted to do the same thing.' Then he opened the bottom drawer of his desk and took out the biggest bottle of whiskey and two glasses and poured an armful into each one. 'Drink it, Lem, we both need it.' I drank it fast 'cause I needed it, like he said. Afterward he sat quietly in his chair staring at me and finally said, 'Now dictate into the tape recorder exactly what happened to the baby, 'cause we're going to bring charges against that bastard and after the police hear your story I'll lay ten to one they wouldn't touch you.' "

Mike drove into the hospital parking lot and pulled into one of the spaces reserved for the house staff.

"Have you heard anything more?"

Lem smiled. "The cops came back the next day at the boss's request, listened to the tape, talked with him in his office for over an hour, didn't even contact me, and that was the last I saw of them. Yesterday I learned that Rosensweig went into court with the tape recorder and testified. The guy who killed his kid got committed to the state mental place indefinitely. And Lem here has got memories of his Goddamn righteous temper almost screwing his career."

"Lem, that's got to be the story of the year." Mike shook his head. "By the way, I'll meet you in the clinic at one o'clock for our home-care visit. Do you know where the street is?"

"Do I know where it is?" Lem chuckled. "Listen, man, that's where this chocolate doctor grew up . . . it's the return of the native."

"I'll follow you then, native."

Mike reached the floor just in time to see the door at the end

173

of the corridor leading into Rosensweig's office closing angrily behind Sheila Plotkin. She stood for a moment, then wiped her eyes and turned in Mike's direction. She was still crying when she stopped in front of him.

"That bastard. That unmitigated bastard."

"Who?"

"Who else? Rosensweig. He's so cruel."

Mike wondered if he should strip the truth from her or if it was kinder just to listen without forcing her to share her humiliation. He had little to do with the decision since she was already telling him.

"He calls me in first thing this morning, so as not to take me away from patients, he said, and sits me down to inform me that he doesn't have a place for me here next year, that I'm not quite ready to assume more responsibility on a higher level at this hospital. . . ." Her voice trailed off and she turned slightly away from Mike as her tears increased. "Then the son of a bitch sits like a gargantuan buddha in his swivel chair and tells me to take a year off and get married and mature and then come back and see him." She took a deep breath, incredulous that she had lived through such a conversation. "Take a year off and get married. Doesn't he know that I've taken my whole life off to get where I am today?"

Mike was embarrassed. He along with the rest of the house staff was inclined to agree with the Chief.

"How did you respond to that, Sheila?" he finally said.

"I merely sat there and like a Goddamn female fool, started crying. I could kill myself for doing that. Then I asked him what he honestly thought I should do. He said he could probably get me a fellowship in something for a year or a residency at one of the smaller hospitals and then we could talk again. . . ." She folded her arms in front of her as if getting ready to ward off a direct blow.

"Mike, did he have to be so damn blunt?"

"Sheila, that's his style. You know that. Whether it works is for you to decide later on, not today. Today is a tough time for you to evaluate anything."

"Yeah, but the question is basically more than that, isn't it? The real question I'm asking you is, Mike, is he right . . . completely?"

Mike knew that this was coming and decided he might as well be honest.

"There was some good advice mixed in with what he said to you, Sheila. You may learn better at a small hospital where the pace is slower."

She stared at him blankly for a minute and then nodded.

"You're right, Mike, and that bastard was right too. It was the way he told me. But you know, I think I was angry because I knew he was right and didn't want to hear it. This year has been a living nightmare for me. There have been times when I doubted whether I belonged in medicine at all. That frightened the hell out of me. All that time and effort, all those things I didn't do, to suddenly wonder if you had made such a mistake. Mike, do you think I've made a mistake?"

"No, I don't think you've made a mistake. We all grow at different rates, I guess. Here in this place you have to make it fast or you end up wondering about yourself like you did." He paused, but she didn't move. "I'm not sure what's better, Sheila. Sometimes growing up so fast causes you to miss some steps along the way. I'm not sure who makes the best doctor in the long run."

She unfolded her arms and smiled.

"Thanks, Mike, I think we both better get to work or you might be looking for a job with me."

She walked swiftly past him and disappeared into an open elevator.

Walking out of the intensive care unit, Sandy saw Mike still standing thoughtfully in the hall.

"Morning, Mike. The Anderson kid went bad last night.

175

She's the one who had surgery for the brain tumor yesterday. She came down from recovery doing fairly well and then about one last night she stopped breathing. Todd had to intubate and breathe her for about ten minutes until Anesthesia arrived and hooked her up to a Bennett. Now she's out, no reflexes, not even corneals. Pulse is stable and the Bennett is working. But nothing much else on her is. Todd speculated cerebral edema and herniation. She needs a physical and her studies drawn this morning. I waited for you because Todd is beat. No sleep, virtually, he looks like a walking zombie."

Mike entered the room where the twelve-year-old girl lay motionless on the bed. Her back was to the door so that the exposed flesh of her back between the separated edges of the hospital gown moved in time to the ominous pumping sound of the machine connected to the tube inserted into her mouth. Her head was shaved, heavy white gauze bandages covering most of the naked skull. As Mike circled the bed, he noted the open staring eyes with the dilated pupils. Bottles hung on tall steel poles, the tubing leading into the motionless body with the usual dripping fluids slowly mixing with her blood in the cannulated vein. The pumping machines, dripping tubes and electronic cardiac monitoring inscribing the peaks and valleys of her heart activity on an unfolding roll of lined paper were the only real activity that existed. The girl lay still with open staring eyes, her lips shoved grotesquely apart by the plastic mouthpiece attached to the respirator.

Mike put the stethoscope in his ears and listened to her back. He stood and folded his instrument, placing it in his pocket.

"She's really filling up. She needs a trach. Wasn't anyone available last night to do it?"

Sandy shook her head. "They had two serious accidents that kept them in the O.R. all last night and asked that we try and wait until this morning."

Mike frowned a moment. "I'm not sure that that was wise. She's loaded in both lungs and needs suction. Call the E.N.T. resident and tell him there's an emergency."

Sandy nodded and left the room. Mike checked the fluids and examined the child's eyes, peering into the retina seeing the hemorrhages and fullness around the nerve head indicating the serious rise in pressure within the skull.

Sandy returned. "He's on his way with the equipment. He'll do it here. I also asked him to bring someone from Anesthesia to adjust the machine after he got the trach in and to breathe her if you think it's needed."

Mike appreciated the way Sandy handled his omission. "She could use something to reduce the edema. What's she getting?"

Sandy lifted up the metal clipboard and read the notes quickly. "She's on steroids and ampicillin." Mike nodded and made a note on his index cards to call the Neurosurgical resident about other means of reducing the increased intracranial pressure.

Sandy walked around the bed and lifted the bottle on the floor checking the quantity of fluid and inscribing the information on the notes hanging on a metal peg at the foot of the bed. "They didn't have an extra electronic cardiac monitor last night. I'll try to get one this morning. Things seemed to happen in bunches around here." Gazing at the still form of the girl, she paused. "Mike, is there anything left?"

Mike stopped writing and looked up. "I don't think so. It's hard to tell but the tumor was malignant anyway."

"Then why are we doing all this, Mike? Why are you extending her life if there isn't much to extend? Why don't we just stop?"

While handling the girl, Mike had tried to avoid thinking about this inevitable question.

"I don't know, Sandy. There must be a valid reason to

177

prolong a life doomed to vegetate until death but no one ever taught me why. They merely showed me the patients and said, 'Go to it, boy.' It's not up to me to make the decision."

Sandy sensed his impatience and discomfort but was dissatisfied with his answer.

"Well, who does make that decision?"

He frowned and pulled out his stethoscope unknowingly and placed it around his neck.

"I don't know. I don't know who has the authority or the right. Someone should but who it is I don't know." He stood listening to the sounds of the various life-sustaining machines. Abruptly he turned and said,

"Since it's not going to be us, let's get to work."

Mike opened the door leading to the Pediatric out-patient department and dodged a small black child scurrying across his path. Blocks were strewn underfoot and the television screen in the far corner barely formed its fuzzy picture. The squeals and shouts of playing children mingled with the coughing and sneezing of the others. A low din of voices hovered over the room, the hushed communication of the mothers sitting on the straight-backed chairs along the tile walls. Mike walked along the aisles until he came to the door with Lem's name scribbled on a white piece of cardboard and thumbtacked onto the scarred wood.

He opened the door and saw Lem leaning over a screaming small black child trying to look into her ears. The mother was grasping the child's arms loosely seeming unaware of the need to hold her child in the proper position for the doctor. She was very young herself and looked up at Mike in desperation. He signaled that he would take over and she sat down with relief. He held the squirming child's arm tightly while Lem peered carefully into each ear canal.

"Thanks, man. She's a tiger." Mike nodded and pointed

178

outside. Lem smiled and spoke. "Be out in a minute. Soon as I talk to her mother."

Mike glanced at the uneasy black girl sitting in the chair, and for a second had difficulty associating the term 'mother' with her. She was so very young, probably about fourteen, he thought, and yet she had all of the responsibilities of this screaming, sick youngster. He closed the door as Lem's deep, warm voice started describing his findings.

Children catapulted out of rooms into the aisle as their parents opened the doors to leave. The nurse threw completed charts onto a growing stack on the metal cart near the wall.

Lem opened his door and the young girl came out pushing her child ahead of her in a plastic bassinette. She carried a slip of paper and nodded as Lem stuck his head out of the door for some final words of advice. She handed the slip to the nurse who patrolled the aisle outside of the offices and disappeared quickly with her baby into the open Treatment Room at the end of the hallway.

A moment later Lem hurried out with his coat on and his black bag in his right hand.

"Ready? This place is wild today. Sometimes I think we're taking care of the whole damn city."

"That's 'cause they heard that you were here today. They all came running to see your beautiful black face."

"Screw, baby. They've seen enough black faces like mine in their lifetime. It's the white uniform surrounding the black face that's a bit of a novelty."

"You're too political, man. I talk about sex and you talk civil rights."

"Sex is easy, man, real easy, but civil rights ain't. So let's talk more about what's not as easy as laying down and spreading."

Mike laughed and shook his head. "Wow, this is gonna be one swinging home visit with you today. I can tell that. What new is eating you today?"

179

"Nothin'. It's just that I feel like we're not making a dent when these black kids come with their sick babies and I gotta talk down to 'em because they can't even understand me. Do you realize that they can't always understand me, and I came from where they are, and they haven't moved any and I have and we have trouble talking. That's when I get upset."

They went to Mike's car, got in and drove to the part of the city where the sun only highlighted the grim undercoating of poverty. The houses were leaning into each other like old people barely able to stand. The steps leading to the houses were wooden, cracked and often missing several slats. Clothes hung listlessly on ropes strung in the yards. A few dogs, their coats lusterless and their bodies thin, roamed freely along the streets, mindful only of their search for scraps of anything that might be eaten. Mike parked the car in front of a store on the corner of one of the streets. The windows had been bricked over and the door was made of dull, heavy steel with several inside locks. A slender, shabby young black sat picking his teeth on the step. He stared suspiciously at the two men with their white uniforms protruding under their light coats. As the doctors walked by, he leaned over and spat on the sidewalk.

"Pretty, ain't it?" said Lem. "Jesus, do you know I could still be here if my mother hadn't beaten the shit out of me every morning to get me off to school, if she hadn't watched everywhere I went and who I went with and lashed me with the fiercest black tongue in creation to keep me goin' straight." He stopped and stood staring at the decay and haphazard chaos of the neighborhood. "You know, it's only because of some tough black woman that most of us have gotten anywhere. We aren't programmed in this country to make it by ourselves. That strong black mother is what counts. Thank God, I had mine."

They passed a house where three small children played in the dirt of the front yard, squealing with delight as they smeared themselves with the dry soil. They were barefooted and clothed sparsely but seemed oblivious of the chilly April afternoon.

Several houses later they stopped in front of a building exactly like those on either side, the only difference being that the wooden steps had been painted a deep red and the paint had worn off in the center where the feet of many agencies had climbed toward the people inside.

"This is it." Lem consulted his small brown notebook. "The kid has been home for two weeks now. Somebody is supposed to have taken care of the plaster and paint inside that gave him the lead poisoning to begin with. Christ, was he sick. We're supposed to watch his development now because he came in convulsing pretty bad and Rosensweig said he was afraid of brain damage."

"This is the one with the fifteen-minute seizure that you and Ed couldn't control? How could he help having something after that?" Over Lem's shoulder Mike read some of the scribbled words on the page. "I appreciate you taking me with you today, Lem. I'm scheduled for home visiting for the next three months and I know nothing about what to do when I go out."

"Just listen, baby, and use your eyes."

They walked up the red steps and looked for a button to press. There was none. Lem knocked firmly on the door. They waited. Nothing happened. No one answered the knock. Lem glanced at Mike and shrugged.

"Hold on. Nobody answers the knock the first few times. If you'll watch the window, you'll probably see somebody checking to see who it is. You gotta be careful in this neighborhood. You gotta protect yourself from the agency people and from your own people, each has its own dangers. . . ."

Lem knocked again and placed his black bag down on the top step. Mike saw the shade on the dirt-flecked window quiver slightly and then a space appeared between the edge of the shade and the window. It remained there for a brief time and then the shade settled back into place.

"See? We've been looked over. Now it will depend on how they interpret our visit as to whether or not we'll get in."

Mike frowned. "But you seem so sure of getting inside, Lem."

"Remember, baby, I took care of that kid and talked to that woman staring at us so she knows me—and one more thing, I'm black." He lifted his large brown hand and tapped again on the door. The knob turned and the door opened just enough for the woman inside to peer out at them. Lem picked up his bag confidently.

"Thank you, sister, for opening the door. Can we come in?"

She stared at his smiling face.

"What choo wan'?"

"I'd like to see Dwayne and check on how he's doin'. And also talk a little with you."

She stood without moving for a time obviously weighing what he had said and then opened the door wide enough for both of them to enter. They walked out of the sunlight into darkness. Mike's eyes adjusted slowly to the change. The woman stood barefooted clutching a worn chenille wrapper around her. Her face had the slack look of predetermined failure; and her hands against the dull pink of the robe were veined and rough. She waited impassively for the men to speak. But neither said anything. They both surveyed the room silently, taking in the unmistakable appearance of futility. An infant of about ten months clad only in a diaper, his knees dark with the grime of the floors, crawled about their feet. He moved toward the woman and grabbed her ankles and clung, crying very softly. She didn't look down but continued staring at the men in front of her. The room contained a good deal of shabby furniture. The sofa sitting against the far wall was ripped open in three places with the cushions sagging from the missing stuffing, some of which was accumulated in the corner of the room. The overstuffed chair against the side wall was worn at the arms and spotted with grease. A wooden playpen was opened against the other wall with sufficient slats missing to make it valueless as a confining place for the infant. A television set had been placed importantly next to the playpen, the rabbit ears projecting upward and striking the fly-specked ceiling. The wallpaper had peeled off in several areas and underneath different colored plaster holes could be seen reflecting the numerous coats of cheap paint that had been applied at one time or another to try to brighten the squalor. The attempts had ceased long ago.

Lem put his bag down on the sofa.

"Where's Dwayne?"

The woman turned slightly and called out the boy's name several times in a bleak voice. There was no response.

"I dunno where he is. I'll go fin' him for ya."

"Sister, may we sit down?" The woman nodded and left the room. Lem sat on the sofa and signaled to Mike to take the chair. The infant boy crawled over toward Lem. Reaching down, Lem lifted the baby up onto his lap. The baby surveyed his face and began to whimper. Lem placed the child on his knee and bounced him and started singing a hymn that Mike had never heard before. The infant stopped crying and sat quietly listening to the deep richness.

The woman returned, dragging a two-and-a-half-year-old boy behind her. Walking over to Lem, she deposited the child at his side. Lem lowered the infant back onto the floor.

"Here he is. Whatcha goin' to do with 'im?"

"Just check him. Hi, Dwayne, remember me? Mrs. Williams, the other doctor is Dr. Hillman who came along to help me. I didn't have much chance to introduce you both."

Mike rose and nodded. The woman stared blankly back at him, not speaking or moving. Mike sat down. Talking quietly to the boy the whole time, Lem checked him. When Lem had finished, he dressed the boy himself.

"Thanks, baby. You're doin' fine."

The boy slid off the man's lap, looked around quickly and

hurried out of the room into the kitchen. The woman still folding her arms in front of her to keep her robe closed, sat on the far edge of the sofa and turned toward Lem, and waited.

"Mrs. Williams, he seems to be doing all right. I can't find anything that says that he still has trouble from his lead poisoning. But we'll want to keep checking him if that's all right with you." The woman nodded without emotion.

Lem pointed to several of the plaster-filled holes. "I thought the landlord was supposed to cover those over. Remember we said that that's where he probably got the lead—from chewing on pieces of that plaster. And you told us it was covered over when you came to take him home."

She looked away and her words were so low that both men leaned toward her to hear.

"I wanted him home."

Lem nodded. "I understand. Did you talk to the landlord?"

She turned and gazed at him incredulously. "Brother, you wanna talk to that man? I tol' him that you said the walls was given' my boy the lead troubles and that they should be covered up. That Jew jes' shook his finger and said, 'Bessie, you make trouble for me an' out you go.' Ya see, I'm three weeks back now. That man can do it to me, put me out, and I ain' got nowhere to go."

Lem waited to see if she had anything else to say. There was silence. "We can force him to do it if you stay here. The boy can start eating the paint again and then we're in more trouble. Mrs. Williams, he could die if he keeps it up." The woman didn't respond. "Have you thought about public housing?"

"Yeah, but they wants to put me across town. I was born aroun' here. My family lives in the nex' block. I ain' movin' away from what I knows."

Lem spoke slowly. "I used to live around here too. I got out. It's not so hard once you try. It scares you early but not afterward."

184

The woman stared at him and shook her head negatively. "I'm not leavin' my folks."

Lem waited. "I understand. Maybe we could find another place around here in better shape. Would you let us help you do that?"

The woman stood up, walked into the kitchen and then came back without announcing what she had done or why she had gone. She walked over and stood beside Lem.

"Why you doin' this? Why you wanna do something for me? I don' understan'."

Lem reached out and took her left hand in his, trying not to disturb her furtive grasping of the edges of her robe.

"We gotta help each other, sister. If we don' help each other, where we goin' to be? You got children here that gotta get ahead. I'm not just helping you. I'm helping Dwayne and the other four kids that you got here."

"Five 'sides him." She walked back to the sofa and lowered herself heavily into place. Lem sat watching her.

"One more thing, sister. How come you haven't dressed yet this time of the day? It's afternoon, the children should see you dressed. It's important for them."

She stared at him and Mike watched her face sag visibly and her eyes cloud and spill over. "Where am I goin'? I ain' goin' nowhere. Nobody's comin' to see me. When I got somewhere to go and somebody to look after these kids, then I get dressed. But where ya think I can go this time of the day with some kids goin' to school on one shift and others comin' home? Anyway, I ain' got but two dresses and I save those for church when I can make it."

Lem stood up and slipped on his coat. Mike rose and did the same. The woman sat, not moving.

Lem walked over, bent down and placed both of his hands on her shoulders.

"Will you let us help with the house?" The woman nodded. Lem straightened up and stood staring down at the beaten

185

figure on the sofa. "Please don't let him eat any more of the plaster, Mrs. Williams." She nodded again. "And we both thank you for letting us come in and visit. May we come again?" She continued to nod and stare down at her lined hands, not responding to their words of good-bye. As they closed the door behind them, Mike turned to Lem and shook his head.

"Christ, I'll never make it. That kind of thing tears me up. I can't face three months of these kind of visits." They moved off of the steps. Lem was smiling.

"How do you think that kind of thing tears her up? She faces it for a lifetime."

They walked silently back to the car, side by side, each lost in his own thoughts. They both felt very uneasy because, for very different reasons, they were anxious to leave this neighborhood behind them.

XVII

MIKE put his suitcase down and looked around at the airport. Sparkling reflections of sunlight ricocheting off the glass walls punctured the bustling activity around him. The glass enclosure with the endless view of the long concrete and green fields gave Mike the sensation that he was standing outside. Bright multicolored plastic chairs lined each wall with people lounging carelessly in them, coats thrown casually over the backs and quiet, intense conversations passing between.

Mike reached into his pocket for the envelope that held his plane ticket. He felt something and brought out the crumpled telegram that had arrived that morning announcing his father's death. He reread the message: *Your Father Dead. Funeral Tomorrow. Mother.* Brief, clear, and cold, as always—never any unnecessary words or feelings.

Mike found himself unable to react. He had used up his tears on his father years ago. But still he was going home, even if it was only to watch them bury a man he had already interred. Perhaps he hoped to find answers, even in the man's death. He shivered and buttoned his coat against the sterile chill of the unfamiliar room.

The minutes passed slowly. Finally a young woman walked past repeating the number of his flight. He picked up his bag; headed toward the gate and walked down the carpeted tunnel and into the plane greeting the frozen smile of the attractive uniformed woman at the door with a smile of similar dishonesty. He sat down and closed his eyes. He was going back. He had promised himself that he would never let their detachment rip at him again. Oh, God, maybe if I can bury him once and for all, i can stop searching. Let me watch him go into the earth and know that I have lost him and there is no other father for me and my angry search must end. Oh, Jesus, it's not that simple, is it? Can I bury myself too and be reborn? Why do I punish myself and go back? I don't have to; they don't need me or want me. I'm too old to try and make them want me again. I'll only cause them pain and give myself new scars. I'm not going, Goddamn it. Let them bury the bastard themselves. They don't deserve the privilege of having me mourn. I'm getting off. He's dead and I'm alive. Fuck them. I'm leaving.

Mike stood up forgetting his seat belt which pulled him forcibly back down. The stout woman peeling an orange next to him turned and looked at him strangely.

"You feeling all right?" She reached toward the paper bag which nestled in the pocket of the back of the seat immediately ahead.

"Yes, I'm just getting off now."

Her mouth opened wide, revealing a piece of orange. She stared at him for a second and then closed her mouth and swallowed. "You're what?" She pointed to the window. The plane was in the air, the houses and streets already reduced to tiny, unreal figures. Mike stared silently at the sight for a long time, not feeling unusual or foolish. Then he turned to the anxious woman next to him and smiled the boyish grin which had calmed most concerned adults in the past. "Sorry. I hadn't realized we had taken off. I'm going to my father's funeral and have a great deal on my mind."

She kept on chewing and patted his hand that held the arm of his seat. Her words were slurred by the orange. "Poor boy. I know how hard it is to face because I've been through it twice myself. The first time . . ." Her voice merged with the drone of the massive engines and he continued to stare at her, smiling, as his thoughts drifted.

Shortly he became aware that the woman's lips had stopped moving and she was watching him. He opened his eyes wider and said simply, "Thank you" and turned away.

He didn't open his eyes again until the plane began to descend. The woman was gathering her books and newspapers together. She glanced over toward him and seeing him awake, patted his hand a second time. "You slept. But you were having nightmares. I'm sorry." Mike frowned and reached over and grabbed her arm. She turned, appeared startled, and pulled roughly away.

"What do you mean nightmares?"

"My goodness, young man, relax. All I could hear throughout the flight was you repeating softly over and over the same word, 'no.' You kept saying 'no,' not loud, mind you, but soft, just 'no.' So I figgered you was having a nightmare."

Mike nodded and turned to look out of the window. She had been wrong. What he had been denying, rejecting, was not a nightmare but his past.

The plane stopped. The woman rose quickly and moved off. Mike sat until everyone else had risen and left and then he lifted his suitcase and coat down. Pulling on his coat, he walked out into the lightly falling rain.

The cab driver talked continually about his son whom he suspected of taking drugs while Mike watched familiar scenes pass quickly by outside of the dirt-streaked window. Little had changed. He marveled at how removed from all of yesterday's scenery he felt at that moment. The driver became silent as Mike's street approached. He apparently sensed that Mike was not interested in his agonies at finding syringes in his son's pockets; and so he had stopped, saving his story for the next

189

passenger who might unknowingly relieve a small part of the burden by just listening. A few minutes later the car came to a halt and Mike got out, watching the car as it turned in the driveway and made its way back into traffic.

Straightening his shoulders, he opened the front door and walked into the dimly lit hallway with the umbrella stand and the large worn rug upon which he automatically wiped his feet. The living-room door was open and low voices murmured out toward him. Two women sat facing each other on the green flowered sofa, the one whose back was toward him obviously doing all the talking. Cigarette smoke circled her head intermingling with the salt and pepper strands of hair held tightly at the nape of her neck by large tortoise shell clips. Her narrow back was straight and her shoulders held firmly back. She resembled his mother dramatically and he realized that this was Evelyn, his oldest sister who had left the house to marry before he had had much chance to get to know her. Her return visits from the nearby city where she and her husband lived always coincided with holidays and represented hours in the kitchen talking endlessly with his mother and sister so that she had become an accepted enigma. Across from her sat his other sister, a plump, somewhat unkempt woman of now indeterminate years. She had gained so much weight during their long separation that the edges of her face and body had become foreign to him. She sat with a handkerchief clutched in folded hands that rested in an overflowing lap, her head nodding sadly as she listened to her older sister. Her face always had seemed to be on the verge of tears, her eyes wide and brimming, her mouth slackly drooping; and now with the loosening of age, her sagging body added to the impression. Mike expected to see moisture on her face as he approached the two of them.

"Hello, Evelyn . . . Hello, Essie."

The thin woman nodded glumly while Essie said, "Mike. It's been some time. Did you have trouble getting here?"

"No, Essie, the flight was fine. You've both not changed very much."

"Don't lie, Mike," said Evie. "We're both older and Essie's fatter. We all change. You must also."

Mike smiled. He had expected that exact answer. Mike looked around. The room was unchanged, only the slipcovers were new.

"Where's Mother, Evie?"

"She's in the sewing room with Aunt Betsy. Go in."

He moved in response to the command. He knew that small room so well. For it was here he had hidden so often from his father's anger. He remembered the warm corners in that room that closeted a young boy's fears without exposure. Now his mother was sitting in the black lacquered rocking chair, her small feet crossed at the ankles, pushing the floor gently with each return of the chair. A knitted shawl lay over her lap dropping down over her legs so that only her ankles and thick black shoes were visible. The shoulders which had seemed so straight for so many years now tilted slightly downward but it was her hair that startled Mike. For it was totally gray. No black graced the wispy strands that were pinned tightly against her head. The only feature of the small woman who sat systematically rocking that had not changed were the clear, bright, determined black eyes that were riveted on the woman seated opposite her wiping her eyes with a scented handkerchief. He heard his mother saying,

". . . and he wouldn't appreciate your crying all over the place. He used to say that tears were for the weak and the very young. He was right, Betsy."

Both women looked up sharply as Mike entered. He stood beside the chair whose rocking did not change cadence for a moment.

"Mike, you finally came," said his mother. "We were waiting for you. The funeral is early tomorrow."

Mike moved from foot to foot, restless as if he were being criticized, not aware of what he had done wrong.

"I came immediately after I got the wire. Maybe it got delayed in the hospital mail room."

"Maybe." Her eyes studied him closely but she didn't move, merely continued pushing the floor with her feet. The other woman stood, noisily adjusting the many disturbed folds of her dress and smoothing down her full bodice.

"I must be going. Is there anything I can do before tomorrow, Mary?"

"No, Betsy. Everything is taken care of. He saw to it that I would have very little to do except grieve. But remember, Betsy, his idea of grieving was to be inside us, not in front of the whole church. . . ."

Her sister-in-law picked up her purse and moved out of the room, stopping long enough to press her dry lips quickly against Mike's cheek and wipe her eyes again before disappearing.

"She's a fool. All that crying when they rarely saw each other except at holidays."

"But, Mother, Betsy is his sister. Doesn't she have the right?"

"What do you mean, 'the right'? I have the right and if I don't feel it's proper then she should have the common decency to follow suit."

Mike didn't reply. He sat down in the cushioned chair previously occupied by his aunt.

"Mother, I feel kind of bad about not getting to see him before it happened."

She snorted briefly and continued rocking. "What's the matter, you don't see enough old people dying in that hospital? What was there to see? He didn't want to be seen that way."

"I know, Mother, but I might have been able to help in some way, give drugs, you know what I mean."

"Look, Mike, I took care of that man practically all my life and I certainly didn't need any help at the end. That was the easiest part."

Mike stared at her with a bewildered expression. "Easiest, Mother? What do you mean?"

Her expression didn't change. She pursed her lips and he noted that her eyes glistened. But no tears emerged.

"It was just him and me. All of you had gone. I could finally do for him without worrying about anybody else . . . I could give him the attention that I had trouble finding time to give before. I could pay him back for those years when you all kept me so busy, that's why I said it was easy. I didn't say it was fun, boy, I said it was easy." For a second, she turned her face away and Mike waited. When she turned back she was completely composed. "Go up to your room and empty your suitcase and then come down for dinner."

"My room, Mother?"

"Of course, your room, what else would it be?"

He stood, his mind suddenly confused with the ambiguities of the situation. He walked out of the sewing room, picked up his suitcase and started up the steps.

He opened the first door to the right of the landing and entered the same room that he had left nine years before. He stopped and turned his head in amazement. Nothing in the room had been changed. The same snapshots were tacked into the fading wallpaper, the prints darkened by age. The newspaper with his picture receiving the scholarship to college was taped to the wall in the same place, the page yellowed and cracked but the tape fresh and recently replaced. The same books that had lined his bureau remained unchanged, dusted and held together by the same china mugs that he had bought on the high school class trip to New York during his senior year. He stood shocked, clutching the handle of the suitcase, his eyes roaming the familiar room. Finally he put his suitcase down on the bed and opened it. He removed his black suit and

walked to the closet door. As he pulled it open, he had a bizarre premonition of what he would find. There hanging on
the hangers were all the clothes that he had left behind when
he went to college. He stood, suit in hand, staring at the old
clothes, noticing that some of the jackets had been recently
pressed and the shirts were starched and clean. He quickly
hung up his suit and closed the door. Then he sat down on the
bed and placed his hands over his face, trying to clear his
mind of this unexpected reception.

For the first time he began to understand his family, particularly the old woman who rocked endlessly in the small room.
The three of them, the three children, had temporarily taken
her away from the sole reason for her life—that being the man
who was to be buried the next day. He was her child . . . he
was her lover . . . everything and everyone else was an intru-
sion. She had reared her children with resentment and they
had responded to that feeling. The girls had married early and
left, not resenting her, only going on to emulate her and destroy the affection of their children. He realized now that he
had been in competition with his father, had learned to hate
the fact that he could never win the affection of either one of
his parents whose need for each other transcended any love
that they could give to anyone else including their children.
And when the three of them had gone, when he as the last had
left, his mother was able to relive the youth of her children
without deflecting any of her attention from her husband.
Mike wondered how often she had come into this room since
he had left, to sit and muse over the son she had lost or
whether she had indeed created a fantasy in which he still existed. What a tragedy, he thought. How unreal I must seem to
her now. The realization of this seemed to release him. He no
longer felt uncomfortably detached. He was a guest in this
room, a stranger in this house, a man who had outgrown his
image and must leave as soon after the funeral as possible to
allow the lives below to continue in their complicated, unnatu-

ral patterns. He glanced in the mirror, smiled at the tired face that stared back, and left the room for dinner.

They sat around the large walnut table eating the spare meal in virtual silence, interrupted only by requests for food or drink. His mother did not mention what Mike had found in his room; and Mike avoided the subject also. After dinner, as coffee was served, Essie began talking about the problems her husband was having with the help in his department store; and she talked continuously through several cups of coffee. His mother rose first and announced that she was going to her room for the evening and would see them all early the next morning. They sat quietly as her chair scraped, and she left the room. Mike turned toward Evie.

"Does she plan to stay here alone?"

"Of course she does. Where would she go . . . or want to go?" Mike didn't answer. The implicit meaning of the response precluded further inquiries. Essie stood and took the dishes off the table. Evie glanced at her watch.

"Essie, I have to leave. Artie will be coming home soon and I have an hour's ride. I'll see you all in the morning." She moved away from the table not waiting for a response. Mike heard the closet opening in the hall, the front door close, and soon thereafter the engine of her car start up as she pulled away. Essie came in holding a towel which she tossed onto the table. "Help me, Mike. I have to get home soon too. The children need to have their homework checked." He picked up the towel and followed her to the kitchen where he dried the chipped flowered dishes from which he had eaten thousands of meals.

"How are the children, Essie . . . and Hal?"

"They're fine, Mike. Hal is very successful, you know, but works much too hard. I worry constantly about him. There are days I call him several times a day to see if he feels all right."

"That's funny, Essie. I remember Mother doing that."

Essie shoved her hands in the soapy water and didn't respond. The room was still. Finally she looked at him and smiled.

"Strange. I never thought of it but she did. How is your work, Mike?"

"Fine, Essie. I'm going to be a Pediatrician, a children's doctor."

"Good, Mike, that's good. We still use our family doctor but being a Pedia . . ." she had some difficulty with the word but struggled, "Pediatrician should be very nice."

"It is, Essie." He ran out of words. He had nothing to share with this woman, this stranger who was part of his early life. He watched her moving heavily about the sink.

"Well, the kitchen's clean, at least. I'm on my way. See you in the morning." She passed by him and disappeared quickly out of the house. Mike walked into the living room and stood in the center of it looking at the furniture feeling like an alien refusing to enter a country he had suddenly found desolate. He stared at the darkness outside of the window for a few minutes, realized how exhausted he was, and started back up the stairs to the room that held his past.

A light rain had fallen overnight so that the ground beneath their feet was spongy and damp. The air still retained some of the moisture and hung in oppressive clouds over the cemetery. Mike stood in the front row, his black suit blending in with the dark dresses and veils surrounding him. Before them the open ground gaped, waiting to receive its contents which was encased in a deep cherrywood box. A priest that Mike did not know stood with his black book open at the foot of the grave intoning prayers in a carefully restrained and uncomfortably high-pitched voice. His young face with its look of earnest devotion seemed out of place at the gathering; his emotions seemed to be so close to the surface, so ready to overflow while the family clustered at his side gave no hint of grief. His mother carried her book with restraint. The handkerchief stuffed within the closed pages had not been removed; no necessity had arisen for its use. His sister Essie sniffed occasionally but it was impossible to tell whether it was from grief or in reaction to the dampness. Mike waited impatiently for the ceremony to be over, to see the box lowered into the ground, to say good-bye finally and completely. The young priest continued to intone. Mike looked up briefly to see several birds immediately overhead. He followed their dizzying flight until he found himself staring in the face of his aunt who stood at the end of the row. She was watching the priest, her teeth biting gently into her lower lip. He could see rivulets of tears dropping quietly behind the black veil. Mike stared at her, wondering why she was crying. What memories was she reliving that caused her to want to cry out in pain . . . what had his father ever done that had touched this woman so deeply that she could openly mourn for him? Mike watched her with mounting curiosity, longing to lean over and ask her, to ferret out something that he could mourn for, even if that something was not his own. The man who was being buried was a stranger. Was he a stranger to all of these other people? Was that why his mother could not and would not mourn? Because she had not been able to reach him. Or was her grief unexpressed because she felt that she had completed her task and done it well? What had they shared? What had they stolen from him, from all of them? He knew he could never ask and if he did he would never be answered.

His back ached slightly and he allowed his shoulders to sag. The rain resumed very gently, dusting their faces with moisture. The words speeded up perceptibly and the sound of the priest's voice increased in pitch so that it seemed to pierce the calm of the family standing stolidly at his side. Mike noticed his mother frowning at the young man. He could hear her dry, flat voice calling him a fool and unconsciously smiled at the thought. How foolish loss of control was to this woman and how much a failing had it been to the dead father he was burying. And how human it seemed to him. How close he felt to a total loss of control in himself. He was a stranger; that boy in that room was the only real child that this woman would remember.

The priest stopped talking. Mike was aware of an uneasiness sweeping the crowd; and he realized that the casket was being lowered by the two black assistants into the hole in the wet earth. Mike grabbed his thighs and held them tightly, afraid that he might faint. He wanted to run away, feeling a terrifying pull toward that opening, a compulsive urge to hurl himself into the grave and beg to be covered along with the box. He wanted to call out, scream for someone to save him from dying, shout for the women in black to save him by remembering him, by recognizing him, shriek for their permission to continue living. His body rocked slightly back and forth watching the earth leaving the spade and falling over the burnished brown wood until nothing could be seen beneath the loam. The only sounds were the soft thudding of hunks of earth as they hit the rapidly filling hole. Soon the grave was covered and his mother turned on her heel and without warning walked away from the crowd of people. Mike stood transfixed, shivering in the mist, staring at the ground where the casket was buried. Gradually everyone walked slowly away from the grave site. The young priest said a few consoling words to Mike's sisters, searched for their mother, and failing this, walked over to Mike. His reedy voice propelled Mike back to the present.

"My sympathies." He extended a hairless hand and clasped Mike's trembling fingers. "I understand he was a fine man. It will be a great loss."

Mike looked at his flushed face with the set, anxious smile. He felt the pressure of the pulpy hand within his own. He shook his head violently.

"Father, he was a bastard. A bastard beyond belief. And my only loss is my own happiness, that was what I lost, that's what

I saw buried today, not that bastard." The young man facing him stood immobile, his face blank, his eyes wide, his hand now limply locked in Mike's.

"Did you hear me, Father? You buried a bastard today and you didn't even know it." Mike released the other man's hand and started to laugh. The priest turned quickly and virtually ran toward his car. Mike stood for a moment, his hand covering his face and laughing softly. He stood that way for a few minutes, those watching thinking that he was hiding tears. When he felt fully released, Mike removed his hands, looked once more at the freshly shoveled earth, and walked toward the waiting car and the silent women. He was free. He knew he would never return again.

XVIII

Ed and Jill climbed up the last flight and paused at the landing. She licked her fingertips and moistened the front of her hair so that it would lie flat against her head. Her long hair had been nervously brushed back over her shoulders. Ed watched her with contained amusement as her hands quickly smoothed down her skirt and blouse. Turning to him, she smiled weakly.

"I hope they like me."

"They will, just don't try to shock them."

"What in the hell do you mean?"

"Just watch what you do. They're pretty straight people."

"Christ, you're making me so nervous I feel like turning around and running down those two flights of steps."

Ed's voice was gentle but pleading. "Jill, don't take out a joint from your pocketbook and fill the whole apartment with the smell of pot. That's what I mean."

"Oh, Jesus, they really are straight. You're not kidding me, they're for real?"

"Very much for real. Just as you're very much for real, but no pot, no dirty jokes, at least not until they know you better. Althea warms slower than Lem so take your time."

She closed her mouth firmly and Ed guided her to the door with the name "Thomas" taped up on a carefully lettered card. He pushed the doorbell and they stood waiting, not looking at each other, Ed smiling in anticipation of seeing his friends, Jill staring ahead, her eyes unblinking and frightened.

The door opened quickly and the whole entranceway was blocked by the massive frame of the man in front of them. His two arms reached out, grabbing each of his visitors. Jill felt herself swept in and spun around before she had had a chance to see Lem's face.

"Oh, damn, it's good to see you both. Ed, it's so good to have you back again," Lem said, wrapping an arm about him and pressing firmly.

"Lem." Ed's voice came out in short gasps from his bracketed position. "This is Jill."

Lem took two long strides in her direction. She drew in her breath and stayed very still. Her hand shot out to greet him but Lem moved against her; and she felt thick, muscled arms circling her in a bear hug. Light diminished and the sound of his voice seemed distant as his greeting penetrated her human cave. Finally she heard another voice, loud and distinct and feminine.

"Lem, let her go. Goodness, you'll smother the child. Let her go."

The arms relaxed and the comfortable cocoon opened. Jill stepped back and saw Lem looking at her with concern.

"Did I hurt you?"

Jill laughed. "Oh, God, no. You are, without a doubt, the biggest man that has ever held me. Did you know that? . . ."

Ed stepped quickly between them. "Jill, this is Althea. Althea, Jill."

Althea's hair was black, kinky and cut close to her head. She wore a plain blue cotton dress which came to her knees in contrast to the very short skirt Jill was wearing. Her body was small, compact and held in tight control.

"Welcome to our home," she said. "I can't tell you how happy we are to meet you. If you'll sit in the living room and I can get my husband to take his eyes off you for a minute we'll have some drinks before dinner."

Lem looked at her and smiled.

"Damn, Althea, if I wasn't appreciative of a pretty girl I'd be near dead. Now you wouldn't want that?"

She laughed, a soft, rolling sound. "No, I wouldn't want that, Lem, and I don't fear for it either. Come along with me." She took his arm and maneuvered him out of the living room.

Jill sat on the print sofa and pressed the space next to her for Ed to join her.

"Oh my God, Ed, he's beautiful. Lem is absolutely beautiful, just like on the posters."

"What posters?"

"Oh, I guess I forgot to tell you. For six months I worked for the Black Panthers."

Ed looked up at the ceiling and cleared his throat.

"Do me a favor, Jill, honey, add that to the list of 'please don't discuss.' "

"Why?"

"I'm not sure, but just don't. Lem and Althea and I have never discussed that before and I don't think tonight is the time."

Jill shrugged and crossed her legs.

"Okay, but you're cutting my conversation down to a few grunts."

Ed threw his head back and laughed. "Hell, that'll be the day."

Jill looked at him seriously. He could see that she was concerned.

"Do you think they like me? You know them, do they?"

"Jill, they just met you, but what the hell. I like you, isn't that enough? In fact, I've come to like all of the different people you try to be."

"Do you know, Ed, you're the only thing I've ever finished?"

203

"Hey, wait a minute, I'm not finished yet."

"Oh, you know what I mean." Her head came down slowly and rested on his shoulder and she began stroking his sleeve. The only sound was the clinking glasses and dropping ice filtering in from the kitchen. Suddenly a loud cough startled them. Lem was in the doorway balancing a tray of ice-filled glasses and juggling two bottles of whiskey in the other. Ed jumped off the sofa to help him, but Lem kept the tray, circling in front of Jill and making faces to make her laugh.

"What's funny?" Ed frowned.

Lem turned innocently. "Just the sight of a clumsy black Pediatrician trying to make like a smart-ass waiter. You know, just because I'm big my wife thinks I can carry twice as much as anyone else."

Althea walked in rubbing her hands slowly on her apron. "Has he made you a drink or is he entertaining you with his stories?" Lem moved quickly to the tray and lifted the bottle of bourbon. Jill nodded. Ed walked over and picked up the other bottle and poured half a tumbler full of scotch over the ice cubes already melting in the bottom of the glass.

"Make me a light bourbon too, Lem," Althea called and sat down next to Jill.

"What do you do?" she asked.

"Go to school. Art school now."

"How far along are you?"

Jill shook her head slightly. "Not far. I just started the beginning of this year. I'm not really sure how far one really goes or plans to go there. I guess I never thought about it until now."

Althea smiled and sipped her drink. Jill moistened her lips and felt the cool moisture on the outside of her drink gathering into droplets on her palm.

"What do you do, Althea?"

"I work. I go every weekday and sit at a desk and play like a secretary."

204

"What do you mean 'play like a secretary'?"

"Well, all I really do is type, type endless meaningless forms and documents that I have serious doubts that anyone reads. But they pay well." Her voice was without rancor, matter-of-fact and even.

"Why?"

"Why, Jill?"

"Yes, why? Why do you do something that sounds so terrible even if they do pay well?"

Ed moved forward in his seat, anxious, but Althea smiled.

"Wait until you have to feed the stomachs of these overgrown boys. Money helps, and a lot of patience." She walked over and stood by her husband.

Suddenly Lem got up. "Is everybody listening? I'd like to make a toast."

Jill looked up and Ed raised his glass, smiling.

Lem's voice took on a tinge of excitement. "Two important things have happened today, one to you and one to Althea and me." Althea moved closer to him and stared anxiously up into his face. "First you two. I toast the first girl that Ed has brought into this house . . . the very first." He lifted his glass and drank. Ed and Jill sipped quickly, but Althea did not move.

"Next and important for us, Althea and me, I did something today. Something that it's taken me a long time to do, too Goddamn long, I know. But anyway, today I called the adoption agency and started the action for us to get a baby. Let's drink to that."

Althea was still speechless. Then she suddenly got up and ran out of the room.

The three people left stared helplessly at each other. Finally Ed spoke.

"Jesus, Lem, you don't spring something like that in a room full of people. . . ."

205

"What people? My friends. I wanted to surprise her. Christ, she's waited so long for me to do this."

Ed shook his head. "That's why you should have told her alone, privately."

"I better go to her."

Ed stood up. "No, let me. She may be angry. I'll try and calm her down." Ed smiled at Jill and walked down the carpeted hall. He paused a second, then turned the knob and eased into the bedroom.

Althea was sitting on the bed, her head in her hands, rocking back and forth. Ed sat down next to her.

"He didn't mean any harm, Althea. He was so proud of himself."

She turned around and looked at him. He was surprised because her eyes were sparkling and her face was relaxed. She smiled.

"Oh, God, Ed, I know my Lem. Of course he didn't mean any harm. I know how pleased he is with his big decision. There's only one problem."

"What, Althea?" Ed frowned.

"Just the small matter that I'm pregnant and he doesn't know yet."

After staring at each other for a minute, they collapsed in each other's arms, laughing hysterically.

Hearing them, Lem poured himself another drink. He was too stunned to speak and walked over to the window and looked down at the traffic. Jill reached into her purse and searched slowly until she found a cigarette rolled in brownish paper with the contents hanging in shreds from both ends. Looking around to confirm her isolation, she lit the unorthodox cigarette, took a very deep breath and held it in. When she exhaled, little returned, and she settled back into the sofa and waited for the surrounding strangeness to recede.

The laughter in the other room stopped, and Ed and Althea came back into the living room. Ed sat down next to Jill and quickly looked at what she was smoking, then at her, smelled the sweet, thick odor of Jill's cigarette and frowned.

"Jill, you promised," he whispered.

"I know. But Ed, things were so tense. I didn't know what was happening and you weren't here."

"Do you feel better?" He made a face at her.

"Yeah. As a matter of fact, I do."

"No more."

"As long as you don't leave me in the middle of nowhere again."

He smiled. "Never again."

She curled her feet under her and smiled dreamily. "You ought to try it sometime. Doesn't solve any problems but who cares?"

Ed looked away as Althea walked to the center of the room and faced Lem's bent back.

"You had your toast, Lem, now I've got one for you. Turn around and listen."

When Lem turned around and saw Althea's delighted face he knew that something special, something special and something good was about to happen to him.

XIX

"MOTHER, I've got a bad headache." Allison stood on the threshold of the brightly lit bathroom squinting at the glare which hurt her throbbing eyes. Her mother leaned toward the mirror staring intently at herself as she applied a thin black pencil to the lids above her eyes. She stood back to evaluate the effect. Allison waited for her to be satisfied. Finally she smiled, ran warm water over her carefully manicured fingers, dried them delicately and turned toward the girl.

"Now, Allison, what were you saying?"

"My head hurts very badly."

Her mother reached over and touched the child's forehead.

"No fever. Did you eat something?"

"No. I was lying in bed reading when it started. It really hurts."

"All right, Allison, all right. I believe you. Tell you what, why don't you take some aspirin? That'll probably do the trick."

"I told Mrs. Hunter first and she gave me two aspirins a half hour ago and my head still hurts."

Her mother drummed her fingernails impatiently against the tile ledge next to the washbasin. She stared at herself in the mirror and then looked at the girl leaning against the door-jamb.

"Allison, I'm sure it's just from doing all that reading." She bent down and slipped on a black patent leather shoe. "Did you take your medicine today?" Allison nodded.

"Is there anything else I can take, Mother?"

"Allison, give the aspirin a chance to work. Go and lie down and close your eyes. You'll see. It'll be better. Tell Mrs. Hunter to give you more aspirin if it doesn't go away." She flipped a jeweled hand suggesting that Allison run along to her room. She was walking slowly away, when her mother called her back.

"Allison, don't tell Daddy about your headache. It just might ruin his time at the theater tonight. It'll be all right, I know, and there's no reason to worry him. All right?" There was no answer.

"Dear, did you hear me? Let's not say anything."

Allison nodded again. She threw herself on her bed and closed her eyes very tightly hoping that she could shut out the pain, but it remained. She reached over toward the night table and opened her eyes just long enough to find the furry owl that sat pompously staring at her. Rubbing it against her cheek, she tried to visualize the little store where she and Mike had spotted it staring at them from the window. The store had been open; the owner was eating a bowl of soup at the counter and stroking a Persian cat. When he brought them the owl, Allison had taken it and rubbed it against her cheek. Mike had paid the man who had carefully wrapped up the present.

Now Allison rubbed the furry coat of the owl against her cheek, praying that her headache would subside. Eventually she fell into a restless, pulsating sleep.

When she opened her eyes again the room was dark. She could feel nothing but the dull pounding within her head. She rubbed her temples firmly against the sheet hoping to erase the discomfort but nothing changed. Her jumper was crumpled; and the creases rubbed against her skin which seemed sensitive to the slightest touch. Her head felt too heavy to lift off the bed. She tried rolling over on her side and felt something pressing uncomfortably into her side. It was the little owl. She held it against her face and tried to go back to sleep, but the pounding increased. Finally she decided to get up and ask the sitter for more aspirin. She rolled to the edge of the bed and gently lowered herself until she was kneeling on the floor. Gradually she was able to pull herself up, holding her aching head as immobile as possible.

Suddenly she knew that she was going to vomit. She bit her tongue very hard and kept swallowing, trying to move as quickly as she could to the door. The sensation abated for a few seconds. Then another wave of nausea swept over her and she felt the bitter contents of her stomach rising in her mouth. Disregarding the pain, she ran down the carpeted hallway and fell over the open toilet bowl in time to disgorge her insides repeatedly until she fell back exhausted against the cool tiles. No one in the apartment stirred.

She sat breathing deeply waiting to see if the vomiting had ceased. Her eyes were closed and her forehead covered with a thin film of perspiration. She pulled a damp towel from the aluminum bar and wiped her mouth. The acrid odor in the room made her gag, but nothing else came up. When she was sure the spell of nausea was over, she got up and walked down the hall.

As she passed her parents' room she looked inside. Maybe it was so late they were back, but the bed was empty. She proceeded cautiously to the living room. A large gray-haired woman lay across the sofa, her stockinged feet curled up under her. The fingers of her right hand touched the pages of a magazine which had fallen to the carpet. Her head lolled backward and she breathed in long audible gulps. Allison stared at the woman hired to care for her. She debated whether to awaken her but decided there was nothing she could do. What she didn't need at that moment was helplessness.

Walking quietly across the padded floor to the kitchen, she

sat down on a stool by the table. The pain was accelerating and she was becoming dizzy again. The clock on the wall said twelve-thirty, which meant her parents had gone out after the theater. That could mean four in the morning.

She found the phone book and turned to the page where the hospital was listed. Careful not to wake the sitter she dialed the number and told the paging operator who she wanted. The pounding inside her head made her press the receiver against her ear in order to hear clearly. A female voice returned sooner than she had expected saying that Dr. Hillman had signed out to another doctor whose name Allison didn't recognize. Allison thanked the voice and hung up. The bitter taste of her bile rose in her throat as she found another number and dialed again.

To Ed, the sound of the phone seemed remote despite the fact that he lay wide awake staring at the ceiling unable to fall asleep. The ringing persisted for almost a minute before he tossed off the covers and swung himself out of bed.

"Yes?" he said at last.

"Mike?" It was a child's voice, breathless and frightened.

"No, this is Ed." He paused only a second before recognizing her. "Allison, is that you?"

"Yes, Ed. Please let me talk to Mike." The voice was small and hesitant now. "Is he sleeping?"

"What's the matter, Allison? What's wrong?"

"I'm sick, Ed. Please let me talk to Mike. I need him."

Ed hesitated a second, then went into the bedroom and began shaking his roommate's shoulder. Mike moved restlessly and turned away. Ed shook him again and Mike opened his eyes.

"Mike, get up. Allison is on the phone . . . do you hear me? Allison is on the phone. She says she feels sick and needs you. Get up and answer the phone."

Without saying a word, Mike threw the covers aside and rushed into the living room.

"Allison?"

"Mike?"

"Yes, Allison, what's the matter?"

"Mike, I feel very sick. My head hurts and I've been vomiting. Help me, Mike. Tell me what to do to make it go away."

"Where are your parents?"

"They're out and some old lady sleeping on our sofa is supposed to be watching us. She's no help, I didn't even wake her. Mike, help me. It hurts terribly."

"Aren't your parents due home, sweetheart?"

"It could be hours, Mike and I'm scared. I've never felt like this before."

Mike's hands were perspiring. Each time she spoke of her pain he experienced a sinking feeling of desperation.

"What do you want me to do, Allison?"

"Come here, Mike, now."

"I'm coming. Leave your front door open so I don't wake your brother. If your parents come home, tell them I'm on my way."

"Mike, they might not want you here but I need you now and that's what counts." The phone clicked and Mike stood holding the dead receiver until Ed said,

"If you're going, you'd better get dressed."

Mike replaced the receiver. Then he reached out and grabbed Ed by the shoulder as if trying to establish the fact that he was awake and not having a bizarre nightmare.

"Ed, am I crazy? Running out in the middle of the night to see an eleven-year-old girl who complained of a headache."

"No, Mike you're not crazy if you really care about her."

Mike's eyes widened. "I guess I do. I'm not sure what I feel, but it's certainly a feeling I've never had before. . . ."

"Then hurry up because she needs you. It may never happen again."

Mike opened the front door to the apartment and looked around for a second to get his bearings. He recalled that Allison's room was on the left. Opening her door he stared into darkness.

"Mike?" The words were pleading. "Is that you?"

"Yes, Allison . . . where is the light switch?"

"Just inside the door to the right."

Mike felt along the wall and flipped it on. Allison was lying propped up in the large bed, her eyes closed and her head leaning back against the quilted leather headboard. One arm was thrown across her face shielding her eyes from the light.

"Really hurts bad, honey?"

Allison nodded and reached out blindly for him. He grasped the outstretched hand and held tightly.

"I'm going to check and find out what gives, Allison. Can you open your eyes for me?"

She did, squinting painfully. Finally she let her face relax and smiled at the blond man sitting on her bed.

"Thank you for coming. Mike, make me better. I know you can."

Mike swallowed and began pulling his equipment out of the black bag. "Presenting Michael, the magician about to perform his daring feats of making his favorite girl completely well." She started to laugh but the effort intensified her pain and she stopped as tears trickled down her cheeks. Mike watched her suffering with despair.

"Okay, honey, no more laughing. We're going to be serious, take this examination in stages. First step is the lady's blood pressure."

She stuck out her left arm and watched as he circled it with the gray cuff and slowly pumped it up. His bland expression did not flicker for an instant. He unloosened the cuff and took it off, saying,

"Right on the button."

"Normal?"

"Uh huh."

"You're not lying to me, are you, Mike?"

"Me, the only honest doctor left in town? Never."

With unusual care Mike took out his ophthalmoscope and directed a pinpoint of light into each of her eyes. As he completed his examination, his expression remained carefully guarded. When he was done, he handed her a bathrobe and told her to put it on.

"What is it, Mike? Is it serious? It hurts like it must be serious."

"Allison, it's a headache probably from the medicine. It may mean a few days in the hospital again but once that's over you'll be great again."

"Mike, what's the matter with me?"

"I told you, honey, a headache from the drugs you're taking, that's all."

"But why am I taking drugs?"

"Allison, everybody told you in the hospital a hundred times. You became anemic from all of those nosebleeds and the medicine is to make your blood normal again. Period."

"Mike, swear."

Mike sat very still, the muscles of his stomach contracting painfully. He could feel beads of perspiration collecting on his upper lip. Christ, he thought, with that blood pressure elevation and those engorged vessels and blurred discs, she's got to have something in her head. Something either from the leukemia or from the drugs, and you have to sit here and lie like a son of a bitch. Well, the least you can do is make sure she believes you.

"I swear. Just a few days and then you'll be back to normal."

"Will it hurt like this all that time?"

"No." He wasn't sure. But he didn't want her to be in such debilitating pain so he lied and tried to believe the lie himself.

He reached back into the bag and pulled out a vial and a

215

paper-wrapped syringe. Then he hunted in the bag and finally brought out a thin foil-covered alcohol pledget and a small paperback book. After thumbing through the book checking the correct dosage he unwrapped the syringe and wiped the top of the bottle with the alcohol gauze.

"The magician is going to take away the pain," he said. "But it'll take a needle to do it. Are you chicken?"

Allison shook her head. "Anything for the throbbing, Mike. The needle won't hurt half as much as my head does now. Will you stay with me after?"

Mike smiled. "I'll stay next to you as long as you want me to, Allison. I promise you that."

She closed her eyes and leaned her head forward, her tears dropping onto the bedspread. When she looked up, Mike was still holding the capped syringe and waiting quietly.

"Remember the owl, Mike? He sits next to me too. Mike and my owl, both so serious and so funny." She put her arm up as Mike wiped it off with the alcohol pledget and inserted the needle quickly plunging the tiny amount of liquid into her upper arm. She winced but he held her firmly, finished, and withdrew the needle.

"Sorry if it hurt."

"I know you are."

Mike threw the syringe away, automatically breaking off the metal tip as he had been taught. God, let the morphine work fast, Mike thought, watching her closely. Allison picked up his hands and held each in her own and laid her head on the pillow. She gazed at him, waiting for his magic to erase her agony. The two people, the girl of eleven and the young man of twenty-five, sat looking at each other in silence. When the child's eyes finally closed, Mike continued holding her small clenched fingers.

After a while his back began to ache but when he tried to change position she stirred and moaned. So he sat watching the steady breathing, waiting for the child's parents to come home and temporarily release her hold on him.

XX

TURNING over in the bed, Ed's bare skin brushed gently against the soft, warm flesh of the girl huddled next to him. The late morning light filtering in from the torn window shade struck his face with unexpected brilliance. He squeezed his eyes shut again, waiting for the prisms of light to settle. When he opened them again a few minutes later, the sun washed his sight more gently and he turned on his side and kissed Jill's back, nibbling on her skin.

"Ed?" she said sleepily.

"Yes, Jill." His voice suggested invitation.

"Ed, is it time to get up?"

"If you want, Jill."

She turned so that she faced him, her unclothed body pressing against his. He stroked her back slowly, moving his hands down over her buttocks and back over her shoulders as she buried her face into the nape of his neck. With unhurried sensuality he began exploring the rest of her body. She murmured indistinguishable words and closed her eyes when he brushed her lips with his mouth and then with his tongue and finally whispered in her ear.

"Jill? Are you ready, Jill?"

Her head was thrown back, her lips parted, her eyes closed; but her arms reached around and pressed against his back, forcing his straining body against hers and together, without words, they made love. . . .

When he awoke again she was sitting with her back against the wall, hugging her knees, looking intently at him. Smiling, he reached out and pulled on the leg nearest to him and eased it down. She slowly drew it up again and touched the top of his head.

"Ed, I've been thinking . . ."

"It's too early."

"Get serious, Ed. This is serious. I've been thinking . . . now don't answer if you don't want to . . . wait a while if you'd rather not answer right now . . . but I've been wondering . . ."

"For Christ's sake, what is it?"

She spat out the next words as if they were bullets from a machine gun. "Why don't you move in here with me?"

Ed, who had raised his head slightly to look at her, now lay back and stared at the ceiling. Jill nervously ran her fingers through her long hair.

"I said you don't have to decide now . . . and if you don't want to . . . what the hell . . . it can stay like this . . . only . . . only, I thought it might work. You know, being together, not just before and after we go to bed, but all the time." Her voice was unsteady.

"We're together at other times."

"I know but . . . Oh, Ed, I'm so tired of trying new things and looking for I don't know what, chasing myself in and out of other people's lives, in and out of my own. . . ."

Ed's reaction was quick and harsh. "And I'm a way out. Something to hold onto."

Her response was gentle, dampening his sudden flare of anger.

"Something I want to hold onto. That's the difference. I've

218

never had anybody to hold onto before, anybody who cared about me like I cared about them. But now you. Is that love, Ed? Is that what other people call love?"

He was cautious and turned slightly away from her.

"It might be, but it might not. If I do move in . . . it's on a temporary basis. The truth is that I don't really know where I'll be after July."

"You can come for as long as you want," she said. "Just come."

Ed watched her fidgeting, first with her ear and then with the sheet that she had pulled around her feet. He ran his eyes over her young, vulnerable body and traced her neck up to her small, vibrant face. He suddenly felt so fulfilled lying next to her; at that moment she was his anchor, precarious, unstable, but hanging firmly onto him.

"Do we split the rent?"

"Does that mean yes?" The words were slow and guarded.

He nodded and she slipped underneath the covers and curled herself against him. They lay quietly breathing, their hands almost shyly held away from each other for a long time before she spoke again.

"Ed, I'm going to bring Henry home with us when he's ready."

"I had counted on that, Jill."

"Where are you going in July?"

"I don't know." His voice changed almost imperceptibly. "I promised the Chief that I was taking a job next year with him, but the kids are getting to me." He stopped.

"If you don't like kids . . ."

"I like kids. I love them, that's the trouble. I dread seeing them in pain. If it were only one once in a while but constantly, all of them, the crying, the helplessness, the parents' faces. I don't know what to do, Jill. I want to give something to them but I don't think I have enough to give."

She tossed her head to the side and pouted. "Well, if I were you and I was so uptight about something like that, I'd get out, do something else for a while."

"It's not that easy. I wish it were. Well, it doesn't make a bit of difference with us, at least not for now. July is a lot of mornings like this from today."

Jill moved quickly out of bed. "Ed, is that the way you felt about Henry, the way you feel about him now? Do you care that deeply about him?"

Ed followed her out of bed. He put his arms around her and stood close to her back. "Yes, and it's the way I feel about you. So please remember that fact before you hurt me, if you ever should."

She was silent. He walked around the bed and picked his watch off the chair and glanced at it. "Jesus, it's one o'clock. I promised to cover for Sheila Plotkin starting at three o'clock today and I wanted to go to church too."

Jill turned to stare at him. "Church?"

Ed grinned at her surprise. "Yes, just one of my idiosyncrasies that you didn't know about. Watch out, I have other straight ways that might make you want to find a different roommate.

Jill lit the only burner that worked on the old stove and put the coffee pot on top. "Don't you have time for coffee? I'll never understand your schedule. Why three o'clock on a Sunday? I can't get used to the crazy hours."

Ed finished dressing. "Time for one cup. Sheila's job hunting this weekend and we're taking turns covering. It's not usually this bad." He walked toward the open card table and stopped halfway. "Jesus, you know, for a minute you sounded exactly like Henry's mother."

They stared silently at each other and then both smiled.

Ed walked steadily through the quiet Sunday afternoon streets. Light May winds disturbed the small bits of paper on the sidewalks lifting them up and then settling them into unusual patterns. For the moment, he ignored the warm breeze flapping his pant legs against his shins. When he stopped at a corner for the light to change he searched the street ahead crammed with brownstone buildings. A tall spire pointed straight up into the cloudy blue sky, challenging the shuffling crowd on the pavement below.

Ed could feel the aura of hushed reverence as soon as he crossed the doorstep and felt the large oak doors close behind him. Light filtered haphazardly through the stained glass windows, lighting up odd corners of the large room. The altar had an air of studied simplicity. Minimal cloth, slight suggestions of color, primarily different shades of woods fitted meticulously into simple patterns so that the aura of serious devotion was unmistakable.

Ed took a deep breath and the musty smells of religion that had always surrounded him as he had entered church came back from his past. Everything has its own smell, he thought. Death, birth, love. Even religion. As he stood musing, a small shawled woman drifted quietly past him and padded softly toward the front of the church. At the porcelain body leaning down from the cross she knelt down and began to pray. Her lips moved and her face became a river of tears which she occasionally wiped with the ends of her shawl. Ed stood caught in the web of her suffering. The two of them, the only visible occupants of the room, remained in this position for a long time. Then the woman rose abruptly, crossed herself, and walked swiftly up the aisle toward the young man. Ed reached his hand out and touched her.

"Is there anything I can do to help?"

She observed him for a moment and scratched her nose silently. "Help? Why help?"

Ed shrugged. "You seemed so upset up near the altar. I thought you might need help."

Her lips pressed together with an expression of resignation. "Help? You want to help? How can you help a lifetime of nothing? Can you go back with me and put something in for me? A good husband, a kid who finishes school, a real friend? If you can do that, then you're better than he is." She pointed her short, bony arm toward the figure on the cross. "If you can help that much, then you belong on that cross, not him." She smiled sadly and patted the young man's arm. "Go get your own help. Mine never came. Maybe yours will." She stood silently for a second and then pushed the heavy door outward and disappeared leaving Ed alone in the cavernous room.

He looked around trying to find the confessional booths. Finally he located them over on the left. Black curtains protected the small cubicles and transmitted a sense of privacy. Ed walked over and slipped inside one of the booths. Inside it was small and stuffy. A stool was positioned next to a ledge, and a round, curtained aperture connected the booth with the clerical room beyond. Ed saw a button to the right of the aperture and decided he had better announce his presence. He pushed it with a tremorous finger, hearing in the distance a small high-pitched bell. For the first time in days he felt a tentative ripple of hope. Nobody came. He wondered whether to press the button again. It was hot in the booth and he began to perspire.

Finally he heard the sweeping sound of cloth and soon, despite the silence, the presence of another person on the other side of the wooden partition became overpowering. Ed felt compelled to speak.

"Father, are you there?"

"Yes." The voice was young. Ed was disappointed but the man was there and he wanted to receive his help. He began reciting the preliminary prayers by rote, remembering times inside other booths when all he had to confess were foolish, childish pranks. The elderly priest had usually been tolerant, chastising gently, allowing easy forgiveness. Now he finished the necessary incantations and sat back on his stool.

"Do you have something to confess?" The young voice tried

to sound involved while trying to identify the voice of the confessor.

"Yes, Father."

There was a pause.

"I'm waiting," said the priest. "Is it that difficult to tell me?"

Ed looked down at his hands folded foolishly in his lap. "I don't want to make a confession, Father. I just want your advice."

"One often leads into the other. Go ahead."

Ed began with medical school, talked rapidly about his ambitions, his fears, his successes and eased hesitantly into his internship on the Pediatric floor. His voice was soft and halting. When he paused, the only sounds were the steady breathing of the man seated on the other side of the booth and his own deep, sighing breath.

"I'm terribly confused, Father. I want so much to stay where I am. I feel comfortable around the children. Father, it's a marvelous world, the children's world, but not when all you see is the suffering, the agony, the loss. Then it becomes a nightmare and Father, I'm not sure that I'm equipped, that I have what it takes to survive."

There was no response at first, just the feeling that another human being sat outside that booth listening, weighing, judging. Finally he heard the priest's voice, slower, more solemn, weighted by the problems that Ed had forced on him.

"Is there anything else?"

"Father, give me a reason to be there, something to get me through the times when I want to run away from the sadness."

"You've asked me to do something very difficult."

Ed frowned. The air inside the booth was becoming stifling. "Father?"

"You've asked me to find your motivation. You've asked me to provide you with the drive, the humanity to continue. That I cannot do."

223

"But Father, I need help. I must come to a decision. I can't keep drifting like this."

"When you talked about running away from the sadness and pain your voice was filled with self-pity. And you want me to tell you the reason to continue?" He paused. "None of us can run away. None of us can turn off the agonies we watch and listen to like a child turns off a faucet. We all must make sacrifices, Doctor." The rustling of the cloth on the other side of the wall suggested a change in position and the voice as it crossed the black velvet covering between the men became more distant, as if the priest was preparing to leave.

Ed stared at the gently stirring cloth and tried anxiously to visualize the man on the other side. "What was the last thing you said, Father?"

The voice was steadier now, full of resolve. "I said that we all must make sacrifices. None of us can run away. Anyone who wants to help gives up something to do so."

Ed leaned forward and pushed aside the smooth black drape and reached his hand through the aperture, wanting to touch the man who had told him so much about himself, wanting to share the mutual resignation to duty that might give him the strength to continue. But he grasped only air; no hand reached out for his and he slowly pulled his hand back inside the closeted booth.

"I'm sorry, Father, we share the same pain, without any solutions for either of us. I'm sorry I tried to burden you with mine. It isn't something that can be shared, is it?"

There was a prolonged, thoughtful silence.

Finally Ed's tired words echoed through the tiny room. "Good-bye, Father. I hope your answers are easier to find than mine have been." He eased himself out of the booth and walked quickly up the aisle not noticing the tall young priest walking slowly around the corner of the confessional booth, his hands folded behind him, his face filled with bewilderment.

The warm, fresh air hit Ed full in the face as he started running down the street, hurtling himself across busy corners, running until his breath and body could stand no more. He stopped, panting, and shook his head, but the tight, constricted feeling that had begun in the church remained. He rubbed his eyes and began walking in the direction of the hospital.

Ed worked side by side with Lem in the tightly cramped Emergency Room, watching and treating the endless procession of weekend illnesses that marched in and out of the congested cubicles. Bottles of intravenous fluids had to be walked around; mothers sagging in exhaustion needed placating; and the sirens of approaching ambulances announced that the day's full potential had not yet been realized. The two interns discussed several of the cases, allowing the surrounding din to act as a screen for their words of anticipation and action. Stretchers slid around corners; voices were raised in anger at the delays; the few nurses on duty wearily walked the hallways trying to cover all of the cubicles; while the doctors worked steadily, listening, culturing, probing, drawing blood, squinting at the chalky outlines on the x-ray, treating, and waiting for the next patient to arrive.

Lem looked over at Ed as he straightened up from checking a squirming infant's ears.

"We liked her, Ed."

Ed smiled.

"Any decisions about next year?"

Ed put down his instrument. "No, but I'm getting very depressed about my own indecision."

"How about a head-shrinker?"

Ed shrugged in a diffident gesture of despair. "Maybe."

The phone rang, ending the conversation, and Ed answered and a breathless voice said, "Is Dr. Erikson there?"

"This is he. What's wrong?"

"This is Miss Wardlow in the premie nursery. One of the infants took a bad turn. Please come immediately, he may be gone."

Ed's heart sank. "Who? Which premie? Who is it?" But the phone clicked and the panicky voice was gone.

Ed bolted toward the door calling out over his shoulder, "Premie went sour. Carry on till I get back." He ran up the flight of steps to the nursery and grabbed a gown. Washing his hands under an already flowing faucet in the hallway, he rapidly surveyed the rooms to find the nurse who he knew would be standing by the sick infant.

His eyes first hit the large glass box where Jill's baby lay. There was no one guarding him and Ed felt his body relax. Then he spotted Miss Wardlow and he moved quickly toward her.

The infant lay in the isolette not breathing, the skin a mottled blue, the eyes staring, the tiny body facing upward with the multiple apparatuses still connected. Ed grabbed a stethoscope from the nurse and listened. No sounds. He began working on the tiny form but none of the prescribed maneuvers evoked any response. Finally he turned to the nurse.

"It's all over. What happened?"

"The baby is only forty-two hours old. Hyaline membrane disease. This was the third time it stopped breathing today."

Ed looked at the still, abbreviated form. "Very premature. God, it couldn't be more than thirty weeks at best."

"Dr. Rosensweig guessed twenty-seven when he saw it about an hour ago."

"Was he here?"

"He always seems to be here when there's trouble. And nobody ever knows who called him."

Ed closed the glass covering of the incubator, walked out of the nursery and picked up the baby's chart. No private doctor, he noted. My job to tell the mother. On his way he stopped outside of Henry's isolette and stared at the infant for a second

226

before leaving the nursery to tell the mother that her baby was dead.

That night in the on-call room Ed found it impossible to sleep. He kept seeing the unresponsive infant, hearing the mother crying. It seemed like days, not hours, since he had been lying in bed with Jill.

Finally he shoved off the sheets and got out of bed. The room was silent. Tonight he was alone. Rubbing his neck where the muscles were aching, he pulled on his pants and shirt and went down to the fifth floor. The bulky figure of Helen Stevens, the night nurse, was the only visible sight in the hall as she pushed her medication cart around checking to see if the nurse before her had given out all of the drugs on the little blue cards.

"Hi, Mrs. Stevens. How you doing?"

"Fine, Dr. Erikson. Almost a full house tonight and some sick kids too."

"Mrs. Stevens, can I ask you for a favor?"

"What's that?"

"I need a couple of phenos to sleep. I have a bad headache. Can I borrow your key to the cabinet and take them? You're busy and I can do it. You can mark it down later."

"Do you know where they are?"

"Sure. They're in the cabinet to the right. You can mark me down for two. The pharmacy's closed and I've got to get some sleep."

The woman reached into the pocket of her white uniform and pulled out a key ring. She fingered several keys until she had located the one she wanted.

"Here. Return the key before you leave the floor. Okay?"

Ed smiled and thanked the woman and walked over to the cabinet as she started pushing her cart into the darkened

rooms. He opened the glass door of the cabinet which was unlocked and placed the key into the small opening in the metal
door to the right. After looking casually over his shoulder at
the empty hallway, he opened the bottle labeled *phenobarbitol*
and placed two small white pills into his palm and then stuffed
them into his mouth. He picked up the water pitcher, poured
a small amount of fluid into a paper cup and drank it, swallowing the pills. He swung the door closed, forgetting the bottle still clutched in his hand.

As he was about to put it back, he heard a voice calling him.
He turned and found himself staring at Allison's tired, anxious
face.

"Ed, please visit me. Mike is off tonight and I just had a terrible dream. I'm so scared. Please come and sit with me for a
minute, will you?"

He took two steps toward the child pleading in the doorway
when her voice stopped him again.

"Please, Ed, I wouldn't ask you if I wasn't very scared. Ed, I
dreamed I was dying. Please sit with me and tell me it was just
a dream. My head doesn't hurt any more since the taps and
the x-rays so I know that Mike was right but I was so frightened by the dream. Please, Ed."

They walked across the hall. Allison was temporarily alone,
her roommate having gone home that morning. As they entered the darkened room, Ed suddenly realized that he had
the bottle in his hand and turned to return it to the closet.
"Ed, don't leave me alone." He stared at her terrified face and
placed the bottle on the table beside her bed, before pulling up
a chair.

"Ed, it was awful. I knew I was dying and I kept trying to
wake myself up to prove that it was a dream but it was so
hard."

Ed's voice was soft and steady. "Dreams can be terrible, Allison. But look around you. You're here, same place. Mike was

right, as usual, look how much better you feel. You'll be home very soon, alive, very alive." He stopped.

"Have you ever dreamed about death, Ed?"

"I dream about it a lot lately, Allison."

"Isn't it a terrible feeling to think that you won't be able to see and feel and hear? I don't like to even think about it because I love doing all of that so much and don't want to lose it now. It was a dream, wasn't it, Ed?"

"Allison, it must have been a dream. And isn't it better to dream all the bad things in life and live only the wonderful ones?"

Allison smiled. "You're right and so smart. Now I know why Reggie loved you."

Ed turned away but Allison's voice continued. "She did love you. She talked about you all the time. She said you always knew what to say to make her understand. I think she did understand, don't you? I think she knew and you helped her know and she loved you, and now I know why." Ed shook his head begging the child to stop.

"Ed, I know it's hard to think about her dying but just think of what you did for her when you knew her. That's what I think about, what we had to share when we were together and I feel better. You have so much inside for us, Ed."

Ed felt his eyes getting heavy from the pills. This child had called his caring for a dying child an act of love. Was that the answer? Was that what he had to give?

"Allison, I'm getting sleepy. Are you?"

"Not too sleepy, but let me have a few more minutes. Put your head on the edge of the bed and we can talk."

She possessed totally and swiftly and the feeling of belonging to her was reassuring. Suddenly he realized what Mike felt. Loving a child was such an uncomplicated emotion and perhaps that in itself would sustain him. Anyway, he would try. . . . The best he could. He would share himself with the children around him. That must be what he had been searching for.

He reached across the bed for the bottle of pills, thinking that he should return them before they were needed. Allison's voice drifted toward him as he closed his eyes.

XXI

LEM hurried into the room leaving the nurse in the doorway silently wringing her hands. Allison lay on top of the covers, her bathrobe still tied around her waist, her silken blonde hair covering the pillow. Her face was calm, eyes closed, lips slightly parted. Beside her, Ed lay bent over on the edge of the bed, deeply asleep. His right arm lay tucked under his head with the palm open as if waiting for something to be placed in it.

Lem reached out and shook Ed's shoulder.

"Ed, wake up." He moved slightly and sighed; but his eyes remained closed. Lem took a deep breath and shook harder. The nurse took a step into the room. Lem's voice was louder though still a hoarse whisper. "Ed, wake up, do you hear me, man, you gotta get up." Ed twisted and tried to move away from the disturbance. "Baby, get up. It's Lem. I have to talk with you."

Ed opened his eyes and looked at his friend's worried face. He shook his head and lifted it an inch off the bed. His neck hurt and his back ached as if he had just lifted something very heavy, the muscles taut and sore.

"Ed, are you awake? Answer me fast, man. How many did you take?"

Ed stared at the dark face, the eyes frantic with concern.

231

What had happened? Why was Lem so upset? He sat up and realized where he was.

"Ed, please, did you take all of them? Helen said there were thirty-one in the bottle. Hurry up, we don't have much time." Ed watched the man standing in front of him with the startled look of unbelievable loss growing in his face and Ed shook his head.

"It's late," Ed said, trying to explain to Lem he wanted to sleep.

"What do you mean? It's not too late, it's only been three hours. Oh, sweet Jesus, baby, how many?"

"Two. Just to go to sleep," Ed said, still half asleep.

"Are you sure? If you don't want your stomach pumped out personally by me, you'd better show me the rest of those Goddamn pills, 'cause, you hear me, you white bastard, I'm not going to let you die."

Ed stood and reached for the bottle on the bedside table. "Die, Jesus Christ, Lem, what did you think I was trying to do. Allison called me and I forgot to put back the bottle."

Lem meanwhile was counting. "Twenty-nine, that leaves two like you said."

Ed was fully awake now and conscious of the nurse still standing tensely at the door and the girl stirring restlessly on the bed.

"For God's sake, how could you think I was trying to kill myself?"

"I suppose it's a usual practice, finding you sleeping on a patient's bed and a bottle of sleeping pills missing."

"I'll be glad when this night is over," said Helen Stevens. "I've aged twenty years."

Ed looked at both of them. His voice was tired. "I'm sorry. She was afraid and wanted to talk and I fell asleep without returning the bottle. Christ, I'm sorry."

The nurse nodded and turned toward the cabinet. She stood there for a long minute and then picked her book off the sink below and wrote several short notes on the open page, ignoring the men behind. Lem understood and pressed Ed's arm, indicating they should leave.

"God," he said, "look at how I'm sweatin'."

"Lem, I'm sorry. Christ, am I sorry."

They were standing by the elevator doors. Lem reached over and pressed the button.

"Lem, I'm staying next year. In Pediatrics."

Lem smiled. "What in the hell made you make up your mind?"

"The kid."

"Allison?"

"Yeah, Allison. It's strange, isn't it? A kid with leukemia convincing me that it was worth hanging in."

"Man, nothing surprises me anymore, but that kid, what has she got? First Mike, now you. Tomorrow I'm going in to make an appointment with her. I got a few problems I'd like to solve."

Mike drove his car into the parking lot the following morning, peering out of his windshield at the luminous day. He sprinted toward the hospital entrance clutching a paper bag in his right hand and hurried up to the fifth floor.

Allison was standing at the sink, her face covered with soap. Her robe was off, and she was on her toes trying to see herself in the mirror placed high above the basin. When she saw him she grabbed a towel and quickly wiped her face.

"You're too early. I was fixing myself up for you."

"Pardon me," said Mike. "Princess, don't behead me. Just turn me into an owl so I can sit next to your bed like the last young man who fell in love with you."

"Oh, Mike, that's wonderful. Our owl, a prince, that's a wonderful idea."

Mike lifted the paper bag. "Guess what's in here and you can have it."

She opened her eyes wide and sucked in her breath. "What is it, Mike? Come on, I can't guess, please . . . All right, I'll guess." She paused and looked at him. He was trying unsuccessfully to conceal a mischievous grin, the same look he had had that night after the ball game in front of the shop when he had noticed the owl in the window before she had seen it. "Mike, you found another. Oh Mike, another owl!"

She ran over, opened the paper bag and pulled out a small furry creature. It was smaller than the first owl and had no wooden body, just fur.

"Oh, Mike, she's beautiful. It's a she, you can tell." She dropped the furry animal on her bed, ran across the room and flung her arms about him, pulling him down until his mouth was level with her uplifted face. She kissed him full on the lips and stepped back. "I love your present, Mike, and I love you for making me well." She stood in front of him looking seriously up at his face. He didn't smile. He just stared down at her as if trying to memorize her features.

Waiting in the rotunda, Mike heard a burst of laughter and turned to see Rosensweig marching down the hall. Todd was trotting beside him.

"Jesus, Todd, since when did you become so funny?"

Then Rosensweig spotted Mike and signaled to the senior resident to go ahead.

"Good morning, Hillman. How's your girl this morning?"

"Which girl, sir?"

"Jesus, Mike, do you think I'm blind in my own department? I may not be dignified enough to satisfy some of my professional friends but I can see clearly. I'm talking about the young girl with leukemia, her name escapes me. What in the hell is it?"

"Allison Reddy."

"Right, well, now that we've got her name, how is she?"

"Her leukemic meningitis seems to be clearing, Dr. Rosensweig. She's still on steroids, and on daily taps with drug injections . . ."

"I know. I know what treatment she's on. Remember I work here too. What I asked is, how is she?"

"Better, sir. She'll probably be going home soon."

"Good." He paused. Mike put his bag down. "Mike, are you being smart?"

"I beg your pardon?"

"Damn it, Mike, I asked if you were being smart. It hurts enough as it is, but getting so close it can destroy you." Mike started to turn away but Rosensweig persisted. "Sometimes I play the fool, sometimes because that's really me and sometimes because it's what people expect. And sometimes because it solves the problem to be that way . . . for me." He paused. "Mike, are you also playing a part with this child because you think it is what you should do or is it what you honestly feel?"

Mike faced the older doctor and said, "It's something I really feel, sir. It's as if I've been turned on to something special."

Rosensweig closed his eyes very briefly and took a deep breath. "Join the fraternity, my boy. After a while you'll get used to the pain. My only advice is, take it very slow at first." He swung his huge body around and went off to his office.

Back in his room, Mike found Ed pulling on a fresh pair of white pants.

"Morning," said Mike. "How was it?"

Ed looked at him and smiled foolishly. "Wild, a wild night. Remind me someday to tell you."

"What's come over you? That's the most relaxed I've heard you in weeks."

Ed tied his tie, watching himself in the mirror. "Mike, I'm moving out of the apartment sometime this week."

Mike stopped changing his clothes.

"Why, Ed? Jesus, you're not chucking the whole thing, are you?"

"No, in fact, I've decided to stay next year. I'm moving in with Jill."

"Hell," said Mike, "I lay half the population looking for a meaningful score and you find it right off the bat."

"You looking for advice?"

Mike laughed. "One good lay and you're an expert."

"She's more than that, Mike."

"I know she is, Ed. Do as I say, not as I do. Make it last."

The two men left the room.

Mike went down to the nursery where he started an exchange transfusion and soon forgot everything except the delicate procedure he was performing on the infant lying in the heated box. Ed had gone to the ward where he had two elective admissions.

In her room Allison felt unexpectedly dizzy. She moved away from the window where she had been staring at the people walking on the windy street below. Her knees felt weak like the last time her nose had bled. Instinctively she reached up and touched her face, but her hand returned without the stain of blood. Suddenly a cramping pain ran through her abdomen and hung, slowly growing in intensity. She doubled over but the pain refused to abate and she slipped to the floor. After a few moments, she pulled herself over to the reassuring support of the bed. The acrid taste in her mouth welled up like vomit; and she gagged, but nothing came up. Sharp thrusts of pain stabbed her abdomen. With enormous effort, she pulled herself onto the bed.

The medicine wasn't working. She felt worse than she had the night Mike had come to her apartment. Mike, you must find something better, she thought. Suddenly she couldn't see, she was plunging into darkness, riding with the pain into a distant country. She reached out blindly for the button that summoned the nurse. Desperate, she tried to cry out, but her voice was only exhaled air without sound. Reaching again for the nurse's button, her hand touched the furry body of her new owl. Her last conscious gesture was to clutch it to her. A moment later the little animal slipped to the floor, falling from the child's limp hand.

Ed finished writing up the new admission. The child had been taken to her room and the parents hovered outside, the mother moistening her lips as she watched her child being made comfortable in the strange room. Ed had tried to allay the couple's anxiety but he knew that only the child's eventual release into the outside world again would dispel their fears.

Putting the chart back in the rack he decided to do something that he had been trying to find time for all morning. He wanted to thank Allison for something which she would never understand, repay her for her unrealized influence.

He was halfway into her room when he stopped, paralyzed. The child lay sprawled on the stained white sheets, blood spreading like a river's edge over the immaculate covers. Her hair was matted with blood and still more flecked her pale lips.

Ed ran over to her and pressed his stethoscope against her chest. Nothing. He stepped back and hollered Sandy's name as loudly as he could. He began pressing the girl's breastbone firmly inward with the fleshy part of his palm in short, firm thrusts. After a minute, he shouted again and Sandy appeared in the doorway, her face stricken with disbelief.

"Get the crash cart, fast. . . . Allison's bled out. . . ."

She disappeared and returned pushing a metal cart, pulling out plastic tubes and laryngoscopes as she ran. Ed reached into the cart and took the cover off the medicine rack. He accepted the extended laryngoscope and endotracheal tube; and together the two intubated Allison's windpipe. Sandy began breathing into the tube while Ed continued his massage. Finally he stopped and quickly placed the end of his stethoscope against the soft flesh of the girl's chest wall. He listened as Sandy continued blowing into the plastic tube, then shook his head.

"Nothing. Call Dr. Breen now for this room. Hurry back and draw up some adrenalin. I'll keep pumping."

Sandy was back in a second with a full syringe which Ed plunged into Allison's chest. When he had injected half the fluid he pulled out the needle and replaced his stethoscope.

"She's not responding. I think we've had it."

Lem appeared in the doorway and rushed over to the bed. His voice was soft.

"I heard the Dr. Breen and recognized the room number. The Anesthesia boys are right behind me. Let them try, Ed. You're shaking too much now." He pulled Ed away as the team of three physicians arrived with the oxygen tank, respirators, and the emergency equipment.

The three, two men and one woman, methodically worked on the child. Ed moved into the far corner of the room, pressing himself into the crease of the wall, his eyes averted. Sandy stood next to the team waiting to help if needed. Lem paced back and forth, his hands thrust into his pockets.

"Where's Mike?" Lem said suddenly.

Ed took a deep breath and whispered, "I think he just finished an exchange. He'll probably be coming to see her on his way back to the nursery."

Lem shook his head slowly. "Oh, sweet Jesus. . . ."

The emergency team slowed their efforts. Finally they backed away from the bed. The woman turned to Sandy, and said, "Sorry, it was too late. Even a transfusion wouldn't have helped." They gathered their equipment, leaving Lem, Ed, and Sandy helplessly staring at the motionless figure on the bed. Finally, Sandy moistened a paper towel and started to wipe away the crusting blood from the dead child's face.

"What's the matter?" A voice shot across the room. "What in the hell is the matter?"

Sandy stepped away so Mike could see the bed.

"Mike, she's dead. She bled, probably an ulcer from the drugs. . . ."

Mike said nothing, just stood in the doorway swaying. Then, after endless minutes, he slowly walked to the bed and lifted Allison's arm, gently placing it back on the bed. No one moved. Finally Mike bent slightly and took the girl in his arms.

"Hi Allison. Hi, honey. I'm sorry I was late today."

Suddenly he began to weep, tears pouring down his cheeks and dropping on Allison's chalky face. He stood in that position, pressing the child against his body until the sound of his crying ebbed and died. Then he carefully laid her back on the bed and silently walked out of the room.

XXII

THE following afternoon Ed was analyzing laboratory slips on the new admissions when he heard his name on the loudspeaker.

"Ed, is that you?" Jill said when they were finally connected.

"Yes, it's me. What's wrong?"

"Wrong? Oh, nothing's wrong. I just wanted to tell you something."

"What, Jill?"

"Don't think I'm crazy, Ed, please don't, but do you know what I just did?" Her voice rose with excitement. "I went out and bought Henry a crib and I'm having it sent here today. Am I crazy?"

"No. I had hoped Henry wasn't going to sleep between us."

"But Ed . . . I bought the biggest crib they had."

"You may lose him in it—he won't be all that big when we get him home."

"You're not mad that I bought such a big crib—crowding us in that small apartment?"

"Tell you something, Jill, Henry has squatter's rights. He was there first."

He laughed and hearing her enormous sigh of relief, continued laughing as he hung up the phone.

"Erikson, is that actually you?" Rosensweig had come up behind him.

Ed's face began burning as Rosensweig gave a low whistle, looked around the empty hallway and said, "You know what that means, Ed. You're getting laid." He began to roar. Then he said in his usual booming voice, staring at Ed with obvious affection, "Come with me Erikson. Now that your mind has cleared, maybe you can help me on a consultation I've been asked to see. Be careful, though. If you give me the right diagnosis, make me think I thought of it myself."

He chuckled and threw his arm around Ed's shoulder, guiding him down the hallway toward a private room.

At the nurse's station on five, Sandy was standing with a new patient, staring at Allison's empty bed. With a sigh she picked up the phone and dialed the page operator.

"Is Dr. Hillman in?"

"Yes, he's here. Where do you want him."

"Children's ward, phone eight."

Sandy hung up and turned to the boy seated in a wheelchair beside her. His mother stood behind the chair grasping its high back with both of her hands. Her voice was sharp.

"Nurse, has Dr. Greenwald called yet? He was to phone in and leave instructions this morning."

"Not yet, Mrs. Simpson. But Dr. Hillman will be down very shortly to see Wayne."

"Who is Dr. Hillman, may I ask?" The tone was unmistakable.

"He's the intern who will be responsible for Wayne."

"I don't want anyone touching Wayne until Dr. Greenwald comes here. Do you understand? Wayne is not to be subjected to a million inexperienced hands."

Sandy took a deep breath and tried smiling. "I'm afraid the rule of the hospital is that Dr. Hillman will have to take a history from you and examine Wayne."

"It's a rule?"

Sandy nodded.

"Well, all right, but just one of those men . . . just one."

The boy huddled in the chair seemed oblivious to the conversation.

The phone rang on the desk. It was Mike.

"You have a new patient," said Sandy. "A private admission of Dr. Greenwald's with possible nephritis. Did you know about it?"

"Are you kidding? He never calls ahead."

"Will you be down?"

"Yes."

Mike came on to the ward, his face showing the strain of a sleepless night. He had obviously combed his hair in a hurry for blond strands stuck up in the back. When he reached the wheelchair he leaned down and shook the boy's hand. Sandy was surprised by his warm, easy smile. She handed him the boy's chart and he began pushing the boy to the Admissions Room. Even after they were out of sight, Sandy could hear the mother's strident voice.

"Now remember young man, in an emergency if anything happens I want Dr. Greenwald and only Dr. Greenwald to touch this child."

Sandy cringed.

Mike wheeled the boy, who was now dressed in his pajamas, ·back to the ward. Trailing behind was the boy's mother folding his clothes into neat piles as she walked. Mike stopped by the desk.

"Where does he go, Sandy?"

She swallowed and ran her tongue over the top of her mouth. "In there." She pointed.

"Allison's bed?" His voice held sadness but no regret.

"Yes."

She turned to the boy who was holding Mike's right hand.

"Okay sport, that's your room. And remember it's a deal, whenever the ball game is on T.V., if I'm here we have a date to watch it."

The boy looked up at him and smiled, hesitating to release his hand as Sandy tried to wheel him into the empty room.

Mike had not moved when Sandy returned.

"Mike . . . are you all right?"

"Yes, Sandy. I'm going to be fine."

"Is there anything I can do?"

"Yes, Sandy, let me try again with you."

"Mike, it has to be different this time." She bit her lip.

"I think it will be. I feel different, Sandy. So much has happened to me. I feel like I've suddenly let go."

"All right, Mike, we'll try again. Come over to the apartment. We'll eat at home."

She smiled at him and walked into the room where the boy's mother stood waiting impatiently.

Mike picked up his scribbled notes, sat down at the desk, and started writing down the life story of the new boy on the ward . . . slowly . . . carefully . . . because his arms were tired and his eyes burned.